WILDSIDE
MAGAZINE GROUP

Publisher
John Gregory Betancourt

**General Manager
& Creative Director**
Stephen H. Segal

H.P. LOVECRAFT'S
MAGAZINE OF HORROR

Editor
Marvin Kaye

Contributing Editors
Sean Wallace
Craig Shaw Gardner
Darrell Schweitzer

Copyright © 2006 by Wildside Press, LLC.
All rights reserved.

H.P. Lovecraft's Magazine of Horror™ is published four times a year by Wildside Press LLC. Postmaster & others: send change of address and other subscription matters to Wildside Press LLC, 9710 Traville Gateway Drive #234, Rockville, MD 20850-7308. Single copies: $7.95 (magazine edition) or $18.95 (book paper edition), postage paid in the U.S.A. Add $2.00 per copy for shipping elsewhere. Subscriptions: four issues for $19.95 in the U.S.A. and its possessions, $29.95 in Canada, and $39.95 elsewhere. All payments must be in U.S. funds and drawn on a U.S. financial institution. If you wish to use PayPal to pay for your subscription, email your payment to: *wildside@sff.net*. The publisher may be contacted at:

Wildside Press
Attn: HPL Magazine
9710 Traville Gateway Drive #234
Rockville, MD 20850-7308
www.wildsidepress.com

Writers and artists: Please query us at *lovecraft@wildsidepress.com* prior to submitting any materials. We invite letters of comment, and we assume all letters received are intended for publication (unless marked "Do Not Publish") and become the property of Wildside Press.

H.P. Lovecraft's
MAGAZINE OF HORROR
Fall 2006

Spotlight on
BRIAN LUMLEY

Nonfiction

Fiction

Missed the first few issues of **FANTASY** magazine?
You can go back in time.

☐ YES! Send me issue #1 of FANTASY magazine for just $7.95 ($5.95 + postage)

☐ YES! Send me issue #2 of FANTASY magazine for just $7.95 ($5.95 + postage)

☐ YES! Send me issue #3 of FANTASY magazine for just $7.95 ($5.95 + postage)

☐ **YES! Send me a 4-issue subscription to FANTASY magazine for just $19.95**

Payment is by: ☐ Check (enclosed) ☐ Money order ☐ Visa/Mastercard/Amex

Name _____

Address _____ City _____ State____ Zip _____

Credit card number _____ Exp. ____/____/____

Signature _____ Email address _____

☞ *Mail to:* **Wildside Press, 9710 Traville Gateway Drive #234, Rockville MD 20850-7408**

...or order online at **wildsidepress.com**

THE OUTSIDER

editorial ☉ by Marvin Kaye

Growing Up In The Dark

What first "hooks" us on fantasy and terror? Do you remember? I do. My own lifelong fascination with the genre traces back to my childhood in West Philadelphia. Radio, movies, comic books, and 1940s issues of *Weird Tales* all played their part. The various creepy EC Comics — *The Crypt of Terror, The Vault of Horror,* etc. — came later, but as soon as I could, I pored over the pages of the *Classics Comics* (later *Classics Illustrated*) editions of *Frankenstein, Dr. Jekyll and Mr. Hyde* and other issues, and of course I loved the superheroic adventures of Captain Marvel (he of the Shazam!), and especially enjoyed the odd humorous tilt that spun off a series of tongue-in-cheek Frankenstein comic books.

Most of the early radio shows I was allowed to listen to were funny, but fantasy was not proscribed for children, and I was enamored of Isabelle Manning Hewson's *Land of the Lost,* though some darker fantasy/crime thrillers also were permitted, notably *The Shadow.* I didn't discover *I Love A Mystery* till a few years later, but was instantly caught up in its classic adventure, "Temple of Vampires."

Weird Tales — every so often a luridly-illustrated copy showed up. I always thought my father bought them, and only found out a few years ago that it was actually my eldest sister Dorothy who shares my taste for ghoulery. And it was she who took me across the street to the Haverford Theater every Saturday for months to watch the inevitable western that looked like the same film over and over again (well, they always chased each other around the same rock) and — the good stuff! — the murder mysteries or, better yet, monster movies. The high point of my movie going, though was when I was visiting relatives in Richmond, Va., and got to go to a matinee with one of my cousins. It was a tough choice because we could have gone to the new Danny Kaye movie, and he was one of my favorites, but though I was only seven years old, I got to see one of the scariest films ever made, Val Lewton's *The Body Snatcher* starring Boris Karloff and Bela Lugosi.

And yet all these influences came after the fact. The reason I turned my attention to darker places and themes is that quite simply, I was afraid of the dark. (Who isn't? Paraphrasing H.P. Lovecraft, it's one of three phobias we are born with: coldness, darkness, wetness. No accident that HPL stories frequently begin at night in winter by the seaside.) I'm not sure when my fear of night grew to an uncomfortable proportion; certainly it was early, but I was not so young that I didn't have a fair idea what was out there to be afraid of: ghosts, murderers, vampires, witches, and a lot of bad things without names, just menacing shadows.

I've been told by a few other fantasy writers that they tried to solve the problem the same way as I did: by pretending to be part of the darkness ourselves. "If I pretend to be a scary, wicked thing," I reasoned, "they'll think I'm one of them and leave me alone." Well, that's how I remember buying into fantasy and terror, and if retrospect makes it seem childishly pathetic, and I think it does, still, back then — it worked.

Today, old fears mostly are things of the past; today's terrorists with their inhuman disregard for the value and compassion of life outstrip the monsters and creatures of the night that, by comparison, seem ever so preferable. Maybe my early let's-pretend stratagem is self-fulfilling, but I'd rather break bread and have a beer with the Frankenstein creature than

> Lovecraft says there are three phobias we're born with: coldness, darkness, wetness. No accident that his stories frequently begin at night in winter by the seaside.

Welcome to issue no. 3.

~

With this issue, H.P. LOVECRAFT'S MAGAZINE OF HORROR returns from a brief hiatus to a regular quarterly publication schedule.

We have retooled and redesigned these pages for your enhanced reading pleasure. Or perhaps "pleasure" is the wrong word for this genre — let us say, rather, your still-horrifying but more delicately cultivated reading experience of terror, disgust and abomination.

In issues to come, readers will discover (and, hopefully, derive some sense of fulfillment from) a number of new features appearing within these pages. Your reactions and suggestions are most welcome — write to us online at LOVECRAFT@ WILDSIDEPRESS.COM with the subject line "Reader Feedback."

In the meanwhile: October is a big month for Lovecraft fans across the nation. On page 7, "That Which Has Not Yet Happened" notes two major upcoming H.P.L. festivals.

FROM THE PAGES OF THE PAST

THE GENTLEMAN FROM ANGELL STREET: MEMORIES OF H.P. LOVECRAFT
by Muriel E. Eddy and C.M. Eddy, Jr.
A collection of photographs and memories of Lovecraft by his two close friends in Providence, RI. An intimate portrait of the man by people who knew him best.

ISBN 0970169914 $9.95

NEW COLLECTIONS FOR THE PRESENT

EXIT INTO ETERNITY: TALES OF THE BIZARRE AND SUPERNATURAL
by C.M. Eddy, Jr.
A carefully chosen collection of short stories from an original *WEIRD TALES* author and member of Lovecraft's circle.

ISBN 0970169906 $14.95

AVAILABLE WHEREVER BOOKS ARE SOLD

 FENHAM PUBLISHING

P.O. Box 767 Narragansett RI 02882   401-788-9803

H.P. LOVECRAFT'S MAGAZINE OF HORROR is looking for a few good college interns
to work at our editorial office in Rockville, MD. For details, contact Stephen H. Segal at segal@wildsidepress.com.

any of those monsters, say, at Enron, Iran, or the White House. Hey, even Dracula, untrustable though he was (is?), was a fascinating raconteur . . . *vide* the second and third chapters of Jonathan Harker's diary.

The featured author in this third issue of H.P. LOVECRAFT'S MAGAZINE OF HORROR is the renowned British fantasist Brian Lumley. He has often told tales of the Lovecraft mythos, and one of the two stories he has contributed to this issue is in that tradition; both are memorably eerie. Thanks to his colleague and countryman Stephen Jones for his overview of Mr. Lumley's career, and thanks to contributing editor Darrell Schweitzer for his interview with the great writer.

Three of the new stories in this issue embody unusual aspects of death. Of the many excellent stories submitted to me over the past few years, Mike Allen and Charles Saplak's eerie nautical tale "Strange Wisdoms of the Dead" is one of the most unsettling. Chelsea Quinn Yarbro takes us inland for the dark peasant concerns of "Sugar Skulls," a story that reminds me of, and compares quite favorably with, Ray Bradbury's tales of death and bare-bones (sorry) survival in Mexico.

A comparably lighter note is struck in Jonathan L. Howard's "Exeunt Demon King", a new adventure of his arcane sorcerer Johannes Cabal that evokes both the spirits of theatre and (albeit earlier than I'd originally planned) Yuletide.

The final tale and only reprint in this edition of H. P. LOVECRAFT'S MAGAZINE OF HORROR is one of a handful of stories written by the late Earl Godwin, brother of fantasy and historical novelist Parke Godwin. "Daddy" is one of the most original horror stories I've ever read — and is also a tale of love beyond imagination.

But Is It Horror?

It was that time again. I had once again begun my Extremely Scientific Method of preparing this column, which meant I had gathered together a pile of likely looking recent releases and was looking for Something of Interest.

I decided when I started this column, several installments back, that I would only talk about books I *like:* novels and collections that ranged from the startlingly innovative to the plain old good read, with the occasional interesting failure thrown in. If a book didn't please or surprise me in some new way, it doesn't get mentioned here.

This column, alas, began with a few unmentionables. I scanned page after page of gut-munching zombies, noble and misunderstood vampires, and people who seemed to enjoy killing others with common household instruments. Now, I'm no high-class horror purist. I like your good pulp read as much as the next guy. But there was nothing new here.

The modern horror novel is, according to who you talk to at the moment, either on the verge of a new breakthrough or teetering on total collapse. Modern horror publishing has become totally schizophrenic, with most genre books either appearing as mass market paperbacks or expensive limited editions — so authors are either read by the tens of thousands, or collected by a few hundred people. There is good stuff coming out of both ends of this publishing nightmare (although I don't see a lot of the high-end stuff, as I simply can't afford it) — and there's some not-so-good stuff, too. But at the moment I realized I needed something different.

The different stuff is out there, waiting for all of us. We've just got to look a little harder.

Some of the most interesting horrific stuff I've found is being published without the horror label. Over the last few years, some of the best horror novels I've read have been called something else entirely.

The most obvious place to look for this sort of thing these days are those fantasy/horror/sf hybrids, the so-called "New Weird" novels, mostly coming out of the UK. **Perdido Street Station** by China Mieville is the one to start with. The brain-sucking moths that dominate the second half of the book are a wonderfully icky invention.

Psychological suspense (aka "mystery") can also veer into horror, especially in the masterful hands of

PERDIDO STREET STATION by China Mieville (Del Rey, mass market paperback, $7.99)

THE BRIDESMAID by Ruth Rendell (You'll have to hunt for it at used bookstores)

COIN LOCKER BABIES by Ryu Murakami (Kodansha, trade paperback, $18)

THE LITTLE BLACK BOOK OF STORIES by A.S. Byatt (Bantam, trade paperback, $14)

Ruth Rendell. Any of the books written under her own name explore this territory. **The Bridesmaid** is the first one I read. It's a good place to start.

There are also a number of apocalyptic novels being written all over the world, most famously in the early and mid-period work of J.G. Ballard (you'll often find these filed under "fiction"). To see a more modern example of the form, I would recommend **Coin Locker Babies** by Japanese author Ryu Murakami, a vision of Japan as the end of the world.

So, temporarily lost in the dregs of the genre, I started to wonder what else was out there these days? And so I began my search for books that sounded like horror, even though they were called something else.

The first book I found was a collection by a Booker Prize winner, **The Little Black Book of Stories** by A.S. Byatt, stories compared to fairy tales and the Arabian Nights on the cover copy. Mostly, though, the five long stories in this collection are flat-out modern horror. These are all stories based firmly on character, and all seem rooted, in some way to the "real" world, although perhaps not the nicest corners of reality. But other things enter into the commonplace, things fantastic and terrible, as the stories range across the spectrum from supernatural to psychological horror, so each tale is something of a surprise.

Byatt's writing is spare and wonderful. The very first story, "The Thing in the Forest," concerns a pair of women who had encountered a very ancient creature in the woods when they were young, and how that encounter affected their entire lives. Here's how the author first describes the creature:

"Its head appeared to form, or become first visible in the distance, between the trees. Its face — which was triangular — appeared like a rubbery or fleshy mask over a shapeless sprouting bulb of a head, like a monstrous turnip. Its colour was the colour of flayed flesh, pitted with wormholes, and its expression was neither wrath nor greed, but pure misery. Its most defined feature was a vast mouth, pulled down and down at the corners, tight with a kind of pain. Its lips were thin and raised, like welts from whipstrokes. It had blind, opaque white eyes, fringed with fleshy lashes and brows like the feelers of sea-anemones. Its face was close to the ground, and moved towards the children between its forearms which were squat, thick, powerful, and akimbo, like a cross between a monstrous washerwoman and a primeval dragon. The flesh on those forearms was glistening and mottled, every color, from the green of mould to the red-brown of raw liver, to the dirty white of dry rot."

This is only the first third of Byatt's description, which is quite terrifying in its layering of specific detail. And it is that sort of detail that give these stories their weight, whether their subject matter is fantastic, as in "A Stone Woman," which is, indeed, about a woman who turns to stone, or the other tales, which deal more with the horror of emotional and physical violence. All five stories are well done, and the collection is well worth seeking out by the horror reader looking for something a bit different.

But my quest for horror outside the genre had only begun. Next I wandered over to the young adult section, where I was lucky enough to find **The Book of Dead Days** by **Marcus Sedgwick**. An author's note at the beginning of the book notes that both the ancient Egyptians and the Aztecs had calendars of twelve months, with each month lasting thirty days. But both these civilizations realized there were a few days left over to the year, and the Aztecs, especially, called these the Dead Days, and thought they were full of ill omens.

The book takes place in a city not unlike London, in an age when magic and science are fighting for supremacy, during those five dead days. It concerns a magician named Valerian, his servant known only as Boy, and a young woman named Willow; but the book is also full of ghosts, and murder, and an unholy pact. The horror is mostly in the atmosphere, the violence just off-stage — this is young-adult, after all — which makes it all the more frightening. This is the first of a series, but it is sufficiently self-contained to be enjoyed on its own. If you're tired of waiting for the next Harry Potter, and feel like reading something with the dread right up front, this book is a great place to go.

Wandering into the world of the small press, I next read **The Lovecraft Chronicles** by **Peter Cannon**, an author I'd known from his earlier *Scream for Jeeves*, a book that mixes P. J. Wodehouse with H. P. Lovecraft to very humorous effect.

THE BOOK OF DEAD DAYS
by Marcus Sedgwick
(Wendy Lamb Books, trade paperback, $15.95)

THE ETCHED CITY
by K.J. Bishop
(Bantam Spectra, trade paperback, $15)

THE LOVECRAFT CHRONICLES
by Peter Cannon
(Mythos Books, trade paperback, $15)

Cannon's new book, is, of all things, an alternate history of H.P. Lovecraft's later life. Over the course of three separate narratives, Cannon introduces us to three people who interact with this Later Lovecraft, as the book asks: What if the author had not died young, and had found success in hardcover, in the movies, and had even traveled to London?

The first, and longest of these three pieces, told from the point of view of an adolescent girl who becomes Lovecraft's typist, and gets rather a crush on old H.P., is the most successful, but all three are fun. The book is rather entertaining, but it is not a horror novel. Rather, it is "about" horror — the Lovecraft circle, and the peculiarities of H.P.'s nature. This is the sort of odd little books that I think is best published by a small specialty press. I think you would need at least a passing interest in Lovecraft's writings and his life in order to enjoy the book. But if you're familiar with Lovecraft and his circle, you'll have a good time with Cannon's speculations.

I had high hopes for the next book on my pile, **K. J. Bishop**'s The Etched City. Quotes on the cover compare it to King's "Dark Tower" series, *Perdido Street Station*, Aubrey Beardsley, Italo Calvino, and Jorge Luis Borges! And, if I hadn't been planning to review the book for this column, I would have had no problem at all.

The Etched City is a very good book. So good that I'm still going to mention it here, even though it's not really a horror novel. It's a great fantasy novel, with small touches of horror: creatures that are half-human, half-crocodile; a strange metamorphosis of a major character; a maybe-dead avenger who wields a weapon fashioned from the essence of his dead wife; an axe that leaves its killing blows filled with flowers. It also contains great characterization, a well-realized culture full of violence, evil and poverty, and glorious bits of magic realism. The author (and this, amazingly, is her first novel) uses horror as a small part of a total package to build a mythic whole.

Horror, after all, is first and foremost an emotional reaction, and is part of a great many books that don't wear genre labels. Sometimes these books are a bit harder to find than books from the usual publishers, but sometimes the rewards are greater as well. I think it's worthwhile to keep on looking. ᛞ

I have concluded that Literature is no proper pursuit for a gentleman; and that Writing ought never to be consider'd but as an elegant Accomplishment to be indulg'd in with infrequency, and Discrimination. -- H.P. Lovecraft

From Pulp to Literature

Lovecraftians have a number of important new books to celebrate, starting with *The Dreams in the Witch House and Other Weird Stories*, the third and final Lovecraft volume in the Penguin classics series, edited by S. T. Joshi. Like its two predecessors, *The Call of Cthulhu* (1999) and *The Thing on the Doorstep* (2001), the collection reproduces on its cover a painting by a macabre artist of an earlier century — *The Nightmare* (1781) by Henry Fuseli — a far better choice for such a dignified edition than, say, a piece of pulp art. Alas, Penguin has recently reconfigured its classics series, so that the design isn't consistent with the previous two volumes with their pale blue, as opposed to black, spines. While Joshi has taken some pains to mix minor and major tales in the series, this concluding collection contains mostly Dunsanian dreamland stories. The big exception is "The Shadow Out of Time," delayed until now, one supposes, because the correct text, based on Lovecraft's original manuscript (which went missing for some sixty years), wasn't available in time for inclusion within either of the two earlier volumes.

Necronomicon Press has reissued S. T. Joshi's *H. P. Lovecraft: A Life* in paperback with new cover art by Jason C. Eckhardt. (The three-quarter view of HPL, hand on arcane book before window with curtain drawn back, appropriately evokes a style of 18th-century portraiture.) In a four-page afterword, Joshi surveys the critical and scholarly developments since the publication of this landmark biography in 1996. He corrects a few errors: pointing out, for example, that new evidence indicates that the poet Louise Imogen Guiney wasn't talking in a letter about the Lovecraft family as undesirable boarders during the winter of 1892-93, as L. Sprague de Camp once suggested. As an economy measure presumably, no corrections have been made to the main text.

The Library of America's *Tales*, edited by Peter Straub, stands as perhaps the most notable collection of Lovecraft's fiction since *The Outsider and Others* (1939), the original Arkham House volume. In the Oct. 31, 1996, issue of the *New York Review of Books*, Joyce Carol Oates in a lengthy essay on HPL raised the possibility of his inclusion in this prestigious series, and now Lovecraft is only the third 20th-century "genre" writer, along with Dashiell Hammett and Raymond Chandler, to be so honored. Due to space restrictions, Straub had to be selective, but he's included all the major work, 22 tales in all, plus a few lesser stories that some may deem unworthy of what many will perceive as a "best of" collection. While one can understand why the author of *Ghost Story* avoided the Dunsanian dreamland stories, I for one wish he had chosen, say, "The Silver Key" over "The Lurking Fear." The chronology at the end states that HPL met Frank Belknap Long in 1920, a mistake no doubt derived from Joshi's biography (which curiously also gives their first meeting correctly as occurring in 1922). One can only hope that the august Library of America will take the trouble to get the year right in any reprint.

The recognition conferred by the Library of America has resulted in a gratifying amount of attention in the mainstream press. Favorable reviews have appeared in the *Boston Globe*, *San Francisco Chronicle*, *The Weekly Standard*, and *The Wall Street Journal*. Salon.com, in contrast, has posted a largely negative article by Laura Miller, a prolific and respected critic, who contributed an appreciative piece on Lord Dunsany last fall to the *New Yorker*. In the snooty Edmund Wilson tradition, Miller attacks Lovecraft for, among other things, his bad style, citing a passage — "a hysterical, hallucinatory outpouring that makes Edgar Allan Poe sound like Jane Austen" — from, wouldn't you know, "The Lurking Fear." I like to think she would have had a harder time finding an example of overblown prose in "The Silver Key." 𝄞

> **Lovecraft is the 3rd genre author honored with a Library of America edition.**

THAT WHICH HAS NOT YET HAPPENED...

>> *With every passing year, it seems more American cities and regions have come to embrace their historic weirdos. In 2006, it's New England's turn to get bizarre with its cultural tourism: A group of H.P.L fans have assembled in Brattleboro, Vt., to produce the first-ever* **Lovecraft in Vermont: The Horror in the Hills Festival** *the weekend of Oct. 20-22, featuring speakers, dealers, and tours of the town featured in "The Whisperer in Darkness." Details are available online at lovecraftinvermont.com.*

>> *This year's* H.P. **Lovecraft Film Festival**, *Oct. 6-8 in Portland, Ore., features a mix of films, shorts, and discussion panels, including a fascinating version of Poe's* The Tell-Tale Heart *(with a long-lost voice recording of Bela Lugosi) and talks by Ramsey Campbell, Scott Conners, and Robert Price. More info: hplfilmfestival.com.*

IN *AUDITION,* EIHI SHIINA DEPICTS EVERY MAN'S WORST NIGHTMARE.

Land of Rising Shadows

When did Japanese cinema become so terrifying?

Wanna see something really scary? That was the subject line of an email the writer Christa Faust sent me three years ago. Unimpressed with *The Blair Witch Project,* she claimed to have found a Japanese movie full of the frissons the *Blair Witch* hype only promised. Did I want to borrow the tape?

Sure, I said, somewhat skeptical. Christa's admirably idiosyncratic tastes did not always match mine. Although she was partly responsible for my addiction to Le Cinema du Hong Kong, I remained immune to her passion for low-budget *lucha libre* epics in which masked wrestlers with disturbingly large nipples grappled with dimestore monsters. While hoping for something as sublime as *A Chinese Ghost Story,* I knew I might find this new enthusiasm as baffling as her last, a Mexican horror-comedy in which a balding, overweight Count Dracula protected himself from AIDS by wearing condoms on his fangs and, rather than a rubber bat, transformed into a real if bedraggled looking turkey (ask Doug Winter if you don't believe me).

While prepared to be either entranced or appalled, I expect to be frightened; no supernatural horror film since Nicholas Roeg's 1973 *Don't Look Now* had done that (okay, there was the bit with the striding figure in white in *The Exorcist 3,* but that was a terrific scene in an otherwise unremarkable sequel). Neither artfully flamboyant nor artlessly tacky, the movie that had so impressed Christa proved to be a subtle, somber ghost story, one that for all its technological trappings and subtext of modern anomie, struck (and still strikes) me as the most successful feature-length evocation of the spirit of M. R. James. It was also damn scary.

I'm talking about Hideo Nakata's 1998 *Ring* (aka **Ringu**), which I'd heard of but knew little about beyond its success at the Asian box-office and that it somehow concerned a cursed videotape. If you've seen either it or last year's glossy but to my mind less effective (despite the terrific Naomi Watts) American remake, you know that a grainy VHS bootleg was an appropriate way to first encounter what seems well on its way to becoming the most influential horror film of the past decade. It wasn't until I purchased my first multi-regional DVD player that I realized that Nakata's *Ring* wasn't an isolated phenomena. Germany may have created the genre in the '20s and the British and Italians largely dominated in the '50s and the '60s, but many of the best recent horror films are Japanese.

Some stateside fans are only just now becoming aware of this fact. Five years after its pan-Asian success, *Ring* has been released on a non-frills domestic DVD by DreamWorks, a belated but commendable move at a time when companies like Miramax buy remake rights to Asian films but do their best to keep the original versions off U.S. shelves. The DreamWorks release is titled *Ringu* (the phonetic Japanese approximation of the English *ring.*) In order to avoid confusion with *The Ring* (note the definitive article), their highly successful remake.

I don't have the space to compare the two films at any length or comment on how both depart from Koji Suzuki's source novel (more of a Crichtonesque medical thriller with elements of Campbellian Psi than a traditional ghost story) or the earlier Japanese TV adaptations.

For that and much more, I highly recommend Javier Lopez's Ringworld website, which is (http://ringworld/somrux.com). Suffice it to say that I prefer the quieter and less special effects-happy

RINGU
Released 1998
DreamWorks Video
$19.98

AUDITION
Released 1999
Lion's Gate
$19.98 (uncut edition)

DARK WATER
Released 2005
ADV Films
$19.98

UZUMAKI
Released 2000
Elite Entertainment
$19.98

approach of the Japanese film and miss its Lovecraftian backstory. (Sadako may be the Kabuki version of an M. R. James revenant; she was conceived under circumstances suggesting "The Shadow Over Innsmouth.") Still, the American version has its virtues. While lacking interesting extras, the DreamWorks disc sounds and looks better than the PAL DVD from the UK's Tartan Terror imprint, which prior to the DreamWorks release was the only way to see the film in nonbootleg form with English subtitles.

At least one other touchstone work of modern Japanese horror is now available on domestic DVD, Takashi Miike's outrageous **Audition**. Unlike *Ring,* its shocks aren't of the supernatural variety (although at one deceptive point it looks like it's going to mutate into a melancholy ghost story). It does, however, feature an embodiment of feminine rage as potent as *Ring*'s Sadako. At the risk of saying too much about a film which spends its first hour as a deceptively gentle comedy-drama about middle-aged loneliness before turning into Something Else, I think that the winsome, delicately sad Asami is the most disturbing screen psychopath since Norman Bates.

Be warned; the climax is so graphic that it caused walk-outs when shown at the Anjelika Film Center in New York. Of all the films mentioned in this column, this release sports the most impressive package. The spiffy, slip-cased DVD from American Cinematheque's Chimera Entertainment includes a 24-minute interview with Miike, a half-hour of commentary from him (lending useful insight into the question of how "real" the final atrocities are) and interesting liner notes by Chris Dejardines.

Those interested in exploring the Japanese horror boom further don't have to stop there, nor must they content themselves (as I once did) with bootleg VHS tapes. While my first all-region DVD player cost nearly $300, you can now buy one for as little as what you'd spend on fourth-generation dupes from a gray-market dealer at the World Horror Convention. I recommend the CyberHome 500, which I found for $69.95 at Best Buy. The salesclerks won't tell you this, but just hit the **Eject** button, hit **Stop** and enter **31999** on the keyboard of the remote and you'll get a hidden menu that allows you to turn off the region coding.

But where to buy the DVDs, if you don't live near a Chinatown or Little Tokyo? Poker Industries (www.pokerindustries.com) is a reliable US-based parallel importer that offers Asian and other foreign genre DVDs at decent prices, and which is scrupulous about listing the technical details of their discs. Even though I'm irritated that the latest upgrade makes it easier to access their site via Internet Explorer than Netscape, I still suggest checking them out. Here are a couple of titles to look for:

HOW CAN SPIRAL-SHAPED THINGS KILL YOU? LET THE JAPANESE FILM *UZUMAKI* COUNT THE WAYS.

Dark Water. Also based on a novel by Koji Suzuki, Hideo Nakata's 2002 follow-up to his success with *Ring* and *Ring 2* is already scheduled for an American remake. Ironically, it appears to have influenced the DreamWorks version of *The Ring,* both via the titular imagery and in making the evil revenant a child rather than a young woman.

Yoshimi, a divorced mother fighting to retain custody of her five-year-old daughter, moves into a dreary apartment building with severe plumbing problems. The rooftop tank leaks down through the ceiling and walls and a child's bright red backpack keeps turning up in unexpected places, despite her persistent efforts to throw it away. Soon, she and her daughter are both glimpsing a small figure in a yellow rain slicker, who leaves very wet footsteps behind.

If Nakata's *Ring* was Jamesian (Montague Rhodes rather than Henry), *Dark Water* suggests Ramsey Campbell. It's a quieter, sadder film than *Ring* and lacks that blockbuster's nightmarish finale, but remains an engrossing ghost story, almost doing for elevators and wet spots on the ceiling what Ring did for late night TV broadcasts. The Region 3 NTSC DVD from Hong Kong's Wide Sight Entertainment is anamorphic widescreen and has removable English subtitles. Poker Industries sells it for $14.95.

Uzumaki (2000), aka *The Spiral* (not to be confused with *Ring 2: Spiral*, the alternate first sequel to Nakata's *Ring*) is a harder film to describe. Directed by the single-named Higuchinsky with a visual style reminiscent of *The City of Lost Children*'s Jeunet and

> UZUMAKI manages to evoke Lovecraft by way of David Lynch and even Samuel Beckett.

Caro, the film's plot manages to evoke Lovecraft by way of David Lynch and even Samuel Beckett.

High school student Enriko is dismayed to find her small town first obsessed with and then transformed by spirals. Her boyfriend's father commits suicide in a washing machine, his body twisted into a spiral shape. One classmate becomes possessed by her own coiling Medusoid hair; several others slowly mutate into giant humanoid snails with spiral shells. The film doesn't quite have enough plot to support its 91-minute running time; there's no third-act complication or revelation, no real explanation for the spiral curse. But while more imaginative than chilling, it's certainly worth a look. The Region 3 NTSC DVD on Hong Kong's Universe label has acceptable picture quality, removable English subtitles, and costs $12.99 from Poker Industries.

As *The Spiral*, the film has played the Sundance Channel as part of their commendable Modern Japanese Horror package, along with Hideo Nakata's *Ghost Actress* (aka *Don't Look Up,* an interesting forerunner to *Ring,* otherwise impossible to find with English subtitles) and surprisingly, the uncut version of *Audition.* ʕ

A typical "Monster Boomer," Ian McDowell grew up reading Famous Monsters of Filmland *and* Castle of Frankenstein. *As a teenager, he performed in community theatre with future make-up effects genius Tom Savini, whose ape suit he borrowed on several memorable occasions.*

There are dark spaces in the world...

...but there shouldn't be any on your bookshelf.

SPECIAL 96-PAGE EXPANDED ISSUE!

Weird Tales

IAN WATSON

CHARLES L HARNESS

STEPHEN DEDMAN

GREGORY FROST

APRIL 2006 / #339

U.S. $5.95 CAN $7.50

Cover by Rowena Morrill

☐ **YES!** Send me back issues of *Weird Tales* for just $5.95 each!
(Postage: $2 per order U.S., $4 foreign)

☐ #340 — stories by Jay Lake, Tanith Lee, Sarah Hoyt, Holly Phillips and more

☐ #339 — stories by Charles L. Harness, Stephen Dedman, Gregory Frost and more

☐ #335 — stories by Michael Bishop and Tanith Lee; interview with Terry Pratchett

☐ #328 — stories by Ian Watson, Stephen Woodworth, Donald Barr Kirtley and more

☐ *Worlds of Fantasy & Horror* #1 — stories by Joyce Carol Oates, Ramsey Campbell, Morgan Llywelyn and more

☐ **YES!** Send me a six-issue subscription to *Weird Tales* for just $24, and start me with: ☐ issue #338 ☐ issue #339 ☐ issue #340 ☐ issue #342

Payment is by: ☐ Check (enclosed) ☐ Money order ☐ Visa/Mastercard/Amex

Name _____

Address _____ City _____ State _____ Zip _____

Credit card number _____ Exp. ____/____/____

Signature _____ Email address _____

☞ *Mail to:* **Wildside Press, 9710 Traville Gateway Drive #234, Rockville MD 20850-7408**

...or order online at wildsidepress.com

Brian Lumley

ON LOVECRAFT AND LEGACIES

interview by Darrell Schweitzer

with a bibliographical history by Stephen Jones

He stumbled across Lovecraft's work as a young man in the '60s — and it shaped Brian Lumley's destiny forevermore. Now Britain's greatest vampire novelist shares his thoughts on the genre, the craft, and the author who revolutionized both.

So, Brian, it's been a long while since you first picked up a Lovecraft book — and it changed your life, did it not? It did indeed. When did I pick it up? I think my first Lovecraft came into my possession in Germany, when I was a young guy, maybe 22 or 23 years old. It was *Cry Horror!* A British World Distributors Ltd. paperback, two shillings and sixpence. While I had hit upon Lovecraftian stories before, Mythos stories, namely Robert Bloch's "Notebook Found in a Deserted House" and others of that ilk, one or two *Weird Tales* stories maybe, this was the first time I'd had a real, complete book by Lovecraft. That was it. That was the beginning. All of a sudden I wanted to write as well. I had tried one or two short stories when I was a much younger guy, maybe fourteen or fifteen year old, but all of a sudden, I had a real incentive. Lovecraft had shown me the way just as he had shown many other people the way.

BRIAN LUMLEY'S NECROSCOPE™

ILLUSTRATED BY BOB EGGLETON

LUMLEY: A LIFE IN LETTERS

BRIAN LUMLEY WAS BORN in the coal-mining town of Horden, County Durham, on England's wild northeast coast in 1937. Initially called up for two years' National Service in the British Army when he was 21 years old, he remained for a further 20 years serving as a sergeant with the Corps of the Royal Military Police.

Although he wrote some "humorous" science fiction stories when he was around fourteen years old, Lumley actually discovered his interest in horror fiction while he was stationed in Berlin, West Germany, in the early 1960s. He had come across a copy of Cry Horror! in a YMCA bookshop. It was a 1958 British paperback reprinting of H.P. Lovecraft's collection, The Lurking Fear and Other Stories (1947), and included several of the Rhode Island author's interrelated Cthulhu Mythos stories.

A few years later, while he was stationed in Cyprus, Lumley read August Derleth's anthology Dark Mind, Dark Heart (1962) and realized that Lovecraft's work had a devoted following of writers inspired by the late author's work. Lumley added to his collection of Lovecraftian books whenever and wherever he could. Around 1967 he contacted publisher Arkham House and started ordering Lovecraft material directly from August Derleth. Through their correspondence, Derleth suggested to Lumley that he should try his hand at creating his own Mythos fiction.

It was not long before Lumley began writing during his night shifts. He sent three of his Lovecraft-inspired tales off to Derleth along with an order for some more books. He was astonished when the veteran editor purchased two of the stories straight away and suggested a revision of the third one. >>

He'd shown you the way in a period in which there wasn't a lot of horror fiction being done. That's right. In England we had Ronald Chetwynd-Hayes, who, I think, had already begun to put together some books of macabre fiction. August Derleth at Arkham House, of course. He was called the Dean of Macabre Publishers at the time probably because he was one of the few Macabre publishers at the time. And there was . . . who the hell was it who wrote *The Haunting of Toby Jugg?*

Dennis Wheatley. Wheatley in England was producing macabre books, and some of them were very good for their time. And that was about it. There really wasn't much happening.

But you just wrote anyway without seriously thinking about the markets. I didn't know anything about the markets. I was in Berlin. Since buying *Cry Horror!* I had moved on to Cyprus and picked up *Dark Mind, Dark Heart,* an Arkham House book, full of Lovecraftian bits and pieces, more macabre stories, really enjoyable stuff. I had started to collect Lovecraft and other Arkham House writers. So, from Cyprus I went to Berlin. In my desk duties as a military policeman, after the last drunk had been locked up and the last would-be refugee had been cut to pieces on the wire or the wall or shot, there was nothing much to do. But you couldn't sleep. It was a very dangerous situation. It was a hot spot. It could be the beginning of World War III. So you had to be awake. So I was reading Arkham House books. Several of these books carried August Derleth's address, which I still remember.

You've often rather forcefully expressed the opinion that the Cthulhu Mythos is still an evolving, on-going concern, and consists of more than reading "The Call of Cthulhu" and "The Dunwich Horror" over and over again. Would you care to expound on that? I think you've just done it for me, Darrell. It's the interest in Lovecraft himself which keeps the Mythos swinging. The reason it is still moving along is because people are still finding Lovecraft as an originator. And of course they always will. There are new generations coming up all the time. Now, I say there always will, but that may not be true. When was the last time you read Edgar Allan Poe?

Rather recently, actually, though I admit I've had to review a lot of it because I've been writing introductions for Poe books. Well, yeah . . . but what happens here is that eventually the stories do become dated. We know they're classics, but they do become dated. I couldn't read Dracula again now, for the simple reason that I found it musty in large part twenty years ago, so I've got no doubt I'd find it even mustier now. They do. They do date. And Lovecraft will date as well, eventually. So, the new guys will come along writing in the Mythos, doing it and Lovecraft a favor, because if people stumble across their books first, before they stumble across Lovecraft — which has happened with me on many occasions. People have read my stuff first. I get any number of e-mails which say, "Brian, I am so glad I found your books because I wouldn't have found Lovecraft if I hadn't found your books first, if I hadn't read *The Burrowers Beneath, The Transition of Titus Crow,* or some of your short stories. Then I went looking for Lovecraft." When I read Lovecraft, I went looking for Robert Bloch and the other writers in the Mythos. So it will go on, but it's going to take a hell of a good writer, now, to write an original, interesting, intriguing Mythos story.

If you're correct that Lovecraft's own stories will date, does that mean that the Mythos itself has some quality which could outlast Lovecraft? Is it possible that the time will come when Lovecraft is so dated that no one reads him, but people read the Mythos in the work of other writers? Yes, it's possible. Let's face it. Cthulhu has become one of the classic monsters. You now think of the Wolf Man and Dracula and the Mummy — and Cthulhu. It's a fact. He is one of the classic monsters.

He's also a plush toy. There again. What was that outfit that was doing the classic monsters plastic kits?

"Let's face it – Cthulhu has become one of the classic monsters. You now think of the Wolf Man and Dracula and the Mummy – and Cthulhu."

Aurora. That was about thirty years ago. They didn't have plush toys back then, but there you go. These things have all had their offspring.

It has been argued that Lovecraft is more powerful than other horror writers because he is writing a genuine anti-mythology, an authentic response to the discovery of the vast universe of billions of galaxies, in which mankind can only have a trivial role. Therefore this is a lot more vital than, say, the Mummy, who is surely a local affair. Lovecraft looks outward to the cosmos, where the older mythologies are local and static. Human beings will always want to read about human beings. If we carried your idea about Lovecraft looking outward to the cosmos, the time would come when we're writing stories not about human beings at all, but about the outer cosmos, where we are in fact minuscule in the fate of the universe. I don't see that happening. Writing and reading is human interest. We won't read anything that doesn't have people in it. Yes, we may read about cats because we understand cats. They're our little familiars. But I think people will always primarily have an interest in people and how the universe affects them, and not the other way around.

Lovecraft talks about achieving total externality, with no human interest at all. One wonders if he was talking through his hat a little bit. You can't have a story without characters of some sort. He may have wanted to write without characters. If you check the dialogue in his stories, you won't find a hell of a lot of it. So, you could be right there. He certainly didn't want to write about women much, because the only women in his stories . . . you had the semi-cretin Lavinia Whateley, who did noxious things with Yog Sothoth. You had the woman in "The Thing on the Doorstep."

Asenath Waite. But she wasn't really a woman, remember. That was her father's spirit animating and controlling the daughter's body. That's correct. Maybe Lovecraft had something about women, which with his childhood, you could understand, I think. I think that Lovecraft might have liked my stories, but I don't think he would have liked me as a person. Hey, my idea of a man-woman relationship is a whole lot different than HPL's.

People don't faint a lot in your stories. No, I don't let them do much fainting! They actually make love, too. They don't hold pinkies and tell each other how much they appreciate each other.

You realize that if Lovecraft had lived to a normal life-expectancy, you could have met him. Yes, indeed. As you know, I was born just nine months after he died. That was a fact that was pointed out to me by Donald Wollheim, when he came across to Germany one time while I was still in the Army. This was a fact which I did not know he intended to use. He put it on the back of one of my early books, that I had "inherited the mantle of Lovecraft," because I was born nine months later. But, you know, if Lovecraft knew I was writing Mythos stories he'd turn over in his grave; not because he wouldn't like the stories, but because they come from a different mindset entirely.

Of course he encouraged all of his friends to write in the Mythos. I know he did, but, I'm saying, would I have been one of his friends? [Laughs.]

>> Despite not having an agent yet or any other contacts within the genre, Lumley's first professionally published story appeared in The Arkham Collector Number Three (Summer, 1968). Entitled "The Cyprus Shell," the nine-page tale was inspired by H.P. Lovecraft's horror of the sea and sea food. At the time Lumley had been writing seriously for less than a year.

His next appearance was in The Arkham Collector Number Four (Winter, 1969) with 'The Thing in the Moonlight II'. It was based on a dream the author had and formed the completion of a fragment which, at least in part, was written by Lovecraft. When the story was published in The Arkham Collector it included some minor textual and layout changes which Derleth apologized for. Lumley's preferred version eventually appeared in Fantasy Tales No.5 (Winter, 1979).

With only two published stories to his credit, Lumley made his hardcover debut with two contributions to Derleth's next Arkham House anthology, Tales of the Cthulhu Mythos (1969). Although 'Cement Surroundings' appeared pretty much as the author had written it, Derleth suggested to the newcomer that he should cut his 14,000-word novelette 'The Sister City' by around 10,000 words! Lumley reluctantly agreed, and over two nights he reduced the story by two-thirds. He later reincorporated all the original material and built upon both tales for his first novel, Beneath the Moors (1974), about the discovery of a hidden city beneath the Yorkshire moors. 'The Sister City' also became Lumley's first story to be published in his native Britain when editor Richard Davis included it in The Year's Best Horror Stories No.1 (1971).

Lumley next introduced readers to his occult investigator Titus Crow in 'Billy's Oak', an unconventional >>

>> ghost story with Mythos overtones, first published in The Arkham Collector Number Six *(Winter, 1970)*. The character returned a few months later in 'An Item of Supporting Evidence' in The Arkham Collector Number Seven *(Summer, 1970)*, a story that was inspired by the fascination of the author's coal miner father for museums and ancient civilizations.

Having quickly established himself as a promising new writer to watch, Lumley turned his hand to science fiction with the short post-apocalyptic tale 'Mother Love' in Gerald W. Page's magazine Witchcraft & Sorcery No.6 *(May, 1971)*, subtitled "The Modern Magazine of Weird Tales". He also had two stories in Derleth's next Arkham House anthology, Dark Things *(1971)*. One of these, 'The Deep-Sea Conch', was written as a "reply" to the narrator of 'The Cyprus Shell', with which it forms a diptych.

Amongst Lumley's earliest literary influences was reading William Hope Hodgson's 'The Voice in the Night' in one of his father's books when he was eight or nine years old. The two stories in Dark Things, 'The Deep-Sea Conch' and 'Rising with Surtsey', along with 'The Night Sea-Maid Went Down' and 'Haggopian', form a loose quartet of Mythos "sea" stories by the author.

It turned out that Dark Things *was the final Derleth-edited anthology of new stories to be published by Arkham House. Following a short illness, the writer and editor who had done so much to keep the work of H.P. Lovecraft in print and inspired and supported so many new writers, died of an apparent heart attack on July 4th, 1971. He was just 62 years old.

More than a year earlier, Derleth had suggested to Lumley that they should put together a collection of the writer's stories to be published by Arkham House. The book eventually appeared after Derleth's death as The Caller of the Black *(1971)*, containing 14 stories* >>

He probably would have been polite to you. The only person who ever really got him upset was Forrest J. Ackerman. Really?

The Lovecraft letters are full of unkind comments about Forrest J. Ackerman, largely because of Ackerman railing about Clark Ashton Smith being no good. There was a great flap about this in a fanzine in the 1930's. It was a little undignified for Lovecraft, actually. Yes, well, flaps in fanzines have been happening since time-immemorial. Lovecraft was having arguments in his early amateur publications, and I suppose it will go on forever. Let's face it. You and I may be the best of friends, but we've had our arguments about the Mythos and writing and science fiction and fantasy and horror in general. It doesn't mean that the world will not continue because there are flaps in amateur magazines.

I don't think we've ever had a heated disagreement. Lovecraft got really upset. He was quite unflappable otherwise. One wonders how things would have been if Lovecraft had lived until 1970. Would he have seen anything of mine, I wonder? My first stories were published in 1968. It's possible — if he had still been lucid. Doubtless he would have picked up little Augie Derleth's Arkham House books. There's no question about that. I suppose he would have been pleased with most of them. He probably would have seen my stories. If he'd seen my first one, it wouldn't have anything to do with the Cthulhu Mythos. "The Cyprus Shell" wasn't a Mythos story. Maybe I would have been overawed by his presence and backed off and never written *The Burrowers Beneath* or "Sister City."

I think there would have been considerably less of a tendency to continue the work of a living writer, even if he let you. But remember that in his lifetime he was encouraging people to contribute to his Mythos, de Castro, Hazel Heald.

Lovecraft actually wrote their stories and put in the Mythos elements himself. I know. Who were the others? C.M. Eddy.

The Mythos writers who really wrote their own work were such people as Donald Wandrei, Robert Bloch, Clark Ashton Smith, Robert E. Howard, and so on. These were the ones who were real writers and could do it themselves. That's right. Then you had Robert Bloch's "The Shambler from the Stars."

Or Frank Belknap Long's "The Horror from the Hills," which is based on one of Lovecraft's dreams. That's right. And Lovecraft obviously enjoyed this, because after Bloch's "The Shambler from the Stars," he obliged by killing off "Robert Blake" in "The Haunter of the Dark." So Bloch came back and did — what was that third one?

"The Shadow from the Steeple." I've written to Frank Belknap Long. I have letters from him. I have written to Carl Jacobi. It wasn't that I wanted to apologize for using his ideas in "The Aquarium." It wasn't that I wanted to apologize for using Frank Belknap Long's *Hounds of Tindalos*. I was so keenly interested in these things that I wanted their permission to use them. I would not have done them without their permission. If Lovecraft had been alive, I would not have done my stories without his permission, and there might be a sixth book of Lovecraft's letters from Arkham House, and there would be certain loud-mouth Mythos authorities who wouldn't be able to decry some of the stuff I've done, because I would have had Lovecraft's permission.

You might have had his cover blurbs too. Yeah. That's right.

I'm sure someone would still say, "Well, Lovecraft is just being polite . . ." Of course. Of course. "He didn't really mean to say that. He hates Lumley, actually." [Laughs.]

Of course it would be a whole different field. There very likely wouldn't be any Arkham House, because it wouldn't have been necessary to memorialize Lovecraft in the late '30s if he were still alive. If he'd lived longer, my hunch is that he probably would not have written much for *Unknown*, but he would have had original stories in *Famous Fantastic Mysteries*. Yes, that's probably about right.

And then some material in *Fantasy and Science Fiction* in the early '50s. Yes, and he would of course have seen the era in which Margaret Brundage's covers would not have needed ripping off the magazines. [Laughs.] But he would have seen a lot of far worse covers —

The grand old days of *Thrilling Wonder Stories* when men were men and women wore measuring-cups. Yes. . . . [Laughs.]

Of course no writer can keep on doing the same thing over and over forever, Mythos or not. You've certainly moved on to other things. How that happened was very simple. Thirteen years in the army, I was writing — and I had no contact with fandom and with the publishing business. Everything I was getting published, I had to send myself to publishers. These were unsolicited manuscripts, until Kirby McCauley came along. After August Derleth died, there was no Arkham House to send the stuff to. Well, there was an Arkham House, but there was no August Derleth, and stuff was mounting up. Come 1980, when I was due to leave the army, it dawned on me that there was a bigger world out there. There were more real publishers. I had to find them if I wanted to continue writing, and I could not keep on writing Mythos stories when the main publisher of those stories no longer existed as such.

It wasn't that I was stuck in the Mythos or that I should find my own voice. I always had my own voice. My stories have females in them. My Mythos stories had S-E-X — filthy words in some of them. "The Return of the Deep Ones" has sex scenes in it. Not explicit sex, but one knew that I wasn't writing from an entirely neutral point of view. There were sexual inferences. So I had to find a new market. I had to do something different. Hence *Pyschomech* and eventually *Necroscope*, when I really found my style, found my mode. But my stories always changed. If you look at the Titus Crow series, the first story is a horror story, *The Burrowers Beneath*. The second one, *The Transition of Titus Crow,* is a science fantasy. I was trying all the fields. The third one, *The Clock of Dreams,* is a pure fantasy. *Spawn of the Winds* is again a science fantasy, and *In the Moons of Borea* is a complete fantasy, and likewise Elysia is the most fantastic of them all. I was exploring the entire field.

It seems that the book that made all the difference in your career was *Necroscope.* This is the one that made you a real household name. What happened was, I was living in a little house down in Devon. I had a mortgage. I had very little money in the bank. I certainly couldn't afford to fly across the Atlantic. Paul Ganley, who had published some of my books said to me, "Come across. I've got a thousand books for you to sign. I'll get your air-fare, because there's a cheap fare going," which he did. And Randy Everts, who was publishing a small magazine, *Etchings and Odysseys*, said, "I want to talk to you about using a couple of your stories, and I'll pay for your room in Providence." So I could afford to take my wife, and they could afford to take me, so I went to the World Fantasy Convention. I found the Tor Books party. I didn't know what Tor Books was —

"If Lovecraft had been alive in 1970, there would be certain loudmouth Mythos authorities who wouldn't be able to decry some of the stuff I've done, because I would have had Lovecraft's permission."

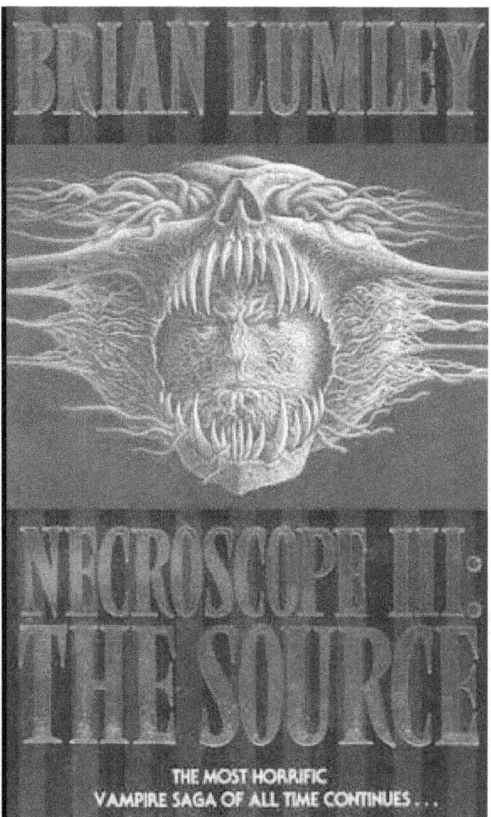

THE MOST HORRIFIC
VAMPIRE SAGA OF ALL TIME CONTINUES . . .

>> and limited to approximately 3,600 copies.

Like other writers before him, such as Robert Bloch and Ramsey Campbell, many of Lumley's Cthulhu Mythos stories updated the eldritch themes for contemporary readers. At Derleth's urging, the author was more than happy to extrapolate such Lovecraftian trappings as the Elder Gods, the Great Old Ones and various forbidden tomes into the modern world. Derleth also prophetically advised him that once he had got Lovecraft's influence out of his system, then he would "really write".

The Caller of the Black introduced Titus Crow's Watson-like assistant Henri-Laurent de Marigny in the character's only "solo" short story appearance, 'The Mirror of Nitocris'. Crow and de Marigny later became the main protagonists of a trio of Lovecraftian novels from Lumley: The Burrowers Beneath (1974), The Transition of Titus Crow (1975) and The Clock of Dreams (1978). Two more Crow stories were also included in the author's second Arkham House collection.

De Marigny was himself the hero of the novel In the Moons of Borea (1979), a sequel to Spawn of the Winds (1978), and a short coda to the series, 'The Black Recalled', was published in the World Fantasy Convention 1983 souvenir book. All the Titus Crow stories were eventually collected in The Compleat Crow (1987, revised 1997).

Despite sporting a title which appears to place it firmly amongst Lumley's series of Lovecraftian pastiches, 'The House of Cthulhu' is in fact the first of a series of high fantasy stories more obviously inspired by Zothique and Hyperborea, the "lost worlds" created by Weird Tales author Clark Ashton Smith. Set in the primal >>

BRIAN LUMLEY

Sorcery in Shad

TALES OF THE PRIMAL LAND

"Lumley deserves a wide audience among those who love Anne Rice, John Grisham, and Stephen King."—VC3A

>> *continent of Theem'hdra – an advanced civilization which existed millions of years before the dinosaurs, Atlantis or Mu – the World Fantasy Award-nominated tale appeared in the premier issue of Stuart David Schiff's influential small press magazine* Whispers *(July 1973).*

Lumley obviously enjoyed writing the Theem'hdra stories, which purported to be transcriptions of manuscripts written by the wizard Teh Atht of Klühn, discovered after a volcanic eruption and passed on for publication to Icelandic professor Thelred Gustau (an anagrammatical homage to August Derleth). Teh Atht's "historical" narratives from Legends of the Olden Runes *were eventually collected in* The House of Cthulhu and Other Tales of the Primal Land *(aka* Tales of the Primal Land Volume 1, 1984), published by W. Paul Ganley's Weirdbook Press in an edition of 1,200 copies. A revised paperback edition appeared in 1991.*

A second series of Primal Land stories featuring swordsman Tarra Khash the Hrossak appeared in Ganley's occasional magazine Weirdbook *and the Italian magazine* Kadath. *These tales of gods, lamias and wizards were subsequently collected in* The Compleat Khash: Volume One: Never a Backward Glance *(aka* Hrossak! Tales of the Primal Land Volume 2, 1991). A novel set in the same milieu,* Sorcery in Shad: Tales of the Primal Land 3, *followed two years later.*

August Derleth had accepted Lumley's first novel, Beneath the Moors, *towards the end of 1970, although it did not see publication from Arkham House until four years later in an edition of around 3,800 copies. The author's third and final volume from Arkham was a second short story collection,* The Horror at Oakdeene and Others, *which eventually appeared in 1977 in an* >>

I knew they existed, but I didn't know what it was. There was a bouncer who stood in the doorway of the party. He said, "Who are you?" I said, "I'm Brian Lumley." He said, "I'm Tom Doherty. Come in to my party. What do you do?" I said, "I write," and I had a dog-eared copy of *Necroscope* in my hand. I said, "You might like to look at this, Tom."

He stood there doing nothing. He said, "Yeah, I'll look at it." So he's drinking his beer and looking at it, and half an hour later when I went out, he's still reading it. He tapped me on the shoulder when I went out and said, "Get in touch with me. Give me a call when you get back home, will you?" I did. Three weeks later Melissa Singer got on the phone and said, not to me, but to my agent, that she would like to buy this one, and *Wamphyri!*, which was also just out and which we shipped over very quickly. My agent said, "There's a third one, *The Source,* which is about a month away from being finished." Melissa said, "We'll buy that one sight unseen as well." So, the next day I didn't have a mortgage and I was rich. I stayed that way every since.

You mentioned once that the first British edition of Necroscope had a cover that didn't work. So they had to recall the book, redo the cover, and then you became rich. Absolutely. The British scene is not as big as the American scene. If you sell 100,000 copies in England, you're doing extraordinarily well. So, the jacket they put on the book in England: there was this rotting skull bursting from the ground. The rotten half was bigger than the fleshy part of the skull. It was a lousy jacket. This was one terrible jacket. And Necroscope, the title, was in Leteraset. You couldn't want for a worse jacket. It wasn't going to sell, and it didn't. So my editor said, "There's something wrong here." So they re-jacketed the book and put a George Underwood cover on it. It went and it kept going, and it still is going. So I was very fortunate. I was fortunate, first of all, to bump into Tom, who has since become a personal friend. Necroscope, incidentally, has sold about 360–370,000 copies in the States alone. It is published in fourteen other countries, including China, Russia, Japan, Greece (of all places), Belgium, France, Germany. I was very fortunate. Yes, this was the one.

You went from there to the very popular subject of vampires — although perhaps it was you who helped make vampires popular. Well, it's possible. I know that Romania is running out of wood. And paper. God knows how many forests have been deforested to print vampire books. In fact they will be printing so many vampire books that there is no wood for stakes anymore. That's why these guys are proliferating. You know that . . . ? [Laughs.]

If you drive a book through their heart, it's not quite the same thing. That's not the same, no.

You've done unusual things with vampires, too. I don't think too many people have taken them to other worlds. Other dimensions. Parallel worlds.

Your vampires don't merely come from an old castle somewhere. They have a much more elaborate background. That's right, but the gate is in Romania. That explains why that place has so many bloodsuckers. In fact there is only one place on Earth that has got more bloodsuckers than Romania. That's Las Vegas.

That's a different kind. Vampire City. I've got a lot of friends there, actually.

You've now made the vampire your own. That is, other people *have* vampires, but there is a distinct *Lumley* vampire. There is indeed, and they are, I am told, unique in their way. They have a real reason for being. They have a real background. There is an explanation of why they have not taken over the world, not even their own world, although they have tried hard enough. Yeah. I changed — well, I didn't change it. I suppose I did what I did with Lovecraft again. I took an accepted mythology and gave it a Lumley touch. But I have not incurred the wrath of orthodox vampire lovers.

You seem to have incurred the wrath of certain Lovecraft critics. Yes, indeed. "Nobody ever erected a statue to a critic." Jean Sibelius.

> "God knows how many forests have been deforested to print vampire books. There are going to be so many vampire books, there will be no wood for stakes anymore."

༄

There are critics who see Lovecraft as a major philosopher, which leads one to a kind of doctrine of Lovecraftianism, and maybe you've become heretical. Oh, he did have his philosophy, which was very real and very genuine to the man. But we're all individuals, Darrell. If we all thought alike and did alike, it would be one hell of a dull, boring old world, wouldn't it?

Do you think there's any influence of Lovecraft in your later works? I've just finished a 21,000-word story, a Deep Ones story. Fedogan and Bremer had remarkable success with *Shadows Over Innsmouth*. It was a good seller. It went into paperback with Del Rey, was picked up by Gollancz in England, done by a Japanese outfit, and still going, doing well. Steve Jones lives by his editing, as most editors do, and it seemed a good idea to do a second book, so Fedogan and Bremer have just signed a contract for a second *Shadows Over Innsmouth*. I don't know what the title will be. It's a similarly-themed book. This time they won't all be English writers. There might be American writers in it as well. I've just done a story called "The Taint," which is an Innsmouth story, set in England. I think it's one of my best. So it's a long time I've been writing Mythos stories. When a good theme occurs, I'll do them again.

Are there echoes of Lovecraft in your non-Mythos writing? Is there a "taint" of Lovecraft which goes through the whole body of your work? Is there anything you've picked up from him? That's an open one —

Certainly he would have been a formative influence. Oh, Heavens yes. Of course he was. I won't say he was profound, the way I've heard some writers say he was a profound influence. I think it was more a desire to be able to write like that. But, having developed that desire and having done it, I very quickly learned how not to write like that. Anything I've picked up from him? I don't know. I sometimes have to fight to stop italicizing the last sentence. [Laughs.] Which I've done, which he did on several occasions. I don't know, a sense of . . . if you can make your reader believe you're more erudite than you really are, you've halfway there. You might be getting there. A love of words, of course. I mean, I never had to scramble to figure out what "eldritch" meant. It was obvious from his writing.

He's kept that word alive. It's one of his gifts to the language. You don't hear it anywhere else. But I'm wondering: "squamous" or "batrachian." Was that Lovecraft who kept those alive, or was that Derleth? [Laughs.]

They're both from Lovecraft, though we tend to use "squamous" only facetiously these days. A lot of these words we use with a knowing sense of irony. I don't think anyone uses "eldritch" with an absolutely straight face anymore. That's right, yes. We no longer see it as a serious thing anymore, do we? [Chuckles.] I can't really say that there is any one Lovecraftian thing that runs through my work. No. I don't think so. I'm not thinking Lovecraft when I'm writing.

You have a very different kind of protagonist. You have a more go-getter protagonist, rather than someone who sits around sifting papers until he sees a pattern eventually. No, no. That's not my people, definitely not.

You have a very different background from Lovecraft. If he had been in the Army,

>> edition of just over 4,000 copies. Despite various references to the Cthulhu Mythos, it was becoming obvious with this new collection that Lumley's earlier incorporation of Lovecraft's concepts into his fiction was beginning to give way to his own distinctive voice as a writer of contemporary horror and fantasy.

However, the author has never completely abandoned the Mythos, and he has described 'Born of the Winds' as one of his favorite stories. It was originally published as the cover story in The Magazine of Fantasy & Science Fiction (December, 1975) and was nominated for another World Fantasy Award. 'The Fairground Horror' was also a Mythos tale, about a run-down carnival and its eldritch attraction, which appeared in Edward P. Berglund's The Disciples of Cthulhu (1976). At this time, writing was still a hobby for Lumley, and if his work was published then that was a bonus.

The author was beginning to build an enthusiastic following on both sides of the Atlantic. In 1976, the fourteenth issue of the British Fantasy Society's journal Dark Horizons honored Lumley with a special edition, and the third issue of the Italian magazine Kadath (November, 1980) was devoted to the writer's work.

Lumley returned to Arkham House with 'The Second Wish' in New Tales of the Cthulhu Mythos (1980), edited by Ramsey Campbell. Lumley re-wrote the ending at the request of the editor but reverted to his original version when the story was reprinted in subsequent collections.

In December 1980 Lumley decided to finally leave the army, after having completed twenty-two years of service, and take up writing full time. Now able to flex his creative muscles, he experimented by producing the ancient Egyptian novel Khai of Ancient Khem (1981) and the science fictional Psychomech (1984), >>

Author of the bestselling Necroscope series

BRIAN LUMLEY
FRUITING BODIES AND OTHER FUNGI

"Should link Lumley's name with Stoker, Rice, and Lovecraft."
—Fear magazine on Deadspawn

>> *Psychosphere (1984) and Psychamok (1985) trilogy.*

However, the author did not forget his Mythos roots. Lumley had cited 'The Shadow Over Innsmouth' as his favorite Lovecraft story, and he paid tribute to the tale with his short novel 'Return of the Deep Ones' which was first serialized in Fantasy Book No.11 *(March, 1984), No.12 (June, 1984) and No.13 (September, 1984).*

Lumley remained in Lovecraftian mode for 'The Statement of One John Gibson' in Crypt of Cthulhu No.19 *(Candlemas, 1984). It was a sequel to the story 'The Diary of Alonzo Typer', which Lovecraft revised from a draft by William Lumley (no relation). 'Cthaat Aquadingen' in* Crypt of Cthulhu No.23 *(St. John's Eve, 1984) purported to be a brief passage from the author's mythical volume of forbidden law.*

One of Lumley's most memorable short stories during this period was 'Necros', a clever twist on the vampire theme that first appeared in The Second Book of After Midnight Stories *(1986) edited by Amy Myers. It was also chosen by editor Karl Edward Wagner for his annual anthology,* The Year's Best Horror Stories XV *(1987) – the first of five appearances Lumley would make in that prestigious series published by DAW Books. 'Necros' was also one of three half-hour pilot episodes adapted for* The Hunger *(1997), a made-for-cable TV anthology series created by Jeff Fazio and hosted by Terence Stamp.*

Despite the popularity of his Cthulhu Mythos-inspired fiction, from this point on Lumley's writing career would be closely associated with all things vampiric. Originally published as a paperback original in Britain with typically pulpy cover art, Necroscope *(1986) was not an instant success. A clever blending of spy fiction and the supernatural, the novel featured Harry Keogh who had the eponymous talent of talking with the dead and the undead. When Lumley's editor suggested that the book be re-jacketed with new artwork the following year, sales began to pick up.*

A sequel, Necroscope II: Vamphyri! *(UK:* Necrocope II: Wamphyri!, *1988) reunited Keogh and the "espers" of the British Secret Service's E-Branch in their battle against the vampires, and the author took the conflict to the parallel Sunside/Starside "Vampire World" for* Necroscope III: The Source *(1989). His fans approved of the change of locale, and the book won the Fear magazine readers' award for Best Work by an Established Author.*

Meanwhile, as a result of an opportune meeting with Tom Doherty at the 1986 World Fantasy Convention in Providence, Rhode Island, Lumley sold the first three "Necroscope" titles to Tor Books in America. The first volume was issued in 1988 with a distinctive skull cover by artist Bob Eggleton and became an instant best-seller. Since that time the series has never been out of print and Lumley's magnum opus has been published in numerous editions and languages around the world.

The author expanded his ever more complex chronology in Necroscope IV: Deadspeak *(1990), but finally decided to kill off his lead protagonist in* Necroscope V: Deadspawn *(1991). However, his legions of fans and canny publishers were having none of it. With the "Necroscope" books now going through multiple printings, the author set about producing a spin-off series. Set on both Earth and Sunside/Starside,* Vampire World I: Blood Brothers *(1992),* Vampire World II: The Last Aerie *(1993) and* >>

things would have been very different, I'm sure. I'm sure. He would have ended up gibbering if he'd been 22 years in the Army. He would have wound up in one of those padded cells he's so fond of.

When Lovecraft actually tried to volunteer for military service in 1917, he said it would either cure him or kill him. But his mother got him first. Yes. She knew it would kill him.

It probably would have, if he had gone to the trenches. I'm sure. No, I don't think he was built for Army rigors. There's a point that struck me, some time ago, about "The Call of Cthulhu." You've read *Dracula*. Lovecraft had read *Dracula*. Now then, how do you see these sensitive dreamers, the Wilcoxes and de Castros and what-have-you? If you will recall, in *Dracula*, Renfield equates very much to these people. Renfield knew the Master was coming. He spoke to him telepathically across the waters. He said, "I'm coming." Renfield was munching lesser things. When the Master came, he'd be eating much bigger things. Your sensitive dreamers in the waking world have been contacted by the Master, who's coming. People in madhouses go crazy all over the world. You'll remember where Renfield was. I'm sure that got through to Lovecraft.

I think what also got through to Lovecraft on that story was Arthur Machen's "The Great Return." But he found the Holy Grail to be way too prosaic, so he supplied something a lot more interesting. You're probably right. I think he learned a thing or two from Machen, and from Algernon Blackwood. Of course he had a great love-affair with "The Great God Pan," didn't he?

He particularly liked "The White People," which you can see coming out in "The Dunwich Horror." His thing against Blackwood, of course, was that he romanticized too much. He had too much of the soppy, soft stuff in his fiction for Lovecraft's taste. But yeah, I think something of Dracula might have gotten through to Lovecraft. But I don't think anything of Lovecraft has lingered in me, really. If I stumble across a Lovecraft theme that needs developing, a Mythos idea that hasn't been done yet, I'll do it. The new one I was talking about, this 21,000-worder for the new Innsmouth book. It's a Mythos story, but you won't find great, old books in it. You won't find long reams of references to Mythos locations and characters. But it's nevertheless a very, very real Mythos story, which you'll find out when you see the thing.

We're still hoping for another "Fruiting Bodies." That's one of the classics *Weird Tales* published. And if an idea occurs which can develop into such a story, you can guarantee that it will be written. Of course. I thoroughly enjoyed writing that one. It wrote itself. I had no struggle at all. It just threw itself on the paper. I suppose every writer does it. They have novels or short stories which some force lifts above the rest of their work. It happens to all of us, and that's one of them. The same for *Necroscope*, of course. It has the same type of force underneath. So it rose up above the rest of my stuff. But it dragged the rest of my stuff along with it. Stories and books which had only been published by small presses are now published in hardback by major presses, on the strength of Necroscope. And they're doing well.

You now have a substantial number of books out there. Indeed I have. It's very pleasant. I need a bigger house now, for my shelves, foreign editions.

I think the best a writer can hope for is to be hit by lightning like that a couple times in his life. Think of Bram Stoker again. He wrote a lot of other books, but if he hadn't written *Dracula*, no one would care about any of them. That's right. Well, lightning has struck me on a couple of occasions. *The House of Doors* did very well for Tor. There were a couple hundred thousand sales there. The Psychomech trilogy did very well for Tor, and for me. A good many sales there too. But I think *Necroscope*, the series, is running about... I must be pushing three million in America alone. Well, I'm not going to run out of brandy or cigarettes in a while anyway.

Has there been any Hollywood interest? Oh, yeah. It's got to be the strangest place on Earth, Hollywood. When I get the right contract with the right people, and it has the right names on it, and they're willing to pay — you see, this is not me being entirely mercenary. I would not even attempt to suggest that they stick to the story. They're probably going to want to get rid of Harry Keogh, for instance. You know, "*Necroscope*. Great book. But do we really need this guy who has his own mode of conveyance between places? How about these vampires? Do we really need this vampire world? Can we make the hero a woman?" If it ever happens, I'm going to say, "The contract's good. The number of zeroes on the bottom is correct. Don't approach me to have anything to do with the script." If the movie's great, then I'll say, "Well, what did you expect?" And if it's a stinker, I'll say, "Well, it had nothing to do with me."

So you take the money and run. Yeah. But not because I wouldn't want it to be successful. But I'm absolutely certain that I wouldn't have any influence on it anyway. Once you've sold it, once you've signed that contract, that's your soul, brother, gone. Look what they did to "Necros," on The Hunger series.

I haven't seen it. They did "Necros," my story, on one of those trilogies.

And what was left of it? You wouldn't recognize it.

The satisfaction of the printed page is that you can control more of what is on it. That's right. It's not a bad idea to accept the money for "Necros." Of course it was very, very good money for a short story. But it wasn't my short story that they did.

I have a theory that what Hollywood often does, to avoid lawsuits, is find the oldest story they can that's vaguely similar to what they wish to make, buy the rights to it, and then ignore it. Then if someone says, "You stole my idea," they can say, "Take it up with Lumley." Yeah, that's right.

Beyond the new Mythos story you've mentioned, what else are you working on these days? There's a science-fiction story I'm working on. It's a novel. It may be the first time that I've had to go back and rewrite. I've set the thing in the Solar System. But there are reasons now why I may not be able to use the Solar System. I may have to go further out, to find or design another star system. So that's at around 120 pages, and it may stay there while I sort it out in my head. It's very Jack-Vanceish, not a pastiche of Vance, but very Vanceish, because I have been in love with his stuff for a long time. Everything that Jack Vance has written, I've read two or three times. If you read his stuff long enough, eventually you'll start to sound like that when you write yourself. Also, of course, I love his style. So, yeah, I would say a cross between Vance and Lumley, with perhaps some horror, a load of horror; but it will be a real science-fiction story.

Meanwhile, I suppose, Darrell, as the ideas occur, I shall try to write some "Fruiting Bodies"-style stories over the next couple of years. I'm not sitting down to write any more novels. There is a new Necroscope book due out in June, a couple novelets and a short story, and a couple other bits and pieces.

But no more novels for a while? Necroscope, no, it's finished. It's done.

You haven't fallen into that temptation that came to Frank Herbert, when they said, "Here's five million dollars. Write another one." If they offered me five million dollars, I would start writing now. Today. I would finish it in two months' time. It would be just as good as the others, because for five million dollars I can make it as good as they want it. But that's not likely to happen, Darrell.

But you can hope. Thanks, Brian.

[*Recorded at Jersey Devil Con, April 27, 2003*] *G*

>> Vampire World III: Bloodwars *(1994)* pitted Harry Keogh's son against his vampiric twin brother. With each of the volumes taking a year to write, the author considered his follow-up trilogy amongst his best work to date.

Although Lumley once again thought about ending the "Necroscope" series, his fans clamored for more. Bowing to the inevitable, he gave them the two-volume set Necroscope: The Lost Years Volume One *(1995)* and Necroscope: Resurgence The Lost Years Volume Two *(UK: Necroscope: The Lost Years Volume II, 1996)*, which covered a gap in the original narrative between Vamphyri! and The Source. He followed up with the three-volume "E-Branch" series, Necroscope: Invaders *(1999)*, Necroscope: Defilers *(2000)* and Necroscope: Avengers *(2001)*, featuring new Necroscope Jack Cutter pursuing a trio of Wamphyri lords around the world.

The success of the "Necroscope" books also spawned an industry of collectible figurines and tie-ins, including various comic book series and a role-playing game. A number of music groups have taken their name or recorded material inspired by the series, and KeoghCon has been held annually in Britain since 2001 for fans of the books.

Lumley returned to the Cthulhu Mythos and the race of ichthyoid Deep Ones in 'Dagon's Bell', a powerful novella that was set on the north-east coast of England. It was published in Weirdbook No.23/24 *(1988)*. 'Big "C"' was a transmutative science fiction story for Lovecraft's Legacy *(1990)*, an anthology of original tales in honor of H.P. Lovecraft's centennial edited by Robert E. Weinberg and Martin H. Greenberg. In contrast, Synchronicity, or Something *(1988)* was a light-hearted novella about Cthulhu Gaming published as a chapbook by Carl T. Ford's Dagon Press in a 350-copy signed and numbered edition.

During this hugely productive period, Lumley also published the stand-alone novels Demogorgon *(1987)*, Elysia: The Coming of Cthulhu *(1989)* and The House of Doors *(1990)*. Inspired by the author's love of the Bing Crosby and Bob Hope series of Road movies from the 1940s and '50s, he set the exploits of his characters David Hero and Eldin the Wanderer in H.P. Lovecraft's exotic Dreamlands for the novels Hero of Dreams *(1986)*, Ship of Dreams *(1986)* and Mad Moon of Dreams *(1987)*, plus the collection Iced on Aran and Other Dreamquests *(1990)*.

The Winter 1989/90 edition of Weird Tales was a Special Brian Lumley Issue that featured an interview with the author and three new stories, while an extract from Necroscope III: The Source in Fear No.8 *(August, 1989)* was voted by the readers as their favorite piece of fiction published in the magazine by an established author.

Then in 1989 Lumley suffered a major heart attack. Although he made a full recovery, it was a warning to slow down which the author heeded. He remained a regular attendee at conventions on both sides of the Atlantic, and in 1991 he was co-Guest of Honor with Dan Simmons and Jonathan Carroll at the British Fantasycon XVI. His science fiction story 'Gaddy's Gloves' was published in the program book. The following year he filled the role of Master of Ceremonies at World Horror Convention II in Nashville.

Fruiting Bodies and Other Fungi *(1993)* was the first major collection of Lumley's fiction for more than 15 years. The book contained "a witch's dozen" tales and featured some of the author's best work published over the previous two

>> CONTINUED ON PAGE 34 >>

ILLUSTRATION BY STEPHEN MCSWEENY

HIS JOB WAS TO NURTURE
THE PLANTS — BUT THEY DIDN'T
APPRECIATE IT MUCH ANYMORE...

The Man Who Killed Kew Gardens

(originally published 2004 in a 100-copy limited edition hardcover by Delirium Books)

by Brian Lumley

The banks of makeshift air filters were whirring away, working overtime in the concrete ceiling of the great Operations Room, once the basement of the biggest shoe store in central London's Oxford Street. At first the monotony of their massed, whistling hiss was an aggravation—not unlike the subdued howling of an airplane's jet engines coming through the fuselage walls, which if you're subjected to it long enough will eventually turn into white noise—and I had been listening to the air filters for quite some time.

I was there early; I liked to have time to myself, to sit and think before my audience arrived. My audience: the flamers, slashers, poisoners, mulchers, and acid sprayers. An army, actually, made up of sections, squads, platoons. I was here in the role of a Commander: to direct and inspire them, warn and forearm them; to issue their orders for the day or, where some of them were headed, for the endless night of underground London.

Why me? Probably because I'd seen the start of it, issued the very first warnings, understood—as best possible—what had happened and was still happening . . . which made me as good a choice as any, apparently. As a conventional general there's no doubt I would be a dismal failure, but until recently I had been the assistant director at Kew Gardens. Enough said.

Rills of dust, dislodged by the vibration of distant jack-hammers, trickled down from the ceiling, were stirred a little by the draft from the air filters. Somewhere up above they were digging out the Green, spraying acid, preparing to lay concrete and gradually turning London grey. And the sooner the better, I thought, but never quickly enough.

The sound of muted footsteps and the scrape of steel-framed chairs on the gritty floor brought me upright in my seat behind my desk on the podium. Two young men, yawning, gaunt-faced, had seated themselves side by side in the third row of four hundred as yet empty chairs. Early birds, new to the game, they awaited their instructions. Well, let them wait. The hundreds were still to come trickling in.

And not only here but all over England, all over the world. For each city had its volunteer army, and each morning the war started all over again. Indeed, it never stopped, couldn't ever stop, daren't stop. Not if we were to survive. The night shifts were coming off now, and the day shifts—the morning forays—were soon to begin. But never a stranger war than this.

The cities: they were our redoubts, concrete islands floating in an enemy ocean. As for the enemy: there were millions of square miles of him . . .

My notes were before me; updated every three or four hours during the night as reports from the battle areas came in, they were as current as could be. My job was simply to read them out loud to the army and then send the men out to their battle locations. But not until the troops were gathered here en masse.

Even as I thought that thought, more scraping sounded from the back of the marching ranks of empty chairs as another bunch of early birds adjusted their seats. And more dust came smoking down as the distant jackhammers started up again.

I tapped my microphone's grid and was reassured by its pop and crackle, then sat back. And with time to spare I let myself slump down in my seat a little, let my mind wander, remembering how it all began.

It was the meteorite, for sure. But it was probably more than just that. It may also have been—just may have been—what they were doing with the crops: genetically modified food. The scientists, botanists, geneticists, had engineered it so that the green things could fight back; fight disease, weeds, bugs, too much sun, hard rains, and yet still prosper in the poorest soil, growing stronger and giving a better yield. We'd made it easier for them to conquer all of their worst enemies, without taking into account that we were their worst enemy. We were the ones—men, and the animals we bred—who ate them for God's sake! And now they're eating us.

Genetic modification, yes, and also the meteorite. In fact, mainly the meteorite.

It was a small thing, three and a half inches long, two and a half wide, like a big egg. A lump of pockmarked rock, seared black at the fat end, convoluted like a morel or a brain coral at the thin end. Not a meteorite shower, like in The Day of the Triffids, just one small rock. And no one woke up blind, and no one was in any way affected. Not at first, anyway.

But that first year: well, we might as well have been blind for all the attention we paid. I remembered it like it was yesterday.

Three years ago; just three years, my God! Two-thirty on an early June morning; a clear starry sky outside my window; something had started me awake. A pistol shot? The echoes of a drum roll quickly fading on the still, small-hours air? Thunder? No, not thunder. No way. So what, then?

I got up, went to the window and opened it wide, looked out and up and away. A vapour trail, curving down out of the stars, was already dispersing, blown on the soft night breeze. A trace of cordite or sulphur stink drifted in the air, also dispersing. And fifty or so yards away, in my next-door neighbour's garden, a thin column of smoke was spiralling up from the rose beds.

Had something crashed? Well obviously, but not an airplane, or it would be visible and there'd be an inferno. Had something fallen off an airplane, perhaps? Or a fragment of space debris, a bit broken off from one of the myriad satellites up there? Or . . . could it perhaps have been a meteorite?

It had taken me one or two minutes to come fully awake, so that by the time I'd thought all these things through the smoke from my neighbour's garden had thinned to nothing, likewise the vapour trail in the sky and the gunpowder plot smell. And everything seemed back to normal.

Except, of course, it wasn't . . .

He was called Gordon Sellick, a retired army colonel whose wife had died several years ago, and he lived next door, mainly in his garden . . . in fact he lived *for* his garden, because that was his life now. But when I say "next door" don't misunderstand me. We were neighbours, but ours were fairly large detached houses, each set in a quarter acre, with long gardens that ran parallel down to the river. A solitary type myself, I enjoyed living in the country a few short miles from my work. Commuting was easy and I didn't have to spend too much time in the cluttered noisy world between gardens, mine and the more extensive, more exotic ones at Kew.

I could see Gordon Sellick at a distance in his garden just about any old time, or close up to talk to on a Friday night in the Olde Horse and Carriage, our village pub at the bend in the river. But this thing from the sky had landed on a Saturday and I wasn't about to wait the week out. Up at eight, I breakfasted and then went round to his place.

He was in the garden, as I'd suspected he would be. And he had found the meteorite.

"So you heard it," he said, beckoning me closer.

"I'd have had to be deaf not to!" I answered. "Is that it?"

Sellick was leaning on his spade in the middle of a bed of beautiful roses, a few in full bloom but many just now budding. At his feet, a small crater was plainly visible, with good dark earth thrown out in typical ray fashion. "Went in about a foot, maybe an inch or so more," he said. And he handed it over, this rock as I've described it, which he'd only just this minute dug out.

"A meteorite," I nodded, brushing dust and dirt off it. "A good job it didn't hit the house. Would have come right through the tiles!"

"Would have been hot, too," he answered. "Gave me a hell of a fright! Rattled the windows like billy-o, but it doesn't seem to have damaged my roses. I'd have been pretty mad about that."

Gordon Sellick was all army. A six-footer in his youth, but beginning to bend a bit now, he still had his curling handlebar moustache and bristling brows—far more hair on his face than above it—and his shiny dome was brown as can be as a result of his interminable gardening. Out in all weathers, ex-Colonel Sellick.

I examined the rock, which was heavy. "This rounded end . . . fried off and blackened by atmospheric friction." I offered my opinion. "And the pointed end . . . hmmm! Looks odd." I frowned. "Might be crystalline. Some metallic ore forged in an exploding star, then pitted and patterned in the frozen deeps of space."

One of Sellick's ample white eyebrows went up, in something of surprise I supposed. "So then, you're a bit of a poet—eh, what? Well, can't complain about that, what with my garden and my roses and what all. Roses? Bloody flowers? Why, they'd have laughed me out of the bloody officers' mess! Funny the things a man can get up to, when he's on his own and there's bugger all else to do."

He was a lonely one, the old colonel.

"What'll you do with it?" I handed the meteorite back.

He shrugged. "Oh, I'll make a few enquiries. Offer it to a museum. Might even try to sell it. See if they can find any of those Martian bugs in it—eh, what? Hah! And if none of that works, I'll sit it in a pot indoors with some of my cactuses."

In fact it went to a museum, into a case behind good thick glass. Best place for it. Better still if it had never arrived here at all . . .

SHOOTING STARS, COMETS, meteorites. The way they've shaped this world of ours . . . it's incredible. And I wonder how many people have thought about it. I look back at all the mass extinctions, at what happened to the dinosaurs, and I wonder.

But for that BIG rock all those millions of years ago, it's even possible that some kind of dinosaur might be lording it in the world right now, living in dinosaur cities, and facing this new unthinkable threat instead of us. Unthinkable in that none of us would ever have thought of it.

But in fact the big rock landed, the dinosaurs were killed off, men evolved, and before you knew it these three kings were following a different kind of shooting star, one that didn't so much shoot as creep across the sky. And didn't that turn things around—"eh, what?" I'm told that some eighty per cent of all the world's wars were caused by religion, but not this current conflict, though it's a safe bet there's a babble of religious lunatics out there right now blaming it all on God . . .

Chairs were scraping again, and had been for some little time. Looking up, I met the massed weary gaze of maybe a fifth of my command—eighty men and youths—drooping where they'd fallen into their chairs. Barely recovered from yesterday's exertions, they slumped there, their legs stretched out before them, their arms hanging limp. But in little more than half an hour's time, ready or not, they'd be joining battle again, trying to avenge the comrades they'd lost yesterday.

Lost comrades, yes.

I THOUGHT OF old Sellick and his garden, the day he called me over, maybe six weeks after the meteorite incident, to show me the ivy growing up the bole of a fifty-year-old magnolia.

"What do you make of that?" he said.

But of what? So-called "expert" that I was, that I am, I couldn't see what he was on about, not at first. "The ivy?" I said.

"It's a decorative variety, probably an Asian strain of Hedera helix, a five-lobed climber that's essentially fragile, and—"

"Six-lobed," he cut in. "Down near the bottom there, last year's growth: five-lobed. But up here, this new growth: each leaf has six lobes. And that's not all. The outer lobes on each leaf have tiny hooks to fasten to the tree. It can grow a damn sight faster if it doesn't have to root itself first. And it's not so bloody fragile, either! This is a mutant strain, or I'm not an ex-Guards colonel. Eh, what?"

I almost laughed, half-laughed, but managed to hold it back while making a mental note to consult the ledgers at Kew. There would be notes on this one, for sure. But still—and perhaps a little flippantly —I couldn't resist saying, "Colonel, you'll be telling me next there are four-leaved clovers on your lawn!"

"Yes." He nodded, deadly serious. "And quite a few with six leaves, too. Eh, what? I've been preserving them for posterity, pressing them under 'flora' in my old gardening dictionary, for at least a fortnight now!" Then he showed me his right forearm: a fresh red scratch deep enough to leave a scar. "See this? Got it from my 'thornless' roses—by God!" He scowled at the sore red gouge. "And what do you think of that? Eh, what?"

I scratched my head. "Something in the pollen? GM rapeseed maybe? I remember they were experimenting with it last year in a field not a quarter of a mile away. Some people from Friends of the Earth and a slew of other so-called eco-friendly groups were down there, ripping it out as quickly as they could plant it. But they didn't get it all. The police were there dragging them away, putting a stop to it. And then, just lately, there's been this problem with the bees."

"Eh, bees?" the colonel queried, somewhat absentmindedly. "Never bother with the little buggers. Eh, what? Got enough on my hands with the greenfly, sod 'em all! I did get stung once, though." Frowning, he sat down in one of his favourite places: a rustic oak bench where it circled the magnolia. And resting his back against the bole, he squinted up at me and asked, "So what's that you were saying? Something about the bees? Come to think of it, I haven't seen a bee in quite a while."

"That would be about right," I told him. "It seems there's something of a scarcity. The local beekeepers are complaining that the workers haven't been making it back to their hives."

Sellick clenched a military jaw, narrowed his eyes, gloomed out over his quarter acreage. "It's not right," he growled. "It doesn't feel the same. This year—I don't know—it's like it isn't my garden at all! Ever since that bloody meteorite! Well, bollocks to it! One way or the other, I'll get my garden back." And starting to his feet: "It's Friday. Do you fancy a pint?"

And I did, so we took the river path and made our way down to the Olde Horse and Carriage . . .

The following Monday I spent an hour looking for Sellick's ivy in the manuals at Kew Gardens. I never did find it, though.

And I never will. It simply isn't there, never will be unless I name it and register it myself; name it after old Sellick, perhaps?

If ever I get the chance.

If we win this war with the rest of the damned foliage: the ivies, roses, and clovers—and the fungi, mosses, and ferns—these and every other botanical order and species that was ever catalogued, all of them changed now and forever changing.

Every damned one of them. Hundreds, thousands of seething, continuously mutating species, most of them hostile to animal life, just as animal life was once inimical to them . . .

MY MIND WENT sideways again. Meteorites and shooting stars.

Those previously "crazy" people who believed that life came to Earth on meteorites or in the tails of comets. I mean, that was something I'd never been able to take on board! Here we had a world of soft oceans and rocks worn down into soils that were simply screaming to be inhabited; an oxygen rich atmosphere and free running rivers of fresh water; black smokers pouring their chemicals into the depths of soupy seas, and lifebuilding ribo-nucleic acids galore. Was it any wonder life happened here?

And then on the other hand we had this "ridiculous" theory of maggots from Mars and other places: space-rocks falling out of the skies to seed the predawn Earth with life. That was what I couldn't get my head around: rocks, without air, water, any-damned-thing at all, cruising the universe's most deadly environment, outer space, with these dormant seeds clinging to them. How in hell did those seeds get stuck on the meteorites, or in the comet's tail, in the first place? Where did they come from?

And that's not the end of it. For then this chunk of interstellar debris comes hurtling down at tens of thousands of mph, gets burned black from atmospheric friction—without damaging the seeds, of course—and slams down with sledgehammer force, releasing, but not hurting, its passenger/s. For me, that just wasn't logical. Not then, anyway.

No, for then I'd believed in Gaia, Mother Earth, Ma Nature, the planet perceived as a living entity. And that was where I'd made my mistake, me and thousands of others. We'd been thinking on a less than cosmic scale —indeed a microscopic scale—that was typical of human egocentricity; thinking in terms of a tiny little mudball Earth-nature, and almost completely ignoring the fact of the great big universe out there. Much like the Inquisition, we'd considered our world as the "Center of Everything," when the center of everything was an entire Big Bang away back at the beginning. What we should have been thinking wasn't Gaia but Galactica, or at the very least Megagaia: not Earth-mother but Galaxy- or Universe-mother.

A nature through all space and time that's just waiting for the right conditions. Planets form around a star; they cool; Ma Nature—Universal Nature—is waiting. She tried before, but her babies got burned up. No problem; she has plenty more; it's just a matter of hitting the right place at the right time. For after all, how many dandelion seeds land on rocks or in deserts or oceans? A very hit-and-miss process, true: trial and error, but they get there in the end. And time is on Megagaia's side.

So eventually the time is right; another rock falls out of the sky, slams down on the surface of this entirely conjectural planet. There are the makings of life on the new world, perhaps even the first amoebic stirrings on the fringes of soupy oceans, and that's what Universal Ma Nature is looking for. That's what she does. She assists. She releases the meteorite's gasses, or whatever it is that those bloody things contain: the catalysts that form chains in the RNA, that bring about life or—where it already

exists—accelerate its evolution!

It was guesswork, of course, science fiction, but . . . just suppose I was right? And now I'm not thinking some conjectural world but Earth again. If I was on the right track, then maybe this wasn't the first time this had happened. Back then, after the big lizards and their killer rock, maybe there was another space pebble, something that balanced things up again, brought about mutations, caused life to continue. The dinosaur survivors became birds, and a certain branch of scared little mammal creatures became monkeys and then men.

And why not? I mean, they're still looking for the missing link. And maybe I can tell them where to find it: behind glass in a museum in a town not far out of London . . .

TWO AND A HALF years ago, that might have been when I poisoned Kew— but accidentally, of course. Anyway, Kew wasn't the only thing that was dying. Lots of things died.

I remember a certain story, a piece of fiction. (I used to read scads of macabre stuff, anything from E. A. Poe to Stephen King.) This one was by an American author whose name I've since forgotten. But he was very good. Coincidentally, it concerned a colour out of space, something that crashed out of the sky on a meteorite. It seems especially relevant now . . . though nowadays I can't think why I chuckled at the idea of malevolent, shining mutant skunk cabbages! Or I can . . . but it no longer strikes me as funny.

IT WAS THE LAST Saturday of summer. I had been down to the Olde Horse and Carriage last night, but old man Sellick hadn't shown up. That was peculiar; the colonel liked his Friday night pint. Something else that was rather odd: the pub's usually excellent menu wasn't nearly up to scratch. Meat, but no fresh vegetables . . . only frozen ones. Fish, but no homemade chips. And then, on overhearing a few snatches of conversation from a group of disappointed, would-be diners, I couldn't help but feel troubled: "Salad days? Forget it! Tried buying tomatoes or a lettuce just lately? Rotten soil, no rain, no spuds . . . not that taste like spuds, anyway!" And: "My apples are blistered to hell and full of yellow shit. Taste like it, too. I caught some village kids scrumping in the orchard. Next thing, they're curled up in the grass crying and puking their guts out. Poor little buggers? I didn't have the heart to give them a hard time. But I'll give you odds they were shitting their pants all the way home!" And: "Don't talk to me about apples. Last year, mine were eaten rotten from the inside out by wasps. This year I'd be pleased just to see a bloody wasp!"

Trouble with the veg, yes, but all very local. The restaurants were shipping veg in! Blame it on the weather or something . . . or something.

So then it was Saturday morning and I gave old man Sellick a call. His phone rang but the colonel didn't answer. Yet from my upstairs balcony I could plainly make out something of him— the odd patch of suntanned skin, tatty jeans, and stained white shirt—stirring under the foliage in his garden. Not fifteen feet from his open door, he must surely hear the phone ringing—I could just about hear it myself—but he wasn't making any attempt to answer it.

Something had to be wrong, so I went round to his place and into his garden to enquire personally.

I couldn't believe how quiet the garden was as I approached down the crazy-paved path. No birds—not a one—and I truly missed the buzzing of bees. As to why I hadn't noticed anything before, I mean in my own garden: that's hard to say. I had been busier than usual, putting in a lot of overtime at Kew. There'd been a great many queries from the public about odd hybrid species; many specimens had arrived, been isolated, were being studied by various botanical specialists. Maybe that's the answer: I'd had too much on my plate to notice what was going on in my own or Sellick's garden, the weirdness that was happening.

But the old boy had noticed it, certainly; and right there and then on that garden path, suddenly I could feel it, too . . . I felt the strangeness, like an alien cloud hanging over everything. Oh, it was very obvious. And the colonel had had it dead to rights the day he'd told me, "It's not right—doesn't feel the same—not like my garden at all!" Dead to rights, yes.

But where was Sellick? I jumped twelve inches when a hedge cutter burst into clattering mechanical life. And there he was, the colonel: under a small mountain of Clematis vitalba, traveller's joy, where his garden shed had used to be. Hell no, where it was now—a considerable wooden structure—but buried deep in the clematis! What in the name of . . . ? Why had he let it get so rank, so out of hand?

Anyway, as a great swath of it was sliced through and toppled to the ground, he saw me framed in the gap and switched off his machine. Then, stumbling over a heap of cut growth as dense as box hedge, finally he confronted me. Grimy, dishevelled, and with sweat rivering his dusty face, he panted a hoarse, resentful greeting and continued, "Meteorite? No, that was more than just any old meteorite. It was the green hand of God, advising us to go easy on the GM stuff! And for the last fortnight I've been fighting this . . . this green jungle that you bloody scientists . . . and *botanists*"—he literally spat that last word in my face—"have conspired to make of my garden!"

"Colonel, I —" I began.

But waving his hedge cutter at me until I fell back a little, the old boy almost literally cut me off. "My roses are far bigger, and more beautiful than ever before," he snarled, "but their thorns are inches long, and for all that I keep trying I can't dead-head 'em. You know how you're supposed to nip their withered heads off to encourage new growth? Well, these things are like bloody rubber: they stretch but they won't break. And as for encouragement—I swear they don't need any! What? They don't even like being touched!" He showed me his arms, his new wounds crisscrossing a great many old ones.

"Gordon—"

"And look at this!" He hurled a bloodied arm to point at his shed where it leaned under the weight of rampant clematis. "Would you believe—could you believe—I cut this lot back just three days ago? You're lucky with your garden, which I'll admit I've long despised: all those flagged paths between segregated beds, more like a piece of fancy tatting than a garden proper! Lucky? Oh, yes: because you don't have half the damned greenery that I've got! Eh, what? Why, right now you haven't a tenth of it! And as for the grass . . . now tell me, what do you make of the bloody grass?"

"Gordon," I tried yet again. "I mean, am I to be allowed to speak, or what?"

He didn't answer, just stood there glaring at me, or if not at me at the world in general; stood there with his chest heaving and the sweat of his uneven fight running down his neck and staining his shirt.

But now that I was able to answer him I could find nothing immediate to say, except: "Grass? What on earth are you talking about?" Where we were standing there was a little grass—a few tufts coming up between the chinks in a small paved patio area—but apart from the fact that it was coarse and needed tending it looked normal enough to me.

"You haven't noticed?" He stared hard at me, then relaxed a little. "Ah, no, but then you wouldn't, would you? You've not got enough of the bloody stuff, not in your pallid little horticulturist's paradise!"

Now I was annoyed and told him so. "You're taking all your anger out on me," I said, "insulting me. But I didn't cause any of this and I don't much care for your accusations. Oh, I agree something is wrong with the vegetation—but the problem isn't special to you and your 'bloody' precious garden! Weird-looking plants, seeds, and fungi are arriving at Kew daily, and there's been some strange stuff happening in gardens all over the southeast. It seems we're right in the middle of this . . . this infestation, whatever it is. And it could well turn out that you're right and our extraterrestrial visitor was its source. I can't guarantee that, mind you. But I do care about what's happening; while on the other hand I don't much care for this tongue-lashing from a cranky old soldier! God, I only came round to see if you were okay! I missed you at the pub last night."

At that, whatever sort of fury—or funk?—he was in, the colonel snapped out of it at once. "Good Lord!" he said. "Oh my good God! Eh, what? But that wasn't like me at all! No, not one little bit. Not to a friend. And you've been a very good friend. But . . . " He gave a helpless, frustrated shrug. "It's the garden. I mean, it's really getting me down. I'm sorry. What more can I say or do?"

"Well, for a start, you might want to flush it out of your system!" I told him. "And first off: what's all this about the grass? Yes, as I've already allowed, there seem to be some serious problems with all sorts of greenery, but to the best of my knowledge no one's so far mentioned anything about grass!"

"Come," he beckoned. And as we walked, skirting the sprawling undergrowth—the rose tangles, and the overgrown brambles that not too long ago were cultivated blackberries—he inquired, "You don't have a lawn as such, do you?"

"No," I told him. "At the front I have a wide gravel drive, ornamental pools and fountains, two chestnut trees over clover, and floral borders—all of it walled. At the back: well, it's pretty much as you described it, except it too is walled, protected. As for grass: grass means work, and it isn't especially interesting . . . er, from my point of view, that is." (I didn't want to start him off ranting again.)

"But I do have a lawn," he said, "or I used to."

"Used to?"

"Just here," he nodded, grimly, "to the side of the house."

But as I went to turn the corner he caught my arm. And: "Go careful, my friend," he told me, very quietly, and in that same moment I thought I felt a shudder running through his hand into my arm. "I think we should go very carefully!"

I frowned at him, glanced around the corner of the house, and saw little or nothing that might be considered extraordinary or dangerous. A square, flagged path surrounded a lawn some ten by ten yards; and central in the lawn a white plastic table supported a floral parasol and was flanked by a pair of folding chairs. After a moment, I looked at the colonel enquiringly.

He gave an impatient nod of his head and said: "The grass—look at the grass."

The grass . . . was green, even, and looked in good health. I couldn't understand why he'd let it grow so long—a good eight or nine inches—but other than that . . .

"I cropped it last Thursday," he told me then. "Just a few days ago; cropped it as short as a bloody billiard table! Nothing normal grows that fast or that even. Every single blade is the same length. No meadow, no golf course or bowling green was ever so uniform. And there's something else. Something really—I don't know -macabre?"

He stepped round the corner of the house onto the path, and I followed in his footsteps, urging him: "Well, go on—what is it?"

"You see that mound," he said. "Near the far corner there?"

The ground had a small but definite hump where he was pointing. We followed the path to the corner in question, and as the colonel halted, crouched, and stared hard at the mound, I said, "Yes, I see it. What of it?"

"Look closer."

I did, and saw something of what he was getting at. Deep in the grass, the last six inches and scraggy tuft of a cat's tail stuck up out of the ground. And a few inches away, a furry paw, claws extended, was also visible.

"You buried a dead cat there," I said. "But not nearly deep enough."

"I did no such thing." He shook his head. "I buried nothing there—but the grass did! Let me tell you about it:

"Yesterday, I was battling with the garden, as usual. Hell, it's my bloody garden, after all! But working late, I was just too tired to bother going down to the pub. As the shadows lengthened I went upstairs; I would have an early night, and get an early start this morning. But looking from the window up there, I saw this manky old moggy come out of the shrubbery. I really hate cats because they piss on every-damn-thing in the garden! Anyway, this one appeared to be on his last legs: he was stiff and scraggy; his eyes bulged; he could hardly walk. But he made it this far before collapsing. I thought: 'Well, in the morning he'll either have moved on or he'll be dead—eh, what? And if the latter, then I'll bury him.'

"But this morning . . . I didn't have to bury him. The grass had done it for me." He nodded at the mound. "I found him like that, which was when I began attacking the foliage again. Damn. it all, I refuse to be intimidated by bloody greenery!"

I shook my head. "Gordon—" (I rarely called him by his forename, though he'd years ago invited its use) "—the grass couldn't possibly have 'buried' this cat. He's actually under the soil—most of him, anyway."

"Under the soil, yes," he answered, "but very shallow, as you've already pointed out." The colonel's voice had fallen to a mere murmur, as if he were talking to himself rather than to me. "And there's a reason for that, why it's so shallow."

"A reason?" Truth to tell, I was beginning to wonder about the old boy's reason. He probably sensed it or heard something in my voice and frowned at me.

"Eh, what? You think I'm losing it, do you? Well, just you step back a few paces and yank some of that grass there. Go on, pull a few blades up by their roots."

I did as he suggested. The grass came out easily enough in my hand, and the roots were white.

The old boy nodded and stepped onto the grass close to the mound. And he too pulled grass . . . from directly over the spot where the cat was buried. Then, again nodding his head—knowingly now—he held the tuft out for my inspection. At which I drew back from him, wrinkling my nose in disgust.

The roots of the grass in his hand were red!

"You're the botanist," he said, very quietly. "Now tell me, what kind of weird morphology is it that uses blood as chlorophyll? What kind of bloody vampire is this—eh, what? I mean, how does it photosynthesize that, for God's sake?"

I could only shake my head . . . but I glanced hastily down, to make sure that I was still on the path.

"And look," he went on. "Look at my feet."

He was wearing tough Wellington boots and had been standing up to his lower calves in the grass by the burial mound for two or three minutes, no more. But already the grass had curled inward, over his boots, and as he moved his feet the grass broke, so that his feet carried some of the severed blades back to the path with him.

Where he had been standing, the earth was almost bare, the grass visibly drawing down into the soil. It was like trying to watch the movement of the minute hand on the clock in the village clock tower—the motion was barely discernible—but the grass was moving!

I backed away down the path and tried to say, "Gordon," but all that came out was a gurgle. At my second try I managed, and said, "Gordon, it's time I made a few phone calls. In fact it's long since past the time! So if you'll excuse me now. . . "

He nodded and said, "And me, I must get back to killing all of this damned stuff. I'll turn it all to compost, start again. That's what I'll do—eh, what?"

"Whatever," I told him. And then I got out of there . . .

The near-distant jackhammers, silent for a while, resumed their clamour, their vibrations stronger than previously. Jarred back to the present—as the generators coughed and electric lights flickered, and rills of dust jitterbugged down from the ceiling—I gave a small start, blinked once or twice, let my audience, my troops, float back into focus.

There, seated in groups, I saw about half of them: some two hundred men, and as many still to come. They'd been arriving in a steady trickle, quietly thinking their private thoughts, automatically assembling with other members of their sections and platoons. Clad in grey coveralls and carrying grey, protective gloves, they were grey as can be and gaunt-faced to a man.

I recognized one of them sitting central in the front row. Yesterday he'd been squad leader of a spore patrol out towards Watford. The fern forest had been making big inroads, mutating as it came. Ignoring the season and propagating like crazy, it was hurling its spores before it, "galloping" over the fields, making exploratory forays up roadside verges and central reservations, and taking root wherever there was soil. Yesterday the winds had been fanning north-west out of London: ideal for the flamers. Whoever could have foreseen or imagined the day would arrive when we'd be burning our fields, our woodlands? And not only the Green but whatever doomed, terrified species of wildlife remained in it.

So there he sat, this squad leader: his hair crisped, hands gnarled and blistered from the heat of the flamethrowers, weary arms a-dangle. Now and then his thin frame would shudder, prelude to wracking fits of coughing. All of that burning must have leeched the air from his lungs and seared them to so much blackened leather. So I thought—

—Until, once again, my thoughts went elsewhere . . .

INTELLIGENCE. WE BELIEVED it was the province— the exclusive province—of the vertebrate mammalia. Well, okay, the cephalopods had the octopus, and two or three other orders had their individual geniuses, but on the whole it was the mammalia, and especially Man. But how does one measure intelligence in species other than or alien to the human variety? And when, at what point, does it take the next step up and become intelligence as opposed to mere instinct?

Consider the Venus fly trap. By what extremes of evolutionary process did this plant develop spiked, spring-loaded leaves to capture its victims? Or take for instance the squirting cucumber, a Mediterranean plant that squirts a weak acid at you if you brush against it. Actually, it's simply ejecting its seeds; but still we have to assume that a dose of acid in the eyes is a warning to wild animals or livestock, to stop them trampling on the plant. To me it's simply another example of weird vegetable instinct. And what if evolution was to take the next step up?

Well, thanks to the meteorite—and to a degree to genetic modification—plant evolution has taken and is taking the next step up. And the next, and the next . . .

AFTER THAT EPISODE with Sellick's grass, back in my own garden —my walled, almost entirely work-free, neatly laid-out "horticulturist's paradise," as he had called it—I went from plot to plot, suspicious as a caged budgie in a house with cats. It seemed the walls might have saved me from any immediate influx. Well they probably had, from most of it. But not entirely.

I found several magnolia corns scattered in the flower beds parallel with the colonel's garden. This had never happened before; the magnolia's seed pods are fairly heavy and usually fall straight to the ground. Moreover, the old fellow's tree was well away from my wall, much deeper into his garden.

So then, had there been a storm which I hadn't especially noticed? I didn't think so. Or (laughingly) had the tree found a way to propel its would-be progeny abroad? Outrageous! And I gave that last thought only momentary consideration. But never-

theless, it was very late in the season to be discovering such as these in my garden, or any garden for that matter. Likewise the dandelions.

I had always been scrupulous with weeds however pretty some may be, and while admittedly I hadn't had much time for gardening recently, I'd never failed to pull dandelions whenever they attempted another insidious invasion. But it appeared obvious I must have missed some, and the ones I'd missed were beauties!

Tall, thick-stemmed, with flowers twice their regular size and as golden as the sun, there were specimens in almost every plot. Some of them were into the seed phase of their existence, once again very late in the season . . . didn't these things know when to stop growing? Even as I stood frowning at them a breeze came up, snatched a puff of parasols into the air, carried them higher and higher, until they whirled away to the south-east. I found myself wondering where they'd land and try to take root: Kent? East Sussex? The English Channel? (No luck there!) Or perhaps some place much farther afield, such as France? Belgium? Germany? And for some reason that galvanized me, sent me hurrying indoors to do my telephoning.

I called Kew, David Johnson, who I knew was on duty that weekend. He was an old acquaintance of mine, an expert on Mediterranean flora who had studied with me twenty years previously.

"Hi," he said, a friendly voice coming over the wires; and yet there was an excited or nervous edge to it. "What can I do for you on this beautiful Saturday morning, when you should be out on the river—or in the pub, or your garden, or anywhere except where I am?"

"In my garden?" I said. "No, I don't think so. In fact I'd rather be anywhere but there! I was already there this morning— and in the garden next door—and I didn't much like either one of them!"

"Ah, you've been neglecting things, right?"

"No, I've been noticing things."

"Oh yes? Well, me too. In fact I've just noticed something— or rather experienced something—that gave me quite a shock! Funny, really . . . and yet not."

There it was once again: that edge in David's voice, more properly an unfamiliar quavering that was quite out of character. And despite that there were things I must tell him, I was suddenly interested in what he patently wanted to tell me.

"What's been going on?" I asked him. "What have you been up to?"

"Well, I'm on my own today," he began. "Gloria Hamilton is supposed to be in, too, but she's come down with something, so there's only me and the security guards; and of course they're doing their rounds."

"Sounds lonely," I said. "In fact you make it sound positively spooky! So what's this: a haunted greenhouse story?"

"Or something," he answered. And after a moment's silence: "Tell me, do you remember that old myth about mandrakes—how they scream when you pull them out of the ground?"

I felt my blood cooling as I answered, "I know the legend, yes." And I was almost afraid to ask, "What of it?"

"Well, I was in the Mediterranean section—my domain, the

hothouse, as I call it—and you know something? That old myth is true! I yanked what I thought was a diseased mandrake—"

"And it screamed?" I beat him to it. And: "David, listen," I continued, in all earnestness. "No, I'm not a bit surprised. I suspect we haven't been nearly as careful or attentive as we should have been, and not only at Kew. By now that entire place is probably contaminated, not to mention the rest of the southeast!"

"What on earth are you . . . ?" he began to ask, but yet again I cut him short:

"No, be quiet, I want you to listen: is Director Hawkworth still in America? I thought so, which means I'm in charge, the man responsible. So: do you have a staff list there? Telephone numbers, addresses? Good, because I want you to start calling them, all of them, and get them in for an O-Group first thing Monday morning."

"An O-Group?" I could almost see the puzzled expression I knew he must be wearing. "Don't you mean a general meeting?"

"No," I told him. "I mean an Orders Group, as in military terminology. You thought a screaming mandrake was odd, David? Well yes, I have to agree. But I suspect that's just one small example of this thing, one small part. As for the whole of it: it's war, David. I do believe it's war!"

Then I had tried to get on to the Ministry of Agriculture and Fisheries. Pointless! Ridiculous! A complete waste of time and effort! At almost midday on a Saturday, no one was there. When I did reach them on Monday morning . . . they already knew about it.

As for the woman I spoke to, not the Minister himself (no, of course not!) but an underling: I sensed she was stalling me, hoping I would go away, just like her bureaucratic superior and a handful of lesser bean-counters in his office must have been hoping "the problem" would go away. And you know, I might have expected it? For of course they were the ones who'd sanctioned all those GM experiments in the first place! And they probably believed the experiments were at the "root" of it—

—Which I have to admit was what I myself still believed, at least at that moment in time. It was my Earth Mother faith, et cetera, which, despite Sellick's meteorite, kept obstructing any positive acceptance of a then inchoate, at best unresolved Galactica or Universe Mother theory.

But the evidence was mounting, and the mountain was like a Welsh coal mine's slag tip in the rain: ready to slip and slide and bury us all . . .

And again the jackhammers, reminding me of where I was. Me and my audience, my army; our eyes turning up almost as one to look at the concrete ceiling, narrowing to avoid the last few trickles of loose dust.

Up there in Oxford Street or nearby, and all over London, men were clearing the vegetation—the remaining green areas, traffic islands, verges, decorative plots—right down to their raw concrete foundations, Then they'd spray sulphuric acid into the gaping holes to kill any roots, fill them with debris, finally level everything and seal their work with fresh concrete.

And as for the parks: God only knows how they were dealing with the parks!

While down here in this briefing room the small army of men waiting for me to speak must be thinking much the same thing as I was: that the city we'd known—the whole world we'd known—was no more and might even be gone forever.

Two or three rows of chairs remained almost empty. I looked at my watch—fifteen, maybe twenty minutes to go. How long had I been here? Some thirty or so minutes? Was that all? I supposed it must be. But then, memory is like that: past events, especially unpleasant ones, hurry across your mind like ripples over a pond on a windy day, eager to get done. Or rather, you are eager to get done with them.

I spoke into my microphone, but softly:

"You're on duty in about twenty minutes, after the briefing—for what that's worth—which I promise I'll keep brief. So we're able to give the latecomers a few minutes grace. That being so, I'll ask you to curb your impatience. I mean, I appreciate how eager you must be to get on with things, but we'll wait awhile longer anyway . . . "

That last was my idea of black humour, if only to calm the nerves and alleviate the tension, but no one laughed. Who could blame them? Not a single man-jack of them was "eager" to get on with any-damned-thing. This wasn't a conventional war, and they weren't conventional warriors. Those of them who were beginning to fidget were doing so not out of eagerness but a perfectly natural fear of the unknown.

Somewhere at the back of the basement a door clanged open and a messenger, a crippled kid whose legs had been shrivelled to useless twigs by mutant nettles, came speeding down a central aisle in his wheelchair. Clamped between his teeth he bore a sheet of paper. Even as I stood up, went down on one knee on the podium to take the note from him, I knew what it would be: a list of those who wouldn't be joining us, those who'd failed to make it through the night, injured or murdered in their own homes while protecting themselves and their families.

As the kid spun his chair about face and went off back up the aisle, I glanced at the typed sheet, saw that I was right, bulldog-clipped the list to the notes I would be reading in a few minute's time.

But before that I let my mind drift again, a sort of guilty "if only I . . . " trip back in time. A futile exercise really, for even back then it had probably been far too late to do anything about anything.

I THINK I MAY have said something somewhere about killing Kew. Actually, I don't think I killed Kew at all. It's just part of this guilt thing I seem to have developed, which I think began after the police contacted me. Contacted me? Well, it was something more than a mere contact.

It was probably the Min. of Ag. & Fish who put the police on to me, to sideline, marginalize and shut me up, I imagine—me and the rest of the staff at Kew. And at first those estimable officers of the law were pretty stiff with us, with me in particular.

Was it possible, they had wanted to know, that I'd smuggled something foreign and illegal out of Kew to give to the colonel or to grow in my own garden? Surely I was aware that the casual-introduction of exotic strains into our finely balanced ecology was a serious offence? Just twelve years ago we had had mad cow disease; hadn't that been enough of a warning not to go messing with nature? What was I attempting to do, sabotage the ecology? Destroy the vegetation and crops that our populace, animals and wildlife lived on?

But then I reminded them about the local GM problem they'd dealt with some eighteen months ago. I told them that if memory served me well it had been they, the police themselves, who had stopped those Friends of the Earth people who had only been trying to avoid this sort of problem in the first place. And there was something else they should take into account: the meteorite that had landed next door. As for myself: I was merely a botanist, a scientist, a man with a conscience who respected the law and knew his responsibilities. Did they really think I would be smuggling forbidden botanical material out of Kew to ingratiate myself with a well known local eccentric? And if they did think so, then why didn't they question the colonel himself? And what items did they think I might have smuggled anyway? There was no more Cannabis indica at Kew Gardens than in any one of a thousand window boxes in Kensington! And anyway, wasn't it entirely legal now?

And so, eventually, I convinced them of my innocence.

At that time . . . well of course I played the meteorite card very carefully. For in light of my former belief—in a Gala as opposed to a Universal Nature—I still wasn't one hundred per cent convinced of what I suspected might be going on here. And as for the police: I didn't for a moment think that these very down-to-earth law officers were ready to subscribe to a Galactica theory—

Not just then, anyway . . .

THROUGH THE AUTUMN and into winter, events seemed to slow down a little. Contra the initial suspicion and police enquiries, I had taken a six-lobed leaf from Sellick's Ivy (as I'd named it) in to Kew to have the real experts look it over. And three days later I was told that the leaf was as fresh as ever; it seemed it didn't want to die! But there was so much going on at Kew at that time—so many peculiar specimens had come in, mostly from within a twenty mile radius of my home in Surrey—and so much work was being done on them—that I simply lost track of the thing, stopped asking after it.

But guilty? For taking that single leaf in? No, the poison was already there in the guise of all those mutant species; my guilt lay in refusing to convert to Galactica! In that . . . and in the fact that I'm a botanist in name only.

There, I've admitted it. And therein lies my guilt: in not having been able to recognize and accept a seedling from space when I was shown one. Oh, I had my qualifications, achieved by sheer hard work and good fortune—by learning things one day and forgetting them the next, after the examinations—but my leanings led elsewhere. My forte was seen to be administration, hence my "exalted" position. And in that position I should have pushed and fought and done more. But as I've already stated, I believe the war was lost before we even started to fight back, lost on the morning that damned thing crashed down in old Colonel Sellick's garden.

So where was I? Ah, yes: the winter, two years ago. And the months passing by, and season following season.

If the winter had slowed things down, the spring accelerat-

ed them almost beyond belief! So that this time when the police called me in it was to act as their local expert!

At last the government had surrendered to increasing public concern and pressure. MAF and their GM experiments had been accused, found guilty without trial, and thrown to the wolves; and as possible saviours of the situation, the botanists had become the new elite. Even then it had been only a "situation," not a full-blown disaster, and despite that I and a handful of others at Kew and similar institutes had been given a free hand, still we were seen by many as nothing more than scaremongers.

In May a resurgent MAF issued a statement: their "experts" were certain that given time, perhaps a year, the alien effects would be "diluted by absorption," or some such claptrap. To the best of my knowledge no one believed them, and rightly so. And all GM experiments were banned worldwide, irrevocably, now and forever.

Well, and it might have had something to do with GM—might just have—but mainly it was Sellick's meteorite. By then they had cut it open; it could be seen that it was most definitely a thing of "alien" or universal nature, spawn of Megagaia.

There were chambers inside: a honeycomb of minute chambers, connected by microscopic tubes to the outer surface. Heat, friction with Earth's atmosphere, would have caused any materials—liquids, gases —that were inside to expand, would have driven the living plasma along the tubules under pressure. And moments before impact the pressure would have shattered a brittle heat-shield sheath, releasing—

—All hell on Earth, as it turns out . . .

A cold breeze blew on my mind, sending the ripples on my mental pond fleeing ever faster. Memories that in the main didn't want to be remembered surfaced, fragmented like confetti shapes in a kaleidoscope, reformed into new, even less acceptable pictures. In June something macabre. I was called to a local cemetery where the police had roped off a twenty-foot perimeter around a family plot: mother, father, and small girl child, victims of a bad traffic accident. They had been buried just five days ago, but already the three graves had sprouted huge fungi, covering them with a canopy of thick fleshy parasols. Mushrooms were my department; I knew more about fungi than anything else in the botanical world. These were boletus, but mutated of course.

Boletus satanus, yes: "Satan's mushroom . . . poisonous when raw." Or in this case just pure poison.

Whereas the more common variety—the original variety—was rarely more than eight or nine inches across the cap, these uncommon growths were up to two or three feet across and leaned outwards from clumps so tightly packed that it was difficult to see the borders of the plot they were shading. . . in which their fat, barrel-shaped stipes were rooted. And they issued a sickly sweet stench promoting dizziness and nausea in anyone standing too close to them. Several relatives of the deceased were present, stretched out moaning on a gravel path, being looked after by a doctor in a gas mask. The police were wearing masks, too.

The doctor, a good distance from this abnormality, offered me his mask; I put it on and was approaching the graves when a man, probably another relative, came staggering down the lanes between plots. He was green, looked ill, had vomit on his shirt and carried an axe. "Bloody bastard things!" he gasped, breaching the cordon.

Then the smell, the alien scent, got to him. He went to his knees, choking, and the axe fell from his hand, the flat of its blade thumping against an outer stipe, one of the fat pink mushroom stems. Then the horror:

The skin of the cap less than twelve inches from the fallen man's face peeled back; a sphincter appeared, opened, hosed out a jet of some vile ichor. The man screamed, shot upright, stumbled away hissing and frothing. His face was melting! He crashed to the ground, stone dead!

The stench must have increased tenfold . . . anyone not wearing a gas mask was driven almost physically back . . . the doctor cried, "My God! Oh God! Oh God! Cadaverine, it can only be!"

I dragged him away, helped him to sit, said, "Cadaverine?"

"That's . . . what . . . it smelt like!" he said, shudderingly, looking at me with streaming eyes, his mouth sucking at air that was at least a little cleaner. "Cadaverine: the loathsome juices that ferment in corpses!"

We called in a spray truck, turned everything to slush with twenty gallons of fungicide, then sprayed the whole area with a fine sulphuric acid mist.

And while all that was going on—thinking of the boletus, of what they must be feeding on—I found myself a place to be sick behind someone's mausoleum. Even back there I had no lack of company; before I was done the doctor and one of the policemen had joined me . . .

IN JULY THE FRENCH closed the Channel Tunnel and banned all imports from the United Kingdom . . . well, what else was new? Remembering my dandelion seeds, however—not to mention an entire year's contact of one sort or another—it was too little, too late. In August the Germans embargoed France, and a week later, right across Europe, everyone else was forbidding contact with everyone else.

Until then America had been just a little complacent, distant, casual; then, suddenly, she was hit! The wheat, barley and maize—all the cereal crops—infected, poisoned by the same disease or "condition." And worse to come: a three-hundred-mile-wide cloud of lethal, choking pollen and granular dust drifting east and south-east from the vast cereal "prairies," taking out entire towns and cities in its darkening path. Quincy, Chicago, Logansport, Lafayette and Bloomington . . . all gone. While fifty per cent of the population in the trapesium of Nashville, Pittsburgh, and the Appalachians was evacuated by presidential order into territory east of the Great Lakes. As for the other fifty per cent: they defied the order, stayed and faced death.

Once again the sleeping giant had been awakened, only this time there was no one to hit out at.

By mid-October millions of sheep were dead in New Zealand, the paddy fields were smoking alkaline swamps across China and the Far East, the Australian Aborigines had wisely chosen to go walkabout, but no longer in the bush . . . now they did it in the desert, the only safe place. For now, at least . . .

Then it was winter again, but you would hardly know it. The weather was mutating along with the flora! Climatic change acc-

elerated by what was happening to the green stuff, by weird new greenhouse gases. But at least the winter gave us a much-needed break, enabling our retreat into the towns and cities, allowing us to regroup, try to sort out some kind of defence. These mass evacuations were like scenes from one of the Great Wars, except there were no tanks in the streets, just tanks of herbicide and acid, and no distant rumbles of man-made thunder. (No, allow me to correct myself: we did in fact bomb several forests, which only served to spread it that much faster.)

And finally it was "spring"—last spring, perhaps the last spring—by which time all Mankind was under siege.

But enough, my mind was almost numb, memories merging, the ripples blurring into a froth on my mental pond. And yet a last few scenes continued to surface, despite that they were things I really didn't want to remember . . .

IN APRIL OF this last year, months after the evacuations, old man Sellick called me at Kew. Most of the land-lines were down (the rampant vines and ivies) but he had retained my cellphone number from the old days. Even so he was lucky to get through; the atmospherics were that bad.

"You're still at home?" I could scarcely credit it. Just a day or two before what was to have been his forced evacuation, he'd told me he was heading north to his sister in Edinburgh.

"Yes," came his reply, almost drowned in static. "I fooled 'em, stayed on. Surrender? Me? No, no! Out of the question! Eh, what? But I've had it now. I'm tired. Can't win. So then . . . I know it's a tall order, but is there any chance you can get me out of here?"

"I'll do what I can," I said. "But I can't promise. You're deep in the heart of it—the very heart of it—and to tell the truth I don't know how you've survived."

"Well I have—until now," he told me, "but now it's fighting back—deliberately! Roots come up in the night, from under the floorboards. Searching, I suppose. I hear them groping. And the garden: I've taken it out, burned most of it to the ground. It'll make for a fine big black helipad for the chopper, that's if you have one. I know I'm asking a lot, but—"

"I'll see what can be done," I told him, before the static overwhelmed us.

I got on to Surveillance and was told that a chopper would be going out that way in a few days time. They picked me up; we sped out over the Green; at Sellick's place they put me down in a flurry of ashes in what had once been his garden. I was in my protective gear: the man from Mars in an NBC suit, gas mask and all. Next door, my old house was invisible under a green mound, sagging under the weight of foliage. Sellick's place, too.

But the colonel's big magnolia was still standing—God, it was still in leaf!—there in the one last patch of what looked like normal garden. I went down the old scorched path at a run, then skidded to a halt under the tree's now ominous canopy.

I just couldn't believe what I saw sitting there. Or rather I could, for I'd seen its like before; it was just that I didn't want to believe. And in that grim gray-and-green wasteland deserted by all animal life, devoid of creature sounds, I stood on rubbery legs, gazing through eyes round as pennies, and reached out a trembling rubber-gloved hand to touch Sellick's mutilated, transfigured face.

Why did I do that? I don't know. Probably to confirm with a second sense the evidence I'd almost refused to accept from the first. But no, I wasn't nightmaring. It was all too real.

Old Sellick. Sometime in the last day or two he must have gone out into what was left of his garden, and as was his wont nodded off to sleep on the bench with his back against the magnolia. Then the attack . . . probably not of the green stuff; more likely the old boy's heart, because he was sitting there clutching his left arm, his head back and mouth wide open. I think it must have been that way—a heart attack—because he wouldn't have just sat there and let all . . . all of this happen.

The ivy: growing up his trousers and bulging out his shirt; entering him somewhere—I hate to think where!—and issuing forth from his dislodged eyes, from his ears, his gaping mouth. And the old colonel all dried up, wrinkled like a walnut—like a kernel!—with all the good sucked out of him, and the veins in the ivy's six-lobed leaves tinted pink with his liquids!

There was no point in staying. I used avgas to set fire to Sellick and the magnolia, returned to the chopper still hovering there, and went back with the patrol to London . . .

INTELLIGENCE. IT'S A CRAZY idea . . . or is it? I mean, how does this thing, or these things, propagate? With no more— or damn few—birds, bees, wasps, flies, how do they do it? Is the wind sufficient, or do they help each other? I remember what Colonel Sellick told me: about roots coming up through his floorboards, searching through the house.

And then there's what happened to David Johnson. For just a few weeks ago, David got his.

He was the last man out of Kew, a rearguard left behind to ensure that everything we had once nurtured was destroyed. Last to go would be that area of his own special interest, of course, the Mediterranean section. But after he'd been left there—on his own, for three days—finally someone remembered that David hadn't called.

So we called him, and got no answer.

We found him in the hothouse, examined him and figured out how he had died. A squirting cucumber had got him in the eyes; the blackened sockets and the blisters on his face told us that much. Backing off, he must have staggered into a patch of previously inoffensive cactus . . . they'd shot poisonous spines into him, and his body was puffed up like a balloon. And finally the mandrakes had got to him . . . they were sprouting in his decaying flesh. I didn't attempt to pull one.

As we opened up with the flamethrowers, the whole place was thrashing and seething— "screaming" if you like—in all its silent fury . . .

I became aware of someone standing at the foot of the podium. A young man, recently arrived, probably a driver. The chairs were mostly filled now; the empty ones . . . would wait until we found replacements.

"Yes?" I said.

"The stores are open, sir," he said. "The toshers are waiting outside, and the transport is ready up top."

I nodded, said, "Good, thank you," and then got on with it. I had promised them I'd be brief, and now I kept my word; kept things even shorter by omitting to read the names of those men they'd no longer be seeing. Why should I drench, or even drown, these already dampened spirits? Instead, the names of our dead, brave former comrades-in-arms would be posted where they could be read privately, allowing the living to deal with their losses in their own way in their own time.

There were eight platoons; I assigned four of them to a continuation of yesterday's work, the other four to an invasion on a brand new front.

"It's the sewers," I told them. "Fungus and a black alga. I don't know how the latter survives without sunlight, but in any case it's your job to ensure it doesn't survive. The fungus is a mutant species of puff- or earth-ball that grows in enormous clumps; it's yellow, warty, and the fruiting bodies are full of black spores. There's evidence that these spores will take root in flesh and produce mycelia, fungus strands that will spread through your tissues like wildfire! We got that evidence from an abundance of dead rats; in fact you won't find any live rats down there! Which just about says it all.

"You'll have gas masks, of course, but with the various gas pockets you are liable to encounter it's obvious that you won't be able to use flamers. So I'm afraid it's algicides and fungicides, and that's your lot. So, if anyone has an even slightly suspicious gas mask, get it changed!

"As for the algae: it crawls, however slowly. So every hour or so you'll surface and get your suits hosed down. Now listen, I know all this is new and strange to you, but you won't be on your own. In the old days—I mean the really old days, back in the 19th century—there were workers called 'toshers' down in the sewers. Scavengers mainly, they searched for valuables that had been flushed away. Well, we've been recruiting toshers, reinforcing our modern-day 'flusher' gangs, the workers who keep the sewers clean and in good order. Now they're working in tandem, but they're not so much treasure-hunting or repairing the sewers as cleaning them out—searching for the Green so that you can destroy it! But I'm not going to understate the danger: there's a lot of this stuff down there, and it's deadly. If we let it get up into our homes and buildings . . . " I tailed it off, let it go at that. And finally:

"Okay, that's it. But always remember: safety first! Suits, masks, equipment—check 'em all out. And tomorrow morning let me see all your ugly faces looking right back at me, just like today."

They began to leave, some faster, more eager, than others. The eager ones would be new to this . . . they wouldn't be quite so eager tomorrow. And I knew I wouldn't be seeing all of their ugly faces.

That thought was like an invocation.

The man in the front row, the squad leader—the man with the crisped hair and gnarly hands, whose coughing had made me think his lungs were suffering from the blown-back heat of the flame-throwers—had lurched to his feet. He coughed yet again, gurgling at me like a drain, and stumbled forward. I saw that his eyes were starting out, his hands clawing at thin air.

I jumped down off the podium, but too late to catch him as he fell over. He writhed on the floor, almost vibrating there, but only for a moment or two. And then he lay still.

Some of his men had come forward, staring transfixed, babbling half-formed questions. Waving them back, I got down on my knees beside the fallen man. He wasn't breathing. I put my ear to his chest. Nothing.

Then something:

A hooked green tendril with a bud at its tip uncurled from his right nostril! It elongated vertically to about six inches in length, swaying there. Then the bud turned in my direction where I lay frozen, with my head on the dead man's chest. And the damned thing opened and hissed at me!

Someone cried out, stepped forward with clippers, snipped the bud off so that it fell on the floor. As it writhed there, other men came forward and dragged me away. More tendrils were emerging from his ears, his mouth; there was nothing for it but to hose him down with sulphuric acid spray, reducing everything to slop . . .

There may be survivors. Maybe the Green won't go into the cold places, maybe it won't invade the deserts. Who can say but that an oasis pool, or perhaps the pack ice, or a black smoker down on the sea-bed, may well be the last refuge of animal life?

Or there again, maybe sixty million years from now another space rock will come hurtling from the sky, and this time it'll kick-start, revitalize the vertebrates . . . though it's possible it could just as easily announce the rise of the insects!

Who can say?

But I have remembered the name of that American author who wrote about a terrible colour out of space: he was called H. P. Lovecraft, and tonight when I go out and look at the sky, I may have a word with him. I may say, "Well, Mr. Lovecraft, wherever you are now, I just want you to know that the stars don't leer. But on the other hand, looking at them and wondering what else is out there, I'm pretty sure I know what you meant . . . ͡

LUMLEY HISTORY CONTINUED

>> decades (including the British Fantasy Award-winning title story). The following year he collected together a number of previously published stories and novellas in Return of the Deep Ones and Other Mythos Tales and Dagon's Bell and Other Discords. Another new collection, The Second Wish and Other Exhalations (1995), contained thirteen stories, each introduced by the author.

Lumley was again Guest of Honor at Fantasycon XIX in 1994, and he carried out the role of Toastmaster at The 22nd World Fantasy Convention held in Schaumburg, Illinois, over the 1996 Halloween weekend.

Published by Call of Cthulhu gaming imprint Chaosium in 1997, Singers of Strange Songs: A Celebration of Brian Lumley was edited by David Scott Aniolowski and included two reprint stories and a poem by Lumley plus eleven other Lovecraftian tales by other writers. In His Own Write: Brian Lumley: Necroscribe collected three previously-published Lovecraftian stories along with a new foreword by to commemorate Lumley's appearance as Guest of Honor at the third NecronomiCon, dedicated to celebrating H.P. Lovecraft and the Cthulhu Mythos in all its forms, held in Providence, Rhode Island, in August 1997.

The following year, Lumley and Tom Doherty were among the Guests of Honor at The 8th World Horror Convention held in Phoenix, Arizona, where Lumley was named Grand Master. Released to coincide with his appearance, the author's themed collection A Coven of Vampires (1998) contained thirteen reprint tales, along with a new foreword by the author plus artwork by Bob Eggleton. Issued in a trade hardcover edition of 1,000 copies and a limited edition of just 100 signed copies, it became publisher Fedogan & Bremer's fastest ever book to go out of print.

With the "Necroscope" series now apparently behind him and no new novels anticipated after the publication of Maze of Worlds (UK: The House of Doors: Second Visit, 1998), Lumley's American pub-

lishers began to look around for other material by the author. As a result, Lumley began compiling fresh hardcover collections for a new generation of readers. The Whisperer and Other Voices (2001) contained reprints of nine stories, including the short novel 'The Return of the Deep Ones', while Beneath the Moors and Darker Places (2002) featured Lumley's complete 1974 novel Beneath the Moors along with eight other tales.

Along with three classic tales featuring Titus Crow and two with Hero and Eldin, Harry Keogh: Necroscope and Other Weird Heroes! (2003) contained three new stories about Harry Keogh which, as Lumley explained in his introduction, were based on old notes and filled in the chronology between The Lost Years and The Source.

Brian Lumley rounded off 2003 with his appearance as Guest of Honor at The 29th Annual World Fantasy Convention held in Washington D.C.

Despite becoming a best-selling author around the world, Lumley has continued to support the smaller presses with his work. Sixteen Sucking Stories (2004) from Delirium Books collected twelve of the thirteen stories from A Coven of Vampires and added a further four tales in a traycased edition illustrated by Alan M. Clark and a CD recording of the author reading his story 'The Mirror of Nitocris'.

Alan Clark also produced the cover art for The House of the Temple (2004), which was the second volume in the Endeavor Press Novelette Series. It contained the title novella plus another reprint story. Illustrated by Allen K (Koszowski), the nicely-produced hardcover was available in both a 300-copy signed limited edition and a signed lettered edition. Brian Lumley's Freaks (2004) was another slim but attractive hardcover volume from Subterranean Press that collected four obscure reprint tales and a new story, 'Somebody Calling', along with a brief introduction by the author and more illustrations by Koszowski. It was published in signed editions limited to 750 numbered and 26 lettered copies.

New from Subterranean is a special edition of the

classic Necroscope, with a new foreword from the author and numerous illustrations by Bob Eggleton. Dimension House is planning a five-volume series reprinting all Brian Lumley's "Dreamlands" novels and short stories, including W. Paul Ganley's concordance of the entire series.

Although best known for his novels and short stories, the author has also contributed poetry to a wide range of magazines, including The Arkham Collector, The HPL Supplement, Nyctalops, Weirdbook, Fantasy Tales, Kadath and Crypt of Cthulhu. In 1982, Ghoul Warning and Other Omens collected 32 of the writer's best poems, most of them original. It was published by Spectre Press in both a 500-copy trade paperback and a signed collector's hardcover of just 80 copies. It quickly became the author's rarest book. Consequently, it was reprinted in 1999 by Necronomicon Press as Ghoul Warnings and Other Omens... and Other Omens in a revised, corrected and expanded edition of 800 paperback copies, a signed hardcover edition of 250 copies and a lettered edition of just 26 copies.

The Brian Lumley Companion appeared in 2002. Edited by Lumley and Stanley Wiater, it included essays, an interview with the author, bibliographies, a photo section and concordances of the novels. And Lumley has made sure it's already outdated: He's still steadily producing new fiction, including 'The Place of Waiting', a major new supernatural novella, and his new Mythos novella 'The Taint'. ͡

Stephen Jones is the winner of three World Fantasy Awards, three Bram Stoker Awards and three International Horror Guild Awards, as well as being a Hugo Award nominee and a 16-time recipient of the British Fantasy Award. His more than 80 books include Shadows Over Innsmouth, H.P. Lovecraft's Book of Horror and the annual Mammoth Book of Best New Horror series. Find him at www.herebedragons.co.uk/jones.

The Hymn

by Brian Lumley

There were six of us—eight, if I include the two men in the cell. Not a cell as in a prison, more a large partitioned room or apartment—or rather a closed, controlled environment with all the necessary life-support systems; also a fail-safe which could be brought into play to cancel the said life-supports in the unlikely event that such action became imperative.

The cell's walls, floors and ceilings were of welded five-inch-thick carbon steel plates, buttressed on the outside; the inlet and outlet conduits, as few as possible, had bores of no more than two inches; the entire structure—its adjuncts and supporting complex—was subterranean in a mountainous region, thus making use of a nuclear shelter left over from a war that had never come to pass. There had been lesser wars, certainly, but not the *big one* that we had all been afraid of back in the early '60s.

Actually, it was during the aftermath of one of those so-called "lesser" wars (as if there ever was any such thing) that the events leading to my current position as director and coordinator of TMI, or "The Mythos Investigation," had taken place—but to speak of that now would be to jump the gun, as it were, and anyway it will come up later, wherefore it better serves my purpose to proceed with my description of the subterrene facility, also to explain something of my fellow observers, and then to let the principal participants in the experiment, our human guinea pigs in the cell, tell the story in their own words.

So, there was myself: a Foundation Member (I'm afraid I can say no more on that subject), also one other Foundation Member, an elderly colleague; there were two men from military intelligence, both high-ranking, inferior only to the highest governmental authorities; there was a female psychiatric specialist; and finally a technician, a man who—having been responsible for the design and construction of the cell, its adjuncts and surroundings—was completely familiar with its workings. He knew how to run the place, and just as importantly how to shut it down. As for myself and my elderly colleague: we were there by virtue of our alleged expertise in certain matters of grotesque myth and legend.

With regard to the names and physical descriptions of the team: I deem these particulars unnecessary; at this late date I see no reason to compromise anyone. And details of the precise location of our sub-sierran venue are likewise out of the question, since I have no doubt it remains a much guarded secret to this day.

And so back to the cell:

The cell had no windows . . . it wasn't required that the men inside should be able to look out. That would be a distraction, and they certainly wouldn't want to see us looking in. We were, of course, "looking in," though not through windows as such; for even one-way viewports would not have allowed total visual access. But recessed into the interior walls, ceilings and various fittings were tiny closed-circuit cameras, each with an exterior screen. Audio was similarly available, indeed absolutely necessary.

The cell was equipped with small bedrooms, bathrooms, cooking facilities, and a large refrigerator containing enough food and drink for several weeks. Lighting was of course artificial; it could be switched off in the bedrooms, so that our subjects might sleep. But even there we were not to be excluded: bedroom cameras could be switched to infrared. It was of the utmost importance that we should be able to see them — and perhaps even listen to them — when they slept.

As to their names: while I am certain that their real names may be found in Foundation archives, where I have no doubt they are kept secure, I shall nevertheless provide them with pseudonyms . . . Letters such as this one may not be as safe as Foundation records. They were Jason and James. On the other hand, I will give them at least something of physical descriptions, if only to enhance the reader's mental picture of them during the discoursive passages to follow.

They were of a height, perhaps five-nine or ten; also of an age, say thirty-two, with Jason the elder by five or six months. Jason was a redhead, outspoken, careless in both dress and attitude, often flippant but never insulting. Lanky and jaunty if a little lopsided in his gait, he had green eyes, a long straight nose and gaunt cheeks. James was quite Jason's opposite. Admitting to a sedentary lifestyle, he had wisps of thinning, prematurely grey hair on a bulbous skull, sharp, permanently narrow and penetrating blue eyes, a small mouth and receding chin, all set on a burly, powerful if under-utilized frame. In short, and if in the near future he did not take up some form of exercise, he could expect to go to seed. Also, where Jason was invariably plain-speaking, James frequently tended to more elaborate prose — perhaps to affect a semblance of personal mystery, an esoteric eclat or occult ambiance.

And why not? Since by his own admittance James was "psych-ically endowed," for which reason he'd become one of our guinea pigs of course. As for Jason: at first he had seemed bewildered by the whole thing. But he had been unemployed, and we had made him an irresistible offer.

Their induction had come following various checks and controls. First: they were just two out of two and a half thousand applicants who answered our ad in national broadsheets. Second: after discarding the sad, mistaken, lying, wannabe, and lunatic two thousand four hundred, the finalists had undergone an exhaustive series of parapsychological tests, which further narrowed the field. Both James and Jason had passed with flying colours, once again to the latter's apparent astonishment. Third: during Zener Card testing at a government establishment, they had been brought into close proximity with an "alien artifact"; this had been caused to occur while they slept in a dormitory unaware of what was happening and under close, covert observation. Both of them had experienced troubling dreams, indeed nightmares.

(Additional to my description of the cell: the "alien artifact" mentioned in the preceding paragraph was fixed centrally in a strengthened glass sphere upon a marble pedestal in the living area, where its influence if any would be unavoidable by the two men.)

Oh, and one other factor conducive to their recruitment: they were both readers of other-worldly romances, with a penchant for the macabre; and so they were acquainted with the speculative fiction facet of matters which the Foundation had been attempting to fathom for several decades. In short, their minds would not be closed to themes, theories, and suggestions which narrower, more orthodox intellects might find unacceptable and immediately refute: they were "familiar" with notions of parallel dimensions, UFOs, alien encounters, and et cetera.

Enough: I have set the scene as clearly as possible within certain limits. So now let James and Jason speak for themselves.

One last point. While the following conversations are accurate (as covertly recorded by myself) I've excised and replaced certain names and references as a further security measure. For as elsewhere stated correspondence such as this — intended only for the eyes of my former Foundation colleagues — may not be as safe as their archive records.

Note: For easy recognition, all such altered sections will be parenthesized.

JASON, YAWNING: "What time do you have?"

James, showing great disinterest: "Does it really matter? After all, we're not going anywhere."

Jason: "I like to be regular in my habits and I'm feeling a bit hungry, so I suspect it's time to eat."

James: "You could regulate your habits by wearing a watch — but since I know you'll only ask again, and since I'm already bored by this meaningless conversation . . . it's six-forty. And before you ask, that's p.m."

Jason, grinning: "Thank you. Most gracious of you. And it seems I was right: time to eat."

James: "I'm not hungry."

Jason: "Then don't eat. Me, I'm frying up mushrooms with a few slices of liver and bacon."

James, suddenly restless: "Then perhaps I will eat, after all."

Jason, going to the fridge: "I'll be sure to set out equal, fresh portions for you . . . unless you want me to cook them for you?"

James, sighing: "Would that be such an inconvenience?"

Jason: "No more than glancing at your watch occasionally, no."

James, changing the subject, staring fixedly at the artifact in its glass sphere, where its pedestal rose through the centre of the circular table at which he was seated: "Did you dream last night?"

Jason, frowning, and squirting a mist of olive oil into a frying pan: "Three nights, three dreams, yes."

James: "The same dream?"

Jason, perhaps slightly troubled: "The very same. But very vague . . . more a set of sensations than a dream proper. Nothing clearly visual, nothing spoken out loud. Mental whispers, or — I don't know — instinctive knowledge? Well, if you know what I mean."

James: "Interesting. And of course I know what you mean! Do you think you're more sensitive to this stuff than I am? I have been living with the knowledge of the truth of all this for . . . for longer than I care to think. Oh, yes. And I was dreaming my dreams long before they sat me in front of this thing." He indicated the artifact, enlarged and distorted by the glass of its globe.

Jason, with perhaps a hint of amusement or gentle sarcasm in his voice: "You have always known you were, er, psychic?"

James: "My ESP skills are different from yours — each to his own mentality — but yes, I have always known. I feel things from afar, and in my dreams they are made manifest. Even though I am not given to understand everything, still I see what is now . . . unlike you who sees what will be."

Jason, nodding, turning slivers of liver and bacon slices in his pan: "Or so I've lately discovered — but I didn't know, not for sure. Or maybe I did, but tried to avoid it — because it worried me."

James, with a snort: "Being able to see the future worried you?

You were too dim to find a use for a skill like that? You scored 78 per cent on the Zener test, yet you were too poor to afford a wristwatch? And if you were 'trying to avoid it,' why on earth did you answer the ad in the first place?"

Jason: "Because I was too poor to afford a wristwatch — or anything else for that matter! We weren't all born with silver spoons in our mouths, you know! Anyway, why do I annoy you? Is there that about me which reminds you of something intolerably nasty that you stepped in at one time or another? Or could it be some kind of jealousy, because my skills are apparent while yours are — let's face it — more or less, er, obscure?"

James, straightening up, narrowing his eyes more yet: "My skills may be obscure, as you put it, but our sponsors saw fit to choose me no less than you. In fact, I have always been . . . chosen. From the very first moment I read of (Cxxxxxx) and the others of the pantheon I knew that they were real; and that one day—when my stars were in the ascendant—I would communicate with them."

Jason, not quite sneering, but with a cynical twist to his mouth: "Why can't you say what you mean?"

James, sharply: "I beg your pardon?"

Jason: "Don't you mean, 'When the stars are right?'"

James, with a cold sidelong glance at Jason: "Interpret my words as you will — and (Axxxxxxx's) if you dare! But he wasn't such a madman, that old Arab. Or if he was, it was what he half knew but could not fathom that made him that way." And, after a brief pause: "Doesn't it concern you that you could be a millionaire instead of a pauper?"

Jason, returning to the table with two plates of sizzling food: "Are you talking about gambling again? How I could have beaten the bookies, cleaned up at roulette, broken the bank at Monte Carlo? But you know what they say about practice, how it makes perfect? . . . Maybe I didn't want to perfect what I might have suspected I could do. Perhaps I didn't want to see things — certain things — any clearer. It could even be that some of the futures I had seen were too clear by half."

The pair, lapsing into silence while they eat. But after a while James asking: "What is it you saw that frightened you so? Myself, I have no fear with regard to the Mythos. I might possibly fear my own imaginings, which are not real, but I cannot fear what is real—and imminent! What is real exists, and what exists will find ways to impinge and may not be avoided. Wherefore what use to fear it?"

Jason, around his last mouthful of food: "But exactly! *Que sera sera!* Ah, but would you really want to know the day, hour, and minute of your own death? And can't you see how knowing it you would try to avoid it?—to no avail. *Que sera sera!*"

James, his eyes fully open, staring now: "You saw your own death?"

Jason, thoughtfully: "Not my death, no—but my brother's, and my mother's. Enough to put me off."

James: "Interesting. Can you tell me about it?"

Jason: "Not now. Some other time, maybe. But now I'm tired. A glass of white wine might help me sleep . . . hopefully not to dream."

James: "But that is why we are here! Surely you've divined that much?"

Jason: "Of course. But still I get paid, whether I dream or not. And I prefer not."

To which there is no answer . . .

JASON TOSSES, TURNS, and sweats in his sleep. He cries out, but feebly, on several occasions. The wine has not helped.

James is similarly affected. But he isn't so much nightmaring as experiencing; which is to say that while Jason is trying to escape from whatever pursues or threatens, James accepts it.

His claim that he does not fear the Mythos (the effects wrought by the artifact) appear to be borne out. Our psychiatric specialist is at least of that opinion: that unlike Jason, James has been having — or perhaps receiving? — dreams such as this for a long time, even as long as he claims, and has become inured.

But he is voluble.

He speaks of a (Shining Txxxxxxxxxxxx): an odd geometrical figure, and of a "prehistoric city, Mnar"—not the ruins in the Deer Park at Benares. He spouts of "the outer spheres" and "star-spawn," and "the lenses of light," before his subconscious ramblings become unintelligible gibberings—a mush and a mumble, defying reproduction by normal human vocal chords, and proving equally difficult to represent, even as writing. Then, after a period of lying perfectly still in an attitude of rapt attention, as if he were listening to something or someone, he states quite clearly, "I shall be your vessel, your gate, your embodiment. And through you I shall visit the farthest places: that roiling lake where the puffed (Sxxxxxxxx) spawn, the spiralling Towers of (Txxxxxxx), the dark light-years twirling like leaves blown in a storm. But . . . this 'great harvest' of which you speak. Pray tell me, what shall we harvest?"

And then a gasp, a cry choked off, his body snapping into a weird rigidity and only very slowly relaxing, and his breathing steadying as his face slackens and he falls more deeply asleep, as if soothed by some unseen hypnotist's persuasions . . .

THE NIGHT PASSES. The pair sleep late, and when they rise they avoid each other . . . James very deliberately, Jason because he can't be bothered with the surliness of the other's moods.

Jason cooks breakfast for himself; James doesn't eat until well into the afternoon when he makes a small cheese sandwich, then sits eating it, scowling at the artifact. And finally:

James: "I believe I heard you call out in the night?"

Jason: "Unlike the outer shell of this place, the partitions between our rooms are thin as cardboard! You could hear a mouse fart on the other side. As for my outcry: well, my dream was a particularly bad one."

James: "Which doubtless accounts for your mood."

Jason: "Oh?"

James: "Your silence."

Jason: "Listen who's talking! We were here for forty-eight hours before you so much as grunted!"

James: "As I recall, you complained to me about the lack of a TV. You asked why not. I did not grunt. I pointed out that as well as the absence of a TV there was no radio and indeed nothing that might interfere with our seclusion, concentration, the immanence of ulterior forces. And incidentally, I don't dislike you. You accused me of disliking you, but that is not so. It is simply that I

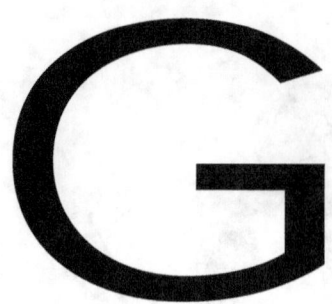

am remote from you . . . my thoughts are rarely mundane. And when I am disturbed — when my thoughts are interrupted — then naturally it becomes an inconvenience, an annoyance. So you see it isn't the case that I dislike you, rather that I despise idle prattle. Not dislike but disinclination, disinterest."

Jason, sighing, shaking his head: "You don't seem to realize just how insulting such remarks are. Now I'm not normally a surly fellow, but I can certainly feel myself sliding that way. Today you were the one who commenced 'prattling,' and I suspect you're not yet done!"

James: "Because while you fail to excite my interest, your dreams are quite another matter. On several occasions I am sure I heard you cry out. This was before I myself fell asleep. Were you dreaming of your brother? Or perhaps your mother? I believe I heard you call a name. But I was only half awake and so can't be sure."

Jason: "Is this important to you? I can't see why. And what with your lack of interest in me—the fact that my presence is 'an inconvenience' and even 'an annoyance'—I don't see why I should trouble myself to talk to you at all, not a single word! And certainly not about my poor dead mother or brother."

James: "But the fact is you were prescient in the matter of their deaths. Could it be that your dreams represent guilt? You foresaw their deaths and could do nothing about it . . . *que sera sera*. And now they come back to haunt you. As to why this is of interest to me: I see the NOW while failing to understand where it is going, while you see what is to be without knowing how to avoid it. I seek to probe deeper, while you turn away from your talent."

Jason, shrugging: "So? Is there a lesson to be learned from these supposed facts? What is your conclusion?"

James, a trifle reluctantly: "That . . . perhaps we ought to work together? After all that, presumably, is why they saw fit to lodge us as a pair."

Jason: "Possibly, but it's a shame they couldn't have found me a female guinea pig partner. That way I wouldn't be spending quite so much time dreaming."

James, raising an eyebrow: "Sex? I have no time for it and never will have. It is an animal activity. Out beyond the stars . . . their procreation is different. More a melding, a substitution, a flowing together, and an explosive multiplication."

Jason, singing: " . . . It's the name of the game, and each generation . . . "

James, apparently aghast: "You would do well not to mock!"

Jason: "Oh, really? I shouldn't mock? When what you've just said sounded like you were describing a clan of alien amoebas?"

James, apparently in disgust: "Pshaw!"

LATER: JASON, SITTING at the table staring at the artifact, then bursting abruptly into speech: "My brother—and especially my mother—bring me warnings. Yes, I'm oneiromantic, but my pre-cognition isn't so much advanced knowledge of what to do or to avoid doing but, as you might have it, knowledge of the direction in which my current position or standing is leading me. In other words, their warnings are useless by reason of the fact that the outcome cannot be avoided. They can warn of my going to hell, but they can't offer me a fire-proof parachute!"

James: "*Que . . .* "

Jason, cutting the other off: "Yes, yes! Of course! What will be will be."

James, nodding sagely: "So then, the dead go on; at least their thoughts: they are not dead who can forever lie. Having undergone their change—knowing more of Being by experiencing Not Being—they attempt to communicate their knowledge, their warnings, to the living loved ones they left behind. In which case I suspect—no, I affirm—that we have this in common with the gods of outer spheres. They too go on forever. Except they don't die but are truly immortal! In my dreams I've seen them; their myriad shapes seeping down from the stars!"

Jason: "I only know of me and mine, which are real things. As for alien beings 'seeping' down from the stars: the nearest star — other than Sol — is four and a half light-years away. That's one hell of a seep! I am convinced it's all a fiction. Think about it. A certain star is a billion light years away. Even at the speed of light your alien 'gods' will take a billion years to get here. And if they are only 'seeping' . . . ?"

James, with a shrug: "As for it being a fiction, our hosts don't seem to think so, else why are we here? And as for 'seeping': a poetic turn of phrase. The Old Gentleman might just as well have used 'filtering,' which is another slow process."

Jason: "Yes, he used 'seeping' — but he meant it like poison in a wound, like pus from an open sore. And remember: the gods of his pantheon were evil. Is that what you crave, the destruction of everything we consider good?"

James, sneeringly: "Hah! Good, bad, love, hate — emotions in general — they are beyond, *above* all that! And anyway, you miss what should be obvious: that they are timeless."

Jason, grunting, and the corners of his mouth turning down: "Timeless — sleeping but not dead — oh yeah, sure."

James, dreamily, ignoring Jason's obvious sarcasm: "Immortal they journey, wandering between the stars, pausing now and then, but only long enough to . . . to harvest their worlds."

Jason: "Immortal? They will be here until the end? Doesn't that imply that they were here at the beginning? How, immortal? Though I'll grant you they would need to be to 'seep' down from the stars!"

James: "Exactly! And that is the point you missed. For when you speak of the speed of light you should not forget that time stands still at such a speed! It is the secret of their immortality: that during their journey they do not age!"

Jason does not answer immediately; when he does, it is only to frown and ask: "Do you think that perhaps we're confused? Do you feel confused? Our conversations, our arguments, seem to go in circles. And personally my mind never felt so cluttered! But . . . maybe I've asked you that before? Or did you ask me?"

James, ignoring the other's question and indicating with a nod of his head and a pointed finger the artifact in its glass globe: "There it is: a 'lens of light,' or so I believe. But do you know where they found it, these people who are using us in an attempt to prove its properties?"

Jason, blinking rapidly, as if to clear his head of confusing thoughts: "No, do you?"

James: "Absolutely! Before I volunteered my person for this experiment, I had them volunteer their sources, their whys and wherefors. Are you interested?"

Jason: "I shall try to be."

James: "It was five years ago, in Iraq, after the war that deposed Saddam the Dictator."

Jason: "Ah, yes! Saddam Hussein and his alleged, er, weapons of mass destruction? I remember."

James: "The American forces stopped a truck on its way to Syria. They found a large amount of gold, a million dollars in hundred dollar bills, and certain items of immense antiquity — including an old book or scroll written in an ancient, indecipherable script. The book contained a map of the desert — with a certain area marked out in the shape of a five-pointed star. It transpired that the book's ancient text was the language of a sunken city or continent lost in Pacific deeps."

Jason: "By any chance, (R'xxxx)? Where (Cxxxxxx) lies dreaming?"

James, nodding: "The same—or so I suspect—though for some reason no one has deigned to confirm my suspicion in that regard. But, learning of the book's existence, a certain esoteric organization took steps to obtain it. Among our hosts are members of that organization;... Do you want to know more?"

Jason: "All very interesting. And by all means carry on."

James: "As you wish. The five-pointed star symbol is well known; indeed its powers, if any, have long been prone to argument among certain savants — "

Jason: "Savants?"

James: "Authorities, such as you and I."

Jason: "But I don't consider myself an 'authority,' merely a reader of weird and macabre fiction."

James, scornfully: "Not to mention someone who catches the occasional glimpse of the future! But let me proceed:

"The map indicated or superimposed this pentagram on a portion of the Iraqi desert. And the most important thing is this, that the desert has not changed in a million years, not to any significant degree. Anyway, the esoteric organization of which I speak sent their agents to investigate, ostensibly to search out elusive weapons of mass destruction said to be hidden somewhere in those great wastelands. But in fact they had predetermined to locate the points of the star symbol — and from these to determine its geometric centre.

"This was not nearly as difficult as it might at first have seemed. The locals offered up information; they said that there were five 'holy men' who occupied the selfsame locations out in the desert. And each of the five — drug-addicted Dervishes, as it transpired, and completely bereft of reason as perceived in our western society — was discovered to be in possession of a star-stone! Alas, they were also in possession of Russian small arms, which they did not hesitate to turn on the investigators. Enter the military, who dealt with these five 'terrorists' with despatch . . . or so I assume since the star-stones were confiscated or 'commandeered.'

"Now we move to the geometric centre: a dried-up well, into which our investigators descend, and down below discover a vast natural cavern, once a waterway — but how many millennia ago? — whose walls are carved with myriad foreign or alien sigils. And upon a marble pedestal at the approximate centre — "

Jason, pointing at the artifact in its glass bubble: "That thing."

James: "Indeed!"

Jason: "I see. And the star-stones kept it secure, turning aside its malign influence. Correct?"

James, shaking his head: "This is not how I perceive it . . . though I can see how such confusion in the Mythos arose originally. No, I believe that upon a time the cavern housed a Being. As for 'malign': I fail to see anything malign in this. What I do see is that there are travellers out there among the stars; not gods, not evil aliens, in no way a threat, but scientists! Different, certainly — our superiors in as many fields as you care to number, and in others that you can't even imagine, you may be sure — but 'kept secure,' yes, I can agree with that."

Jason: "Secure against what?"

James: "Secure against being disturbed! It is a marker, and perhaps even a Gateway, for those who wander the star spaces."

Jason, whose sneer no longer carries conviction: "Sure, and who perform their wandering, seeping, or filtering at the speed of light, eh? As for these five Arab madmen, these zealots: why were they so protective of the star-stones, or rather, this so-called 'lens of light?' Why would they lay down their lives for it? Were they protecting it as some kind of holy relic, or were they in fact protecting us, humankind, from it?"

James: "Bah! Your thoughts are mired in fear! You're a pronounced xenophobe!"

Jason: "Possibly, and on a cosmic scale at that! But in the light of my precognizance, ask yourself this: what do you suppose I am most afraid of?"

James: "Of the (Gxxxx Oxx Oxxx), the Outer Ones, of course. Of the thought of Them in the spaces between the spaces we know — in the stellar voids — riding the gravitic waves of exploding stars! Of their superiority!"

Jason: "Wrong! But you've mentioned two things that do concern me. One: you spoke of Them harvesting their worlds — "

James, starting, blinking, obviously taken aback: "Eh? Did I? A harvest? Yes, indeed, I seem to recall saying something of the sort. I may even have dreamed something of it. But now . . . I can't seem to remember what it was about."

Jason: "There are beads of sweat on your brow. Are you now feeling confused?"

James, wiping his forehead: "Quite right. It's suddenly hot in here. Whoever controls the temperature is not doing his job. But confused? I'm not sure." Then, after a moment's thought: "And two?"

Jason: "Two?"

James: "The second thing I said that concerns you. What was it?"

Jason: "Ah yes! You called the lens a 'Gateway.' And if so, well, wouldn't that be something to fear?"

James, throwing his arms wide: "For thought! A Gateway that allows my thoughts to reach out to Them . . . and theirs to reach me—to reach us, if you would only help me, assist me in opening up our minds to them!"

Jason, thoughtfully: "I think we've both been somewhat confused ever since being put in this place. I certainly have not been thinking clearly, and you've blown hot and cold — contradicted yourself — on several occasions. But if what you say is right: that the lens is a Gateway for mental communication . . . well, perhaps that would explain it."

James, snapping his fingers: "And there you have it! Their thoughts are incompatible with ours, or at best only marginally readable. Can we explain ourselves to sea snakes or gibbons? No of course not! Likewise their purpose — their messages — come unclear, distorted, and misunderstood by us."

Jason: "You admit it, then? That we are being influenced by that thing in the globe?"

James: "Is there any need to admit what was obvious to me from the start? It is why we are here; to enable our observers to discover to what degree we are influenced. For after all, we are the guinea pigs — the ones with enhanced psychic senses — whereas they are merely . . . observers."

NOTE: In this James was only partly right. I was not lacking in certain psychic sensitivities myself; not as intense as James's or Jason's, true, but certainly I had experienced and was still experiencing something of the lens's peculiar influence, a sort of mental confusion—as had the Dervishes in the Iraqi desert, to the extent that prolonged exposure was probably responsible for their madness. It was not our intention, however, to allow so grave a deterioration in our subjects; the experiment could be brought to a close at any time. No, our main interest lay in whatever other properties the lens might or might not possess.

JAMES, CONTINUING: "So then, shall we work together rather than continue to constantly needle each other?"

Jason: "If I have needled it was only or mainly in riposte. And I think I'll sleep on the idea of working together. Perhaps someone will advise me in that regard."

James: "Your . . . relatives?"

Jason: "Perhaps. My mother was clairvoyant, and my brother . . . was my twin. We were all three in a traffic accident. I saw it coming but could do nothing about it. In the moment of their deaths . . . maybe something transferred to me. It strikes me as possible that they had seen it coming, too. As to why that may be relevant to our current situation: I have been experiencing similar feelings of imminence."

James: "You are worried that you're going to die?"

Jason: "I feel . . . a sense of transference, metamorphosis—as if I were about to take flight!"

James, nodding: "Light-headedness. I can feel it, too—the pressure of my thoughts."

Jason: "Ah yes, thoughts! Which reminds me of something you said earlier. On that same subject, tell me if you will how you intend to exchange thoughts with alien Beings who could be billions of light years away? That is, assuming the speed of light to be the ultimate reach of material things."

James: "But you have supplied the answer to your own question! Thought is not material. It may take time and myriad small electrical impulses to cogitate, but once a thought is set free it exists everywhere. The lens amplifies thoughts, directs them and makes them accessible. But a thought in itself, in its immanence, is as far-ranging as the entire universe!"

Jason: "Accessible, but not understandable?"

James, nodding: "Hence the confusion, our confusion. We are less than successful at comprehending the incomprehensible, the mental emanations of minds that think in a great many more dimensions than our pitiful three."

Jason, tiredly now: "Well anyway, let's sleep on it . . ."

BUT OF COURSE the observers must sleep too. We were taking the watch in shifts; that night it was the turn of our psychiatric specialist and myself. The technician slept as best possible on a couch in a room adjacent. It was not the best of times for my mental processes; I was feeling the strain; indeed, the thought had crossed my mind that, despite the strength and thickness of the cell's walls, I too was in close proximity to the lens.

The lens:

Three inches across, a scalloped, faceted disc of what appeared to be smoky quartz. Its constituent elements had not been analysed for fear of damaging its as-yet-unknown properties. It seemed inactive; had never shown any kind of activity; might as well have been some not especially elegant paperweight.

I asked my companion of the night watch for her thoughts on the subject.

"The lens?" She brought the object in its glass bubble into focus on one of the screens. "I find it . . . disturbing."

"Its looks, shape, opacity?"

"Its presence."

She meant its proximity, of course. "Do you feel in any way . . . confused?"

She smiled. "Tiredness, that's all. Leading to a perfectly natural lack of concentration." Which confirmed what I had suspected . . .

JAMES, HIS EYES hollow, red-rimmed: "Well, we've slept on it — myself, badly. And frankly, I have had enough of this so-called experiment. I suggest we put our minds to it, see or experience what we see or experience, and however it goes we call it a day and demand to be out of here. As far as I am concerned they can keep their money. I know what I know, and that must suffice."

Jason, cooking breakfast, his voice far-distant: "I dreamed of dinosaurs; herds of them, thousands of them, stampeding."

James, with a start, his sore eyes blinking rapidly: "Why, so did I!" And then, recovering himself and rather more calmly, "What do you suppose it means?"

Jason, having apparently failed to hear, or having ignored James' question: "I also dreamed of my mother and brother. They didn't say anything and looked sad, but in any case I knew what they were thinking: that I wouldn't be joining them."

James: "That you are not going to die? A good omen, eh?"

Jason, shaking his head: "No, just that I won't be joining them. I also heard a song or a chant . . . no, it was more properly a hymn or song of — I don't know — thanksgiving? Possibly." And giving himself a shake. "Breakfast is up. We might as well enjoy it." Then, as they commence eating: "We always assumed it was a meteorite or comet that took out the dinosaurs, right?"

James: "So?"

Jason: "What if it was Them?"

James, nodding: "I know what you mean, but it just doesn't fit the picture. You're talking about prehistory. Who was there here to call them down from the stars? Man's earliest ancestors hadn't as yet crawled up out of the oceans, let alone come down from the trees!"

Jason, bringing the food — eggs and bacon — seating himself close to James and handing him a plate; then absentmindedly, or even fatalistically picking at his own food: "What if They were already here? Or maybe they just happened to be passing by, and saw how rich it was — the planet, I mean. Personally, I believe that one of them was here, alone in a crazily-angled city maybe something like (R'xxxx). And he/she/it called through a lens to its friends in the stars. And the closest of them came — "

James: "— To the harvest? Is that what you are saying? But even if I thought you could be right, still it might have taken them millions of years to get here."

Jason: "But the dinosaurs were here for millions of years — for a whole lot longer than we've been here, anyway."

James: "And that cavern out in the Iraqi desert? You think it's all that remains of that prehistoric city? Forget it! That cave is recent by comparison. A million, or perhaps two million years old, but no more than that."

Jason: "I agree. No, I think who or whatever was there in the Iraqi cavern got called away long ago, perhaps to a harvesting somewhere out in the stars. But he had seen the beginnings of Homo sapiens, and he left the lens for us to find. Maybe old (Axxxx) was something of a dreamer—maybe he was gifted, that old Arab — like us, but he got it wrong. Maybe the stars don't 'come right' until some intelligence finds them and takes them away! Because they aren't stars in the sky after all but star-stones buried deep in the earth! Too many maybes, I agree, but maybe, just maybe . . ."

James, scathingly: "And maybe, just maybe, you want to give in, quit right now—right?"

Jason: "Quit? On the contrary. I think we should go ahead, speak to them through the lens. Why? Because we can't avoid the unavoidable. And I know you'll do it anyway, because you're ignorant, arrogant and pig-headed. And what the hell . . . *que sera sera!*" He shrugs, again fatalistically.

James, tight-lipped: "Putting insults such as that aside—if only because contact will probably be easier with your help—when do you propose we do it? Tonight?"

Jason, shrugging: "Tonight, tomorrow night, next Friday . . . what difference does it make down here? Why not right now?"

James, turning to stare at the lens in its glass globe, the lens that Jason has been staring at from the moment he sat down at the table: "Right now? Are you sure?"

Jason, putting his plate aside: "It's all . . . all very confusing, isn't it?"

James: "Do you feel you're being lured?"

Jason: "Lured? Let me think about that." And a brief moment later: "Yes, I believe I can feel that thing tugging at me. But mainly I just feel as I think you feel—that come what may we have to know. Or we have to know come what will."

James, also pushing his plate of untouched food aside, and resting his chin in his cupped hands: "Very well then, let's do it . . . "

NOTE: FOLLOWING OUR night shift — myself and our good lady psychiatrist — we could by now have been asleep; but something had kept us at our stations, where we had been joined by our military companions and my Foundation colleague. Our technician was drowsing in a room close by, but such were my feelings of — of what? Uncertainty, confusion, imminence — of interference with my thinking, that I had known I would be unable to sleep. Which was probably also true of my night's companion.

I have mentioned my own somewhat shallow extrasensory perceptions; but now through the medium of this ESP I "perceived" a current that was almost electric, a faint tingle in my scalp. And I was aware that on my viewscreen the forms of the two men in the cell had taken on a kind of rigidity. Their eyes—and their sensitive minds, obviously—were now rapt upon the lens in its bowl atop the pedestal.

And that was when I fought back against my own feelings of almost hypnotic lethargy to send one of our military number to wake the technician . . .

JASON, HIS EYES wide open, staring; his mouth agape; his voice little more than a whisper: "I can hear them singing. The same song or hymn I heard in my dream. It's dark, yet somehow joyful . . . a strange dark joy."

James, excitedly, but at the same time oddly dull or vacant of volume: "Then rejoice in the contact! Out there in the stars, they have heard us!"

Jason: "In the stars, or between the spaces we know? Is the lens a telepathic transmitter, or is it in fact a true Gateway? What if They . . . what if they're extra-dimensional?"

James, a bubble of foam forming at the corner of his mouth: "How far away is an extra-dimension? 'Beyond' the universe?"

Jason, twitching, his knuckles turning white on the table's rim: "But what . . . what if . . . what if it's parallel?"

James, beginning to shudder violently: "I hear the singing, too! And although it's alien, I believe there are parts that I recognize or at least understand."

Jason, his body jerking, threatening to topple his chair: "Their thoughts are merging with ours; either that or they are translating them for us, making them recognizable. And the lens . . . it is a Gateway. And they're using it! They're coming!"

James, dead white, foaming at the mouth, his eyes bulging, entire body vibrating: "I think ... I think we should stop now. I think we should . . . think we have to withdraw. I sense chaos. And the lens: it's glowing, blazing, opening! Ah! Ahhh! Ahhhh!"

NOTE: IT IS DIFFICULT to describe what we saw happening on our screens from this point on. But I shall try.

The lens in its globe was shimmering, emitting lances and arcs of bright white light that came through the glass to dart around the cell like living things, like snakes of fire. These dozen or so streamers or coruscations were certainly sentient; they appeared to be searching, or perhaps surveying, the immediate vicinity, but in something less than five or six seconds they converged into two main beams that struck unerringly home at the heads of our subjects. It happened that fast, literally with lightning speed, and "confused" as we four observers were (our technician and the military man I had sent to awaken him were only now returning) there was nothing we could do to stop it. And on our screens—

—The pair appeared to be melting! Their faces were showing extraordinary agony; they glowed until their eyes and gaping mouths were black sockets in bright, luminous silhouettes; their shaking seemed to be tearing them apart, so that glowing bits were drifting from them like fiery snowflakes . . . and yet they were still singing!

Over and above a high-pitched, alien keening—a blast of noise I can only describe as a battle of unknown elements, the sound of waves breaking on some cosmic shore—came the words of that song driven into their shattered minds and out through their mouths, that "hymn" translated from its original form by who or whatever they had contacted. And in my own mind I heard or sensed something of that original form—that hideous cacophony that human vocal cords could never hope to duplicate — and I knew its relevance!

"Stop it!" I cried then, to anyone who was listening — if anyone was listening. "Shut the thing down!"

My companions were reeling — shocked, numbed, made useless, by what they, too, were receiving from the lens, that now fully open portal. But as for the physical intruders, those shafts of alien light or sentient fire: they were only the vanguard. For what was coming through now was more properly the stuff of our most terrifying nightmares.

They moved too quickly, too strangely, to be viewed in any kind of clear detail. But in colour they were a pulsing yellow-veined or marbled purple and black, and in shape reminiscent of spiders, scorpions, octopi or dragons . . . all these things from moment to moment, and others utterly indescribable. Yet I knew that even these were only a squad of advance troops.

James and Jason: they were beginning to slump into themselves, like slowly collapsing columns or candles of intense white light; but even so, quite beyond pain as we understand it, they continued to sing their joyful song.

"Shut the damn thing down!" I yelled again, this time right in the ear of our technician, who was looking at his instrument panel as if he had never seen it in his life before! His confusion was apparent from his gaping mouth and bulging, stupified eyes. While in the cell a nightmarish metamorphosis was taking place.

What was it James had said that time, of alien procreation?

Something about, "A melding, a substitution, a flowing together and explosive multiplication?" Well, what was happening in the cell may not have been procreation — unless it was by assimilation and duplication — but it was certainly everything else he had spoken of. The scuttling insect-octopus-dragons were invading the radiance of our disintegrating guinea-pig subjects only to emerge in a stream of yet more fantastic shapes and figures; and as James and Jason melted to nothingness, so the star-spawn multiplied in number, bursting forth from those — consumed? — human remnants to come nosing, thrusting at the tiny cameras.

They bloated large on our screens; they knew we were looking at them, scrabbled to send hairy, spiked and multi-jointed legs right through the audio and visual systems — through the screens themselves — into our control room! While in the cell the globe containing the lens shivered to shards and something huge, black, bloated and baneful began to squeeze through from some Other Place, some other space, into ours.

One of our military men was leaning forward, his hands supporting him on the ledge in front of his screen, hypnotized by what he could see but scarcely believe was taking place in the cell. A vibrating black spider-leg eighteen inches long stabbed through the screen into his mouth and out the back of his skull — and he jerked like a puppet as he hung there suspended on it.

I cried out—a gurgled shriek, something quite inarticulate — and aimed a blow at the back of our technician, catching him between the shoulder blades. Driven forward, he flailed his arms; his hand came down on one of the controls . . . sheer luck!

Five pipes or shafts, pneumatic conduits descending at different angles to locations buried in the steel walls, hummed and pulsed. And from up above five star-stones hurtled under pressure down these channels to form the points of a pentagram surrounding the cell. With which it was over.

The alien insect things shrivelled to nothing; the cell exploded with such force that the walls were actually scarred and even buckled in several places; the gonging reverberations were such that my eardrums burst and I lost consciousness. But I was fortunate, for the others with me lost a lot more than that . . .

From then until now I have kept mainly silent, and from time to time I've mimicked the conditions of my four surviving colleagues, which has meant spending time in various institutions. But I did not want anyone questioning me too deeply; I did not want to become any kind of guinea pig in my own right; I had no more interest in any facet of The Mythos Investigation.

You see, I know why I was the sole survivor — the only one to live through it with his person and sanity intact — for I, too, had heard their singing; They saw me as a possible future vessel, or as a radio signal, or a lighthouse to guide them in to harbour. Which is why it is only now, as my cancer kills me and I have mere days to live, that I'm able to report the occurrences of that time as they happened.

As for the lens Gateway: it was vaporised in the blast, of course. I can only hope no other device of that sort exists in our world. The star-stones were likewise destroyed; I hope and pray others have been discovered, or that you, my once colleagues in The Foundation, are at least seeking them out.

And meanwhile:

I have come to believe in God and would even be a regular churchgoer . . . except I cannot bring myself to attend services in the harvest time. There is a certain hymn they'd be sure to sing, and I know I couldn't abide it. Even now I find it difficult to think about it, and even harder to write the words of the song down. But since this is probably the best way to make you understand:

Waiting for the harvest, and the time of reaping,
We shall come rejoicing, bringing in the sheaves.
Bringing in the sheaves, bringing in the sheaves,
We shall come rejoicing, bringing in the sheaves.

Sometimes I dream of great lizards — dinosaurs stampeding in terror through tree-fern forests — and then I wonder about all the other mass extinctions our planet has known. But —

— I long ago retired to Dublin, Ireland, where I discovered that while white wine doesn't help a lot with my sleeplessness, Guinness does the trick every time . . . ๑

Our interview with Brian Lumley appears on page 12.

ILLUSTRATION BY SPECTRAL

THE DEAD WERE WALKING ABOARD SHIP.
BUT THIS WASN'T THE CARIBBEAN,
AND NO ONE WAS LAUGHING.

Strange Wisdoms of the Dead

by Mike Allen and Charles M. Saplak

John Starkey pulled a funeral shroud from one of the corpses stacked on deck, wrapped his shoulders against the chill. He bent the corpse forward to free the shroud; it stayed slightly bent at the waist, and seemed to stare at Starkey, eyes wide but without lustre, hands frozen in a gesture of clutching.

Starkey returned to the wheel of the *Saint Catherine*, and barely gave the corpse another glance. He was cold, he was busy. "Laying to" the one-hundred-and-forty foot sloop was ticklish, even with a full watch onboard; Starkey was the only one alive on this creaking, half-rotted vessel.

He needed to take her out the channel, and northward about three miles. There he would lash the mainsail over hard port, and the wheel over hard starboard, as close to simultaneously as possible. At nightfall he would fire the pitch and straw in the ship's hold. The burning ship would drift south with the current. Starkey would be safely aboard the dinghy he was towing, rowing back to collect his fee. The good citizens of Bliss, those not dead from The Plague, nor taken to the hills for fear of it, would see the ship burn down to the waterline, and would know that more than one hundred and seventy of their stiff, cold brethren were being sent to the next world — and so would be off the streets, with neither smell, nor raw bone, nor ichor to bedevil the living.

The city fathers would give him seventy pieces of the local coinage — two years living, come what may. But coin was only part of the reason Starkey was here . . . .

The channel behind him, Starkey turned the *Saint Catherine* into the northern current. He was making the maneuver more complicated than it had to be. He needed a certain amount of extra time.

He would set the rigging first, since the wheel would be easy. He already had the ragged mainsail at full trim, and had a six-to-one block rigged to take a strain on the traveler, necessary to move the massive sail himself.

He was glad he was alone. He wouldn't have to share his pay. And what he wanted to do, no one could see . . . .

He sweated with effort, despite the chill. The air began to mist over. Strange, thought Starkey. Not the right time of day for fog to form. He glanced at the surface of the water. The normal gray translucence of early winter seawater was now a crystalline blue, a blue like the glaze on porcelain. And above it, thickening fog.

It isn't right. A current from the north, with thick fog? In late afternoon, well before nightfall? Could the blue water be that warm? Nothing makes sense . . . .

But this was not the time to puzzle. He pulled the end of the block rigging over to a ratcheting windlass on the port side amidships. He had the bitter end of the rig made around the windlass, and took up a wooden pin he could use as a lever. He inserted the pin, and leaned into it.

On deck, the stacked and shrouded cargo shifted a little as the boom tensioned and began to shift.

The fo'c'sle and jib entered the fog. Wispy fingers of mist curled 'round slowly, stroking the ship.

Starkey continued to crank the windlass, taking more and more strain. The block tightened some more, and the mainsail boom complained, but continued to swing.

The wind grew, and fog slid like snakes of smoke along the deck. The rigging creaked and complained, and the windlass shivered in his hands. Through his sailor's calluses he felt that something was wrong. Damn this old condemned stack of splinters! The rigging was rotten, the mechanisms were rotten, the hull was rotten . . . .

A rogue wave from the north punched the *Saint Catherine*, she lurched port, and the stack of corpses shifted. One corpse tumbled to the deck, and its shroud fell open, revealing pasty skin and caked blood. Starkey had no time to think, as rigging groaned, then sang, then snapped. The mainsail boom swept the deck, and Starkey could only watch as things unfolded with unreal speed.

And then he was struck, and darkness.

TWO

Starkey knew nothing but cold: a deep, invasive chill that frosted his bones, stung his eyes, and filled his head with visions of eternal snow. He slowly realized that his eyes were open. He lay face up on the deck, staring at a torn sail that flapped soundlessly within a shroud of fog.

He tried to rise and groaned as a knife of pain sliced his temple from within. When his eyes focused again he ran fingers through his hair, and drew them back bloody. Nausea coursed through him. He remained still until it passed, his gaze falling on one of the wrapped forms stacked nearby, on a calloused and dirty hand free from the swaddling shroud.

When he could breathe steadily again, he rose, this time more gingerly, and peered seaward.

He couldn't tell if it was twilight or dawn. The fog was so thick here on deck that when he held out his arms, his hands blurred in the haze.

He could see no horizon. *Saint Catherine* was still in the current of blue water, but there was no wind. Fog rose in columns like "sea smoke," the fog old sailors talked about encountering in the seas where Polaris was at its highest in the night skies.

And the quiet. Yes, of course there were sounds — the ubiquitous slapping of the waves, the groaning of the ship's wooden body, the clanking of the tackle, and a distant, low creaking from far over the water which seemed to resonate in Starkey's very bones — but these sounds were hollow and muffled, as if the fog had wrapped around the world like wool.

He needed to survey the damage. Despite his throbbing head, he made his way across the fog-shrouded deck. He stumbled once on a tangle of line ripped loose from the mainsail, but kept his feet and moved aft, making mental note of each piece of standing rigging he passed, barely noticing how the fog flowed over and around the corpses on deck as a stream dances through rocks. In a minute's time, he was at the quarterdeck.

The wheel was tied over, hard starboard. He was relieved, but forced to search the mists of his own memory. When had he tied the wheel over? After the boom struck him?

So much was blank. *Had* the boom struck him? Had it come free? It was made fast now, with the mainsail over hard port. He'd heard of memory fleeing a man after such an event . . . .

No matter. He had to anchor himself in the here and now. So the ship had survived, the rigging was relatively undamaged, and the hull was as intact as could be expected. There was one last thing to check.

He went to the aft rail, and as soon as the painter, the line to which the dinghy had been tethered, came into view, Starkey could see that something was terribly wrong.

There should have been a strain on the painter as the dinghy was towed behind, but the line lay slack.

Starkey pulled it in hand over hand, and the fact that it offered no resistance confirmed his worst fear.

The painter had been a stout rope, two inches round. Starkey examined the bitter end. Broken? No, breaking lines unravel. Cut? No, cut lines showed uniform marks from a blade. These marks were strange . . . as if it had dissolved.

This was not the end of the world. The ship would drift southward with the current. Two knots current. In three or four hours the ship would run aground in the salt marsh south of Bliss, somewhere between Whitestone and Greater Saltburn.

He could torch it right there in the swamp. It would be the decent thing to do. He may have argument back at Bliss about his seventy coins, but payment was less important than having the time to do what he had come to do . . . .

He stepped carefully through the fog and torn rigging, skirting sprawling bodies. He stooped over a small, tightly wrapped form, the body of a woman, propped against the deckhouse, where he had set her hours ago. He cradled her in his arms and carried her aft and down, through the hatch into the captain's cabin, where he set her on the bed.

In the pale light which bled through the ladderwell and through the aft portholes, he examined her.

Tenderly, he pulled away her shroud.

"Mary," he said, fighting back tears.

"Mary."

He peeled the veil away from her face. Her golden hair spilled free. Her delicate features appeared flush and hale. Her eyes were closed, her expression serene — she could have been sleeping.

Starkey felt breathless. He closed his eyes, leaned over and kissed her cold, swollen lips. They had wrapped her in bedding of lavender and pennyroyal, and their herbal aroma almost, almost masked the scent of meat.

The memory of her skin against his ached in him, tortured him, like a starving man's memory of his last meal. He wanted so much — her musical laugh, her throaty whisper against his ear, the salty taste of her flesh.

Starkey undid the lace at her collar, revealing red sores which stared at him from her bosom like accusing eyes. Her flesh below the collar had become gray and black.

For the first time in many, many years he closed his eyes, and prayed for his very soul.

He could not bring himself to leave her. Her weight in his arms was a comfort, as it had been far too few a night. He gave himself up to sleep, and dreams, and at times it felt that Mary pulled herself closer during the night, listening to his heart as she used to do.

THREE

The sun glittered against the calm sea, its light a trillion shards of brightness.

The good gentleman, Master John Starkey, stood on the quarterdeck of a strong ship. Although he wore the fine clothes of a wealthy merchant, the deckhands didn't mutter beneath their breath as he watched over them. He'd been one of them, he had, and although he had coin now he still knew his rocks and shoals. Even the Captain nodded to him as he passed. Starkey was a man to know.... And his pretty young wife....

There was Mary on deck now, in lace and ribbons, and fine weaves which hugged her shape. She stood with her right hand on a line of fancy rigging, her fingertips delicately curled around it, not clutching it with fear, nor with the unsteadiness of the lubber. Graceful, she was . . . .

Starkey walked up behind her, reached out to put his hand upon her shoulder. She was looking at the village of Bliss, their destination, sitting as peaceful and balanced within the rocky shore as if God had just placed it there Himself, and was watching it with His all-seeing eyes.

"Is it not beautiful, my Mary?" Starkey asked. "Is it not everything I told you it would be?"

She didn't turn around, but Starkey heard her speak.

"It is good," she said. "So good to feel again."

With infinite tenderness, Starkey put a hand to her hair; stroked the wheaten gold.

And as she turned to him with closed eyes and expressionless face, Starkey noticed that the lock of hair he touched had come off, and was tangled in his fingertips.

Starkey sat bolt upright in the captain's bed, gasping.

The bed beside him was empty, although in the lamplight he could see dust, flakes of dried blood, threads of gauze from a funeral shroud — all lying in the faint impression of a slender woman.

Twisted around the fingers of his right hand was a wispy lock of blonde hair.

Starkey calmed himself, folding the nightmare into managable sections, and placing it away.

He swung his legs to the deck, gave his blood time to settle, gave his eyes time to adjust to the dim light. Everything was as it had been when he'd passed out, except that Mary was nowhere to be seen.

Had someone come in as he had slept and taken her? That thought could have filled him with shame, but instead he felt anger.

Starkey cocked his head, listened. There was a commotion on deck. People were moving around. Were these the people who had dragged Mary from his bed?

Starkey headed up the ladderwell toward the hatch which led to the quarterdeck. Moving around within the ship he could see that night had fallen. At the hatch to the main deck he steeled himself. So they had seen him entangled with Mary. Perhaps they were just waiting for him to emerge, waiting with torches, iron eyes, a lash to shred the blasphemer's back, or even a noose rigged to the yardarm.

Well, damn them all! Had these unworthy beasts laid hands on Mary . . . .

He gritted his teeth and pressed against the hatch, swinging it up and open.

The fetid below-decks air gasped out around Starkey, and was whipped away in the breeze which ran fore to aft. The fog was still there, but stars slid through patchy gaps of clear sky above the rigging. Starkey heard the infinitely familiar rhythm of water breaking against the sides of the ship.

As his eyes adjusted he made out not a howling mob with torches, but figures moving silently about the decks. A solitary lantern in the lee of the deckhouse cast long shadows, but little light. He could barely see, and almost bumped into someone not an arm's length away from him.

He peered into the darkness, and realized just what he was seeing. Lips whithered back from dry teeth, lidless eyes, hands clutching as if searching for a stolen shroud.

The corpses were no longer stacked on deck, but were moving about the ship.

Fear welled in his throat like frozen blood. Something within his mind, something normally steady and equalized, pitched and yawed just as the *Saint Catherine* did on this dark sea. Dreams within dreams — what was real?

Immediately, he knew what he had to do. He ran to the solitary lantern, and pulled it from its sconce. Flame was reassuring. Its light and heat were natural, worldly.

And now to the pitch and straw. This ship had to burn. No, he couldn't escape, but that was no matter. This ship, and these walking things, these undead, had to burn.

He was almost at the hatch leading to his below-decks pyre when slender fingers gently, coldly, touched his arm.

He turned, and it was Mary.

Her eyes were open, but dry and unfocused. She took his face in her hands with unnatural strength and pressed her mouth to his, her cold, dry tongue against his teeth, and when he pulled way she loosed a long, rasping sigh.

"So good to feel again," she said.

She then knocked the lamp from his hand, and it rolled across the decks and disappeared overboard.

"Onward," she whispered, pulling away into darkness.

FOUR

A corpse — but was it right to call it that? — stood skeletally tangled in the ship's wheel like a scarecrow on its stake. As the deck rolled, the corpse flexed at the knees, stiffly, but no less rhyhtmically than would a living man. It clutched the spokes and rings of the ship's wheel. In the dim starlight it could have been any one of Starkey's old quartermaster friends, standing watch through the deepest part of a dark, foggy night.

The corpse slowly wound its head over its right shoulder, and the wind plucked a lock of dry, weedy hair to one side, like an invisible hand drawing aside a curtain, showing Starkey a face of split skin and empty eye sockets.

"It is right that he should be there," said someone behind Starkey.

Starkey turned on his heel.

A man, a dead man, stood there, stiffly trying to stay still on the rolling deck, closely examining a rust-encrusted, but still sharply pointed, iron rod.

"Is this my sword?" the corpse asked.

"That's a marlinspike," Starkey said. "We use it to weave lines. Why do you say it's right that he should be there?"

"For he was a sailor," the dead man answered, not looking up from the marlinspike.

"Am I dead?" Starkey asked.

"He remembers. Or something about him remembers. He went back to the ship's wheel. He was a sailor." As he spoke he held the marlinspike before him, making stiff hacking motions, parrying motions, as if it were a sword.

"Where is my shield?" the man asked. "And where did you put my chain mail? And my helmet?"

"I've never seen those things," Starkey said. "Maybe the people who brought you in took those things away. Anything of value . . ."

"I want to meet The Christ dressed correctly. I picture myself kneeling before God, holding my sword before me . . . . The people who brought me in?"

"Do you remember being sick at all?" Starkey asked.

"I was on Pilgrimage. I was headed to Jerusalem. There was a village, not much of a place. A tiny dot by the sea. 'Bliss,' it was so named. I got sick near there. Fever. And blood."

"Am I dead?" Starkey asked again.

"What are you?" the knight asked, looking up from the corroded marlinspike, squinting at Starkey as if looking at a living man was too bright a sight for his dead eyes. "What were you?"

"Are we headed to God?" Starkey asked.

"We are headed where we are headed," the knight answered. "I'll prepare myself. You simply prepare to fire the ship."

"Why do you want the ship to burn?" Starkey asked.

The knight shrugged. "The hero is put to sea in a burning ship. He crosses over to the other side through the flames, and there I'll be greeted by God. That's what I've always dreamed of. Of course, I didn't expect to have to coordinate all of this myself."

"I'll start the fire," Starkey said. "I just need to find someone first. You can rely on me."

The knight nodded.

"God relies on you, Starkey."

FIVE

Starkey finally fired a torch. It was difficult; no hearth was burning on the ship, no cook's stove, no smith's forge. Yes, he'd scrounged flint and iron, but all the torches were damp from the infernal fog.

Starkey prowled the decks as the night wore on, his torch held high. The raised dead moved about, most in stoney silence. Some worked the rigging, others manned the rails. Some clutched their shrouds, others were naked and glistening with the fog.

Starkey went first to the quarterdeck. A figure sat there, hunched over in the darkness, its hands rhythmically moving amidst a tangle of cloth.

"Mary?" Starkey called.

The figure didn't look up.

Starkey walked to a spot over the right shoulder of the figure. The dim light of his torch revealed boney hands moving like spiders amidst a tangle of threads, tying knots, pulling bitter ends, looping bights.

"Weaver," Starkey said, "I look for a young woman. Mary is her name."

The "weaver" slowly turned her head. Her eyes were cavernous, and the dim torch found no irises to illuminate.

And then the weaver spoke, a voice as dry and distant as a desert of ice.

"Look for her here," the weaver hissed, tapping the cloth

before her with a cracked and yellow finger nail.

Starkey peered at the cloth, a half-completed tapestry. He could see where parts of the sails, parts of rags left onboard the ship, parts of shrouds from the corpses themselves were being broken into their component threads then reborn into this knotted world of gray and blood-brown.

Tiny figures danced across the shroud, hand in hand with humorlessly grinning skeletons.

"This is where we all end up," the weaver said.

Starkey turned away. He had no time for these philosophies. He needed Mary — where had she gone?

Starkey padded up toward the deckhouse. Perhaps she was there, sheltered from the fog and spray. Starkey held his torch high with his right hand while he opened the aft hatch of the deckhouse with his left.

The deckhouse was still as empty as when the salvers and looters had left it, but someone was sitting on the roughhewn bench along the starboard bulkhead. Starkey knew immediately that it wasn't Mary.

When he had died he had been an old man, with wispy white hair on his temples, a bald and spotted pate, and jaws left slack by absent teeth. He sat and rocked and mumbled to himself.

Starkey didn't even consider asking this man about Mary. He proceeded toward the forward hatch of the deckhouse, edging past the mumbler, loath that he should try to reach and touch him. As he passed him he could make out the man's words:

"Whilst I traveled to my master's house I stopped and here I rest; whilst I traveled to my master's house I stopped and here I rest; whilst I traveled . . ."

But Starkey also heard something else, something separate from the whispers of the sea and the creaking which had grown to a dull and constant rumble like distant thunder. Not the calls of dolphins nor whales, nor any other sea creature . . . . There was a feminine voice, coming from beneath a hatch which led from the deckhouse to the main hold.

Starkey raised the hatch, and, without hesitation, descended into the hold. The air there was stale and cold. He could smell the pitch and coal tar. He'd have to be careful with the torch. As he made his way amongst the bales of hay and the molded stanchions and beams, the feminine voice, mouthing things he couldn't immediately understand, led him like an invisible cord unwound within a maze.

And then he was upon them.

Normally the sight of a man between a woman's legs,

pumping away, would be exciting and devious, or at the least, humorous.

But these two . . .

The man was rhythmic in his movements, but awkward. It was as if he knew what he was doing and how to do it, but could not remember why.

The woman bleated occasionally, but her voice was dry, passionless.

"I almost felt that...," she hissed into the man's ear.

Disgusted, Starkey left them behind, climbed up the ladder-well out of the hold.

Mary. All things were Mary. He needed her. Would she have returned to the captain's cabin? He hurried there.

He paused outside the captain's cabin. Lamplight shone around the edges of the hatch. Someone within moved around.

He hesitated. Would he see lovers there? Would one of them be Mary? Mary, bleating and moaning beneath some rutting carrion? He couldn't bear the thought....

He decided that if he saw that, he'd fire the ship right away. And he'd hang himself before he watched it burn. He wouldn't even have to think.

Armed with that resolve, he swung open the hatch.

There were no lovers there, but a man hunched over the chart table. As the hatch opened he glanced up at Starkey. The man had arranged his shroud into a dignified cloak. He was bearded, with reddened eyes, dark grey lips, a prominent, furrowed brow.

A chart was stretched across the table. In the man's hands were dividers fashioned from sharpened finger bones, and a straightedge made from a thighbone ground and jointed down on one side.

The man only watched Starkey for a moment, then went back to work on the chart.

Starkey started to chuckle.

"Is there something you want to share?" the man asked, quietly.

"You're using our known course and speed to chart our position?" Starkey asked.

"Yes," the man answered.

"I believe we call that 'dead' reckoning," Starkey said, grinning.

The man gave no indication that he found it funny, or even understood what Starkey was talking about. He shrugged and went back to the chart.

"Where are we?" Starkey asked. "Why are we here? Who set this course?"

The bearded man smiled. As he spoke he took up a sharpened bone, and dipped it into a jagged bowl made of bone, and drew on the stretched parchment on the chart table before him.

"You question carries its own shadow. What about you, John Starkey? Think of yourself as a ship. Your life as an ocean. Where did you go and why? Did you set your own course? Were you driven? Did you drift?"

As he spoke he scratched the bone splinter around the surface of the parchment, describing a lazy curve which spiraled inward.

"My life?" Starkey asked. "Short. But relentlessly long, too, day by day. I rarely had enough to eat. When the Black Death began mowing the countryside down, I was too tired to care to lower my head. Now all I want is a woman named Mary. I don't have time for your riddles. If you know where she'd be, tell me. If not, I'll leave you to draw your snail shells."

The bearded man smiled. "You don't understand this? So many things I didn't understand. I thought the stars were points on a dome above the plain of the sea. Now I can hear the whispers of green creatures who walk the shores of orange seas under blue suns. I can look at a dot of light in the night sky and see a 'snail's shell' made of millions of suns. Do you know why I draw this spiral? Look at this."

He took up the parchment and then reached back onto the captain's bed to take up a skull. He brought the two things together, wrapping the skull with the parchment.

"See this curve, this spiral? It's a loxodrome, John Starkey. The chart is flat, but the sea enwraps a round world, a sphere. Does not a ship's sail disappear over the horizon after her hull? And this loxodrome straightens out, as our course. Oh, so many things I've gained, so many things to understand, and such a short time."

Starkey noticed that the chart bore a traditional compass rose. A nice touch. But when Starkey looked closer, he saw that the compass rose was a tattoo, and the parchment of the chart was really skin.

"What were you in life?" he asked. "A butcher?"

The "navigator" laughed, pulled the chart away, and turned the skull so that Starkey could see the face. The skull still had eyes, which were whole and aware. They focused on Starkey and he recoiled.

"He serves now as he did in life," the navigator said. "It is right that he should be here."

"I leave you to your blood and riddles," Starkey said. He was almost out the hatch when the bearded man called after him.

"Riddles, Starkey? A riddle thus: 'Where is the most beautiful woman onboard a ship usually located?'"

SIX

She stood before him at the eyes of the ship, balanced and delicate, only holding the rigging with her slightly curled fingertips, standing without fear or unsteadiness, peering into the mists ahead. The skies ahead seemed to be lightening, as if with the approach of dawn. The sound Starkey had earlier considered as a distant creaking or rumble was now a distinct thing, a maelstrom of breaking waves, yet muffled, strange in its timbre.

The wooden figurehead was gone, taken by the salvers before *Saint Catherine* had left port on her funerary mission. Working now as an effigy before some shop, or gracing some tavern. Now Mary had taken her place, looking for all the world like the real Saint Catherine, beautiful and grace-laden, yet bloody and broken at the wheel . . . .

Starkey set his torch in a socket for a belaying pin, and approached her.

"Mary, we're headed North. We'll fall off the ends of the Earth. These dead things. They're taking us to Hell. I'm going to fire the ship, Mary. I want you in my arms as it burns. Fire will cleanse us."

Mary glanced back at him briefly. She was smiling.

"An old ship, but a strong one, John. Old and strong, like you. It served its purpose. Be still, and take your place in the sails. Be still for the journey."

"I was more than a deckape, Mary. I had skills. Many a day I spent hours onboard some ship, earning my keep, at work on the sails, nothing there but myself, a biscuit, and a needle."

"No one doubts you, Bonnie John Starkey. You were a good man. But why would that world have a good man in it?"

But stop for a moment. Something that he said. Myself and a biscuit. When had he eaten last? Did he feel hungry? Why didn't he feel hungry?

He couldn't be distracted. Mary stood there, idly tasting her fingertips, looking forward.

Cold. He was so cold. He breathed out to see the puff of breath he knew would come in the cold. But there was no breath visible. Mary was talking to him, but no breath was visible from her lips. It occurred to Starkey that he had seen no breath from anyone onboard. Yet it was so cold!

"Mary," he called. "I just want to be with you. I realize now what a terrible mistake it was."

"What was a mistake?"

"Everything. Everything which wasn't taking me to you. Every moment I spent away from you."

"She loved you, John Starkey," Mary said, turning to look forward, her eyes scouring the mists like a lookout.

"Who do you speak of? 'She' who? Mary, talk to me!"

She turned again to speak to him, as if he were a child demanding attention.

"It's behind us. It shrinks in importance. You want to be with me. That want is an echo, an illusion. You don't want for anything. Forget."

Her face brightened as she heard something in the distance. "It's closer, now, John! It's closer!"

John Starkey moved carefully. He needed to keep his footing. He looked down at his bare feet stepping along the rough planking of the deck. He couldn't feel the wood on the skin of his bare soles.

Finally he was beside her. He reached out to wrap his arms around her, pull her against him. He would close his eyes and not let her go, and think of nothing but her warmth and softness against him.

But she eluded him, and stepped out on the bowsprit. "Alone, John Starkey. Each alone. I don't remember," she called. The rumbling in the distance intensified, as if to punctuate her thought.

He didn't want to step out after her. He couldn't feel his feet or legs, and was sure that he would fall, or worse, knock her off into the ocean below. They would never be reunited.

He tugged at his hair. There had been blood. There had been blood before, but now there was dry, brown powder.

"Why did you leave me?" he cried.

"Now? On the ship? Or when she was alive?" Mary said.

She didn't turn around, but continued to strain forward, into the mists, from which the grinding sound was now constant.

"We each must be alone," she continued. "I can't even feel close to the one inside me."

Starkey watched her casually gesture toward her belly.

"Inside you?" Starkey mumbled, stepping forward onto the bowsprit.

"The child was yours," Mary said, then jabbed a finger forward, pointing, her eyes wide.

"Closer, it's closer!" she screamed. "There! There it is!"

SEVEN

Mists parted before the *Saint Catherine*. Starkey realized what he was seeing, and all the great moments of his past — when as a child he had first noticed the beating of his own heart, when he had crossed the equator and seen coal-black men and strange constellations, when he had first looked into the blue coolness of Mary's eyes — these moments faded like shadows eaten by the fall of night.

Within the mists — and he was at the very source of mist and winds and strange currents, he knew that — fog and rain themselves were the very breath of this thing he was seeing — here was an island of ice. Waves broke against its crystalline shores, ran back to the sea in howling rivulets. Sections of shore calved away and formed ice floes even as Starkey watched.

And even as the shore deteriorated beneath the onslaught of the waves it instantly rebuilt itself; the all-encompassing cold of the thing took the seawater and froze it into arches, bridges, and delicate spires, decorations in a wild landscape.

The sun — or some great light — had topped the horizon behind the castle, so that its rays shone through the ice, splitting into trillions of shards of brightness and color.

As wondrous as was the island itself, most amazing was what Starkey saw there in the island's center. A castle of sheer ice, thousands of feet tall, greater than any cathedral, greater than any city, dominated the island. And yet . . . .

Any castle was a structure, an arrangement, a static stack of stone and beams and earthenworks, existing as is. This was no dead, static structure. Even as Starkey watched the castle constructed itself, pumping the icey seawater upward through great capillaries. Far overhead, seawater was expelled in huge spouts, freezing into gracefully curved walls and ramparts and castellations.

So many details Starkey couldn't recognize in the distance. For a moment he thought this castle to be ringed around with gargoyles of ice, then he thought these figures were human bodies, washed clean of their faces, and then he saw these bodies writhing. He couldn't be sure what he was seeing. The castle was so far beyond the measure of his mind, no details were apprehensible.

Behind John Starkey, all came forward.

Corpses abandoned their places at the rails and in the rigging; the skeleton who had held the wheel tottered forward; the couple Starkey had observed humping in the hold were no longer intertwined, but stumbled forward separately.

The mumbling man was in the crowd, toothlessly mouthing, "Master, Master!"

The weaver attempted to tie her tapestry of a Danse Macabre to some standing rigging, to fly it like a battle flag.

The navigator had some instrument like an astrolabe rigged from bones, and through this he sighted the castle, noting its dimensions.

And there was the knight, bedecked in armor and helmet scrounged from bones. He still held the marlinspike; as Starkey watched he stepped to the rail, shouting, "I'm ready for Thee!" He then leapt overboard and disappeared beneath the ice and waves.

Starkey grabbed the torch from the socket where he'd set it. He had to fire the ship. That he knew. He touched the flames to the rails, the deck, to everything he could reach, but no fire would start.

"Is it not beautiful, my love? Is it not everything I told you it would be?" Mary, her face decorated with geometric webs of frost, hissed into his ear.

No fire would start. The ship lurched beneath his feet, and ice and blue water spilled onto the deck. The castle and its island were expanding, reaching forward, encompassing the *Saint Catherine* — a harbor of ice moving toward the ship.

Snow and mist and freezing rain fell on all like the breath of a mysterious god, and ice began to cover all.

Sprawling, slipping, Starkey dropped the torch, and desperately reached for Mary.

There she stood. All was becoming dark. Starkey felt nothing.

Supreme effort, and Starkey's fingertips touched Mary's hand.

She glanced at him. There she was.

Above all, a yawning chasm. The *Saint Catherine* was drawn into the castle.

Darkness completed itself.

His fingers were touching Mary.

There was nothing else.

For precious seconds, eons, he was touching her.

Then, finally, that touch also disappeared. ⟲

Mike Allen lives in Roanoke, Va., with his wife Anita, two comical dogs and a demonic cat. In his spare time, he's both editor of the poetry journal Mythic Delirium *and president of the Science Fiction Poetry Association. By day he's a newspaper reporter; his favorite assignment to date remains his interview with the inventor of* The World's Only Ass-Kicking Machine.

Charles Saplak has published fiction and poetry in numerous magazines and anthologies, including Alfred Hitchcock's Mystery Magazine, Weird Tales *and* Writers of the Future. *When not writing he likes gardening and woodworking. He lives in Roanoke, Va., with his wife Karen, daughter Charlene and son Marshall.*

ILLUSTRATION BY SERGUEI KOVALEV

NECESSITY WAS THE MOTHER OF
INVENTION — AND *HE* WAS
ITS FATHER.

Daddy

(originally published 1984 in the Doubleday anthology Shadows #7*)*

by Earl Godwin

I stay away from singles bars. I never was good at clever small talk, and I'm at my fumbling worst when the whole idea is to strike up a relationship with a woman. That's why I choose neighborhood haunts where the serious drinkers gather to pass the evening in comfortable ambience. However, the thought is always tucked away in the back of my mind that I just might meet a special lady who could laugh aside . . . my clumsy, inarticulate style and find charming the rather eccentric limitations of my bachelor life.

I met her in spades.

It had been raining and there was a chill in the air, so I sat in the back of the crowded bar in my raincoat nursing a straight bourbon. There were a lot of women in the place, some very attractive, but not that special one with whom I'd consider dancing through a night's fantasy. In life I've settled for some very ordinary women. In my dreams I always go first-class.

She came in with a man, and they threaded their way back through the crowd until a waitress seated them in a booth right next to my table. The man hung up their raincoats and she stood next to me, shaking the water from her dark, shoulder-length hair. A drop landed on my upper lip; I slowly licked it off, staring at her.

They weren't happy: this I could see right away. Worry traced its path across her darkly beautiful features. This was a queen, not just worthy of my idle fantasy, but one for whom I could work my whole life to wash the torment from that exquisite face and replace it with happiness. I don't say that easily, because I consider myself an accredited critic of beauty. I'm a photographer, and even if my sexual successes have been among the mediocre, I have a sharp eye for real beauty, and this creature with her eyes that leaped out and grabbed you would steal the heart out of a polar bear. The man? Who knows? I wouldn't remember him if he fell on me.

I tried not to stare. Her eyes flicked over me for a preoccupied instant and then away. I listened to the soft, tense tone of their conversation. He was saying things like, "Tired of it . . . had enough . . . impossible." I couldn't make out much. Most of it was in whispers and I don't hear well. They raised their voices slightly. The conversation was becoming more intense. The man leaned over the table, his face strained and angry, hers desperate and afraid. She hissed something that sounded like an ultimatum. He jumped up and shouldered his way through the crowd to the front door. I looked quickly at the woman. Her expression was one of weary defeat. It seemed to add years to her face.

Alone and nervous, she fumbled her way through several matches until she managed to light her cigarette. I caught her eye and raised my shot glass in a sympathetic toast. She started to raise hers, but the glass was empty. "I seem to be abandoned and the gentleman had all the money." She flashed a vulnerable smile.

I signaled the waitress. "May I join you?"

"By all means." Her confidence had returned, but there was still that air of vulnerability about her that excited me. I prayed I wouldn't overplay my hand.

I have a book at home called *How to Pick Up Women*. There are hundreds of opening lines for starting a conversation; I couldn't remember a single one of them. We looked at each other for an awkwardly long time until I blurted, "Was that your husband?"

"No."

"He sure ran off and left you like a lone duck."

"No, just a friend. It's not important now. Do you have the time? I have to go soon."

I felt my hopes plummet. "It's nine o'clock. Please — don't go. I love talking to pretty ladies."

She looked at me sharply, with an appraising glance. "Aren't you the charmer." Then she fumbled with another match. I leaned over to steady her hand.

"*Eres muy caballero.*"

"You're Spanish?"

"I've been a lot of things. Do you live around here?"

I hadn't expected that. My pulse started to hammer faster. "Yeah. I've got a studio apartment a couple of blocks from here. I'm a photographer," I added for no good reason.

"Oh?" Her fingers drummed lightly on the table.

"Yeah. Uh . . . I'd like to take some pictures of you." Oh Jesus! I winced inwardly to hear that tired old line come out of my mouth.

"I'll bet you would." She ground out her cigarette in the ashtray, stood up, and reached for her raincoat. My heart sank; she was leaving. She put her coat on and fluffed that wonderful hair out around her shoulders. I sat staring up, hypnotized by her. She was older than I thought at first, pushing forty but still

an incredibly beautiful woman. I would have said younger when she first came in, perhaps a trick of the light. But now she was leaving, the kind of woman ministers leave home for, and I'd never see her again. Jesus.

She smiled at me. "Your place?"

I couldn't believe it.

I was all thumbs and stupid remarks as I tried to appear suave while attacking the suddenly impossible task of putting on my raincoat. She leaned against the booth with a tired patience and glanced up at the clock. She finally helped me with the coat before someone had to cut me out of the damned thing. We walked out of the bar with her in the lead, and I gave a few friends a debonair wave, as if leaving with the finest fox in the house was old stuff for me. Taking her hand, I couldn't help thinking how I'd almost let her get away from me.

My studio apartment was quite naturally a mess. I turned on a light and watched her as she picked her way through a maze of light stands and reflectors. My furnishings were rather sparse, but I did have a studio couch and a couple of easy chairs. The kitchen area was in the rear corner of the big room, away from the window. The sink was full of vintage dishes and maybe some new life forms.

She moved around and studied the pictures on the walls as I fixed a couple of drinks and turned on the stereo. "Very pretty women. How many have you slept with?"

"All" would have been a great answer, "half" would have been half true. "None of them," I muttered.

"I love honesty," she laughed. Then in a husky whisper as she came to me: "It makes me feel so warm toward a man."

We were standing in the middle of my front-room studio with the stereo low and the dim light struggling against the chilled gloom of the big room. She took my hand and guided me to the bedroom in the back of the apartment.

I kissed her full lips. They felt soft and full of promise, parting under mine, searching with her tongue, bringing me to quick readiness. I didn't rush. I'd been waiting a lifetime for this and I was going to enjoy the hell out of it. We undressed each other, pausing to caress favorite parts. Her large breasts were straining to be touched. She stroked and teased me and I pushed her gently back onto the bed — not in a hurry. Hell, I could have foreplayed with her until the cows came home. She was the one in a rush. She cried out then, a sound of relief and hope and something like fear, wrapping her legs around me as we rocked together in abandon. She held me like a vise with her arms and legs, squeezing me tight.

"No, honey, stay. I want it all."

I came and felt a surge of relief flood through me. For her that was it: show's over. She rolled me off her and stood up. "Thank you."

Odd thing to say after an interlude like that. I rolled over and found myself staring up into the wickedest gun barrel I'd ever seen.

"I don't get it. We were having a good time. What gives?"

She stood naked before me, unsmiling, with the pistol leveled at my head. She looked stricken. "Please. I haven't much time and I'm going to need your help. Don't ask questions, I don't have the answers. You have to deliver my baby."

I must have looked classically stupid with my jaw down around my ankles. "You're not pregnant."

"I am now and you're the father."

I managed a laugh like a choking gargle. "Aren't we a little premature? I mean like this stuff usually takes nine months." I laughed again, feeling ridiculous, sitting on the edge of the bed naked as a baseball. But there was nothing funny about her rage or the fear it came out of.

"Stop laughing, Goddamnit! I —" She gasped in pain. The pistol dropped from her hand and she fell face forward, curling into a fetal position, holding her stomach. I picked the gun up and dropped it into a drawer. Rolling her over onto her back, I couldn't help notice that she looked even older than I thought the last time. I couldn't explain any of it, the whole thing was beyond me, but I had the feeling that what was happening here was as unique as it was awful.

I showered and dressed. She was moaning and rubbing her stomach when I got back to her. I stood by the bed looking down at her. There was a grotesque aspect to the situation now. I watched in helpless horror as the woman's belly began to swell — a little at first, then faster, as if someone were blowing her up with an air pump. And all the while her hair was graying like flickers of light in the dark mass of it. Sagging, wrinkled skin and brittle bones, long past the ability to stretch against the obvious labor pains, punished themselves to do what they were made for. She looked — she was now — sixty years old, the sound of her breathing like a saw in wood.

"Help me, please! Oh God, it's almost too late!"

She gave a low animal growl and drew her knees up against her breasts, her hands clamped on the headboard. The gasps were coming every couple of seconds — and then I could see the first sign of a small head.

She'd asked me to help. Me? In a normal birth I would have been useless as pants on a bird. Here I was a blithering idiot. I could only stand frozen and helpless as the nightmare unfolded in front of me. The baby's head and shoulders protruded now; the woman writhed like a trapped fish. Unintelligible gibberish

escaped from her withering lips. Then, somehow shaking out of the trance, I grasped the slippery little shoulders and began tugging, pulling life out of death. The woman was actually shrinking now, falling in on herself, seventy-five, eighty years old. She'd stopped moving by now, gone stiff, gone beyond that, way beyond it, and the smell emanating from the decaying mess of her was almost too much to bear. I had the baby almost all the way out. Only the feet were inside. By the time I cleared them, the thing on the bed had been dead a very long time. The smell was sickening. I fought the need to vomit, stumbling into the bathroom for a fresh razor blade to cut the umbilical cord binding the baby to something that didn't quite make it out of the body.

It was a girl. Remembering old movies, I held her up by the little feet and gave the tiny buttocks a sharp smack. Her gasp and yowl started her breathing.

My daughter.

I carried her into the bathroom and washed her down with lukewarm water. Then, messed with blood and other matter I'd rather not think about, I stared at my reflection in the mirror. He looked like I felt, every bit of it. And he was a father.

I wrapped the baby in a blanket and bundled up the now unrecognizable remains of my date in the sheets. What to do with the gruesome bundle was a problem. I couldn't take it to the police . . . Sure, they'd believe me. Sure they would. . . .

The baby was crying. It was hungry. I collapsed by the picture window in the front-room studio with her in my arms as she nursed at the makeshift bottle I scrounged from my photo equipment, some milk from the icebox and — hell, why not? — an unused condom from a pack in the dresser.

What the hell was I going to do? The shock was wearing off, replaced by exhaustion. I wearily placed the bundle on the floor next to my chair, adjusted the bottle for her to work at it, and sat back with a very deep sigh. I'd had a hard night.

I watched the rain sifting past the streetlights as the drops splashed on the pavement. Cars plowed through puddles and sent sheets of dirty water up on the deserted sidewalks. The clock across the street said midnight. I yawned and looked down at the baby. She was happily pulling away on her bottle, watching me with clear blue eyes. A little while ago they were barely open and still milky, unfocused. God help me — she'd grown.

I fell asleep in the chair, lulled by the soft drumming of the rain against the window. I must have slept for over three hours when I snapped awake suddenly, more out of a sense of guard duty than from any particular noise. The rain had stopped but the streets were shining wet, and I caught the reflection of the stoplight on the corner in the damp sheen of the sidewalk. I remembered and sat up.

The blanket was empty and the bottle lay next to it. Behind me I heard faintly the soft tread of tiny feet. Turning, I could just make out the small form coming toward me out of the dark. My hair rose; I jumped up, knocking over the chair. She approached with careful child-precision. She was wrapped in a sheet that trailed behind her, and her dark hair was tousled down around her bare shoulders, and she pulled at my pants leg, urgent and trusting.

"I'm hungry, Daddy."

I went into the bedroom, picked up the bundle of bedding, and carried it down to the dumpster in the back alley. And I disposed of the remains of that thing I had made love to. The mother of that thing in my apartment. I wasn't thinking; clearcut thought was impossible. I walked back into the apartment. The little girl was standing by the window, peering out.

"Where'd you go, Daddy?"

"I just threw your mother in the garbage. From what I knew of her, she ought to feel right at home."

Her eyes weren't that young any more. She pulled her curls away from her shoulders and shook her head. A beautiful child. She didn't look anything like me. I made her a sandwich and a glass of milk, watching her as she ate — six or seven years old, only I knew better. She wasn't that many hours old. I retreated to my chair by the window and stared hopelessly out into the wet streets. Then she was at my side.

"What was my mother like?"

"I don't know. We didn't spend much time cultivating a relationship."

She giggled, pressing my hand in her two small ones. "I love you, Daddy. You talk funny."

She leaned over and kissed me with a little hug. I felt myself go soft but I couldn't let her know it. We held onto each other as a fresh sheet of rain beat against the windows and made little wet rainbows out of the blurry neon signs across the street. We talked together about nothing much until finally, just before daylight, we both drifted off to sleep.

The roar of a bus outside the front window woke me with a start. I yawned and stretched; a glance at the clock across the street said it was a little after 8 a.m.

"You want something to eat, Dad?"

A pretty adolescent girl carried a plate of eggs into the dining area. "C'mon, Dad. I know you're hungry. The one without the sausage is mine. I hate sausage."

I wasn't in shock any more but still not ready to accept this thing as it was. She sat down and scraped eggs off into her plate from the skillet.

"What are you staring at, Dad? You act like you've never seen me before. C'mon — eat up before it gets cold."

While I ate, I studied her: seventeen or eighteen now, well formed, rapidly becoming the woman I had been with the night before. She devoured her food hungrily and downed a glass of milk in one pull, leaving a white mustache on her upper lip. I leaned over and wiped it off.

"Thanks; I'm always so messy. Okay if I do the dishes later? *All Quiet on the Western Front* is on TV, and I've never seen it. It's a classic."

Whoever, whatever, or from wherever, these things were born with some memories. I waved my hand helplessly. She could do whatever she wanted as far as I was concerned. The only thing she couldn't do was leave this apartment. I'd have to see to that. Until whatever was going to happen . . . happened . . . I'd just sit tight.

The morning passed in front of the television as we watched Lew Ayres in a dated but vivid story of a doomed German infantryman in World War I. She sat with her eyes glued to the screen. I couldn't help admire the beauty budding,

blooming in front of me. She was fullbodied now, the woman I'd loved and watched give birth to her about sixteen hours before. The same woman.

The movie ended. She stood up and stretched, her breasts straining against the sheet that fit her a lot better now. She caught my glance. "Like what you see?"

I felt the surge of heat. I must have blushed. "Sorry. You're very beautiful. But I shouldn't have been staring."

"Were you in the war?"

"I was in Korea," I mumbled, glad for the change of subject.

She sat down again, drawing the sheet up around her. "Men don't have much to look forward to, going off to war all the time. I'm glad I'm a woman."

I thought, Honey, they've got a lot more to look forward to than you do, any way you slice it.

In a moment she went over to the stereo, sifting through the records, smiling over her shoulder at me. "Got an idea." She put on a record and came to me, holding out her hands in invitation. "Let's dance, Daddy."

I moved with her to the music, feeling the same power begin to sap at me as the night before. She pressed against me and hummed in my ear. I wrapped my fingers in that lush head of hair and pressed my face to hers, completely lost to the moment. She tilted her head back and looked up dreamily through seductive half slits of eyes. Her lovely mouth was so close to mine.

"I love you, Daddy," she whispered.

Her mouth came up and I mashed mine down on it. That one second none of the sick, bizarre truth of this thing was going to rob me of the one moment a guy like me remembers all his life. Then, as she writhed her body against me, I felt something else, something cold. As if I were detached, across the room watching, I saw myself pressing back against her urgently thrusting body, sucking at her mouth, the mouth I remembered. A flash of her mother darted through my mind, the woman, the old woman, decaying before she was even dead. The same woman kissing me now. I saw the whole monstrous thing for what it was and pushed away from her so hard that she fell backward onto the floor, frightened.

"Get off of me!" I screamed. "Don't touch me. What are you? I don't think there's a word for you."

Tears of fear and rejection welled up in her eyes, a last piece of the fast-fading little girl in her. "I'm sorry," I said at last. "I shouldn't have done that. But . . . do you know what in hell you are?"

She sighed resignedly and got up, adjusting the sheet around her, slipped over to my liquor cabinet and fixed us both a drink. She handed me the glass, holding me with those eyes, the total woman now, cycle complete. "Yes. I know what I am. Does it matter? I know you want me."

"You're my own daughter."

She sipped at her drink. "I've been a lot of men's daughters. Does it bother you?"

"Damn right it bothers me. You can't possibly think I can treat this like your everyday affair."

I saw the lost look in her then, the same as the night before, only now I knew what it was: the sense of too little time already running out. "You'll just let me die."

"I don't know what I'm going to do."

I collapsed in the easy chair by the window. She moved to it and looked out at the rain. It was still blowing against the glass. The watery reflection did sad things to her face. She already looked much older. I felt I had to say something.

"How long has this been going on? How could it ever start?"

"Does it matter?"

"You've got to admit it's an awful lot for a man to accept."

"I don't remember how it started. A long time ago, hundreds of years. You wouldn't believe it." I heard the despair, saw it in her maturing face. She knew this was going to be her last night. I wasn't going to let her out of the apartment.

With a set of handcuffs sometimes used as a prop, I cuffed her to the radiator in the bedroom and made sure she was comfortable. She didn't fight it; maybe she figured it was time. I wasn't actually killing her, only allowing her to die. I guessed about six more hours would do it.

I'll say one thing for her, she never begged. While I cuffed her to the radiator, she just watched me with a weary resignation. When I started to leave the apartment, she was crying — softly, trying to hide it from me. Somehow I couldn't just close a door on her.

"Look . . . I'm sorry."

"I love you, Daddy."

"Don't say that."

"Why not? That's part of it. Can't there be that much beauty to it, and can't you believe that much?"

I closed the door between us.

Mostly, I just walked in the drizzling rain, stopping now and then for a drink in one of the bars I knew. I wanted to get drunk and blot out the whole impossible thing.

I ended up in the bar where I'd picked her up the night before. I realized now that it wasn't a different woman at all; she was always the same. I sat nursing my drink, glancing at my watch now and then. Two hours . . . a long time yet. I couldn't even feel the drinks.

Just going to let her die, aren't you?

A friend came over to my booth. We talked for a while, how's business, that sort of thing.

How does it feel to be God?

I played the juke. All the songs sounded the same, but who listened? The hallway to the men's room was crowded with drunks. I fumbled my way through. Clear the way for The Lord Who Giveth and Taketh Away.

The mirror in the john was the sort that really tells you what you look like. I never should have looked. Hey, you've seen it all before, a guy doing all the impossible things to keep a beautiful woman.

I love you, Daddy.

What kind of guy would deliver a baby and dispose of a corpse every night for the rest of his life?

I love you. That's part of it. Can't there be that much beauty?

I walked out of the bar and headed up the street toward my apartment. It was raining harder now, and I pulled the collar of my raincoat up around my neck as I turned down my street, knowing when I got up in the morning I'd have to raise a little girl to womanhood. I climbed the stairs and walked down the hall to my door.

And then at night, make love to your own daughter so she can live one day to do it all over again. The full cycle of life a man goes through once, three hundred and sixty-five times a year. But the guys I knew, those guys back in the bar, how many of them ever found a woman like this?

You tell yourself: nobody is God. They can call it what they want — incest, Dracula's daughter, whatever. Me? I was going for it. I opened the door to my apartment and shed my raincoat, dropping it on the floor, and walked over to the stereo to put on something soft and dreamy. I walked into the bedroom; there she was, still wrapped in the sheet, the most beautiful woman in the world at the late end of her prime, still . . . the impossible best. Her head came up when I entered the room. She looked at me uncertainly a moment, reading me surely, reading me right, then a slow smile curled that seductive mouth. Hell, I'd need a decent nursing bottle and baby food.

"Hurry, Daddy, or we'll be too late." *⌒*

"Daddy," a masterful blend of horror and pathos, is the only short story published during the tragically brief life of Earl Godwin (1933–1986). Earl was a resident of Brownsville, Texas, and brother of Parke Godwin, who writes, "Earl was a sharp critic of his own work and he destroyed most of his manuscripts. However, he left two other completed short stories with me and I hope to present them to the public someday."

ILLUSTRATION BY GEORGE BARR

Exeunt Demon King

by Jonathan L. Howard

Christmas comes around but once a year. To Johannes Cabal, this showed shocking over-familiarity and ill-breeding.

Winter as a whole was a trial to him, forcing his attention from his work and to the necessities of running a house as the mercury dropped and the pipes threatened to burst at the first frost.

Even when his house — a three-storey building apparently stolen from the middle of a row of late Victorian townhouses and dropped on a remote hillside, intact down to its small front and back gardens, woodshed, and ingrained soot — even when his house was in good repair and proof against the December cold, there was little he could do professionally but bring his notes up to date and plan new experiments for the thaw. It was, after all, terribly difficult to rob a grave when the soil was frozen. Johannes Cabal's profession was analytical necromancy.

It wasn't a calling that attracted adoration or even tolerance. It seemed ironic to him, while escaping one torch-bearing mob or another, that doctors were regarded so highly for their stumbling and short-termed treatments when all he wanted to do was surpass their greatest efforts. The man who attempts to cure the common cold is a popular hero. The man who tries to defeat death is hounded from pillar to post. He appreciated that the practicalities of necromancy might be unpalatable to some; but really, what was a robbed grave here, a summoned demon there, compared to the possible gains? Oh, but no. The public could never see past the occasional and unavoidable mistakes, bleating on about how the science of necromancy was somehow intrinsically evil just because some of the higher profile failures had ended up wandering the countryside with a hunger for human brains. Sanctimonious fools, the lot of them.

Still, Christmas Eve, Cabal thought as he looked at the calendar on the parlour mantelpiece. A family time. Usually, his solitary lifestyle was not only necessary to his researches, but very much his preference. Sometimes, though, just sometimes . . . He sighed heavily. He wasn't entirely alone, strictly speaking. There were the things in the garden, and the things he kept in the woodshed, but he would rather open a vein than have them tracking grave-mould and pixie-dust onto the carpets. He'd been forced to take action against the things in the skirtingboards some time before so that only really left the thing in the box. He looked up at the wooden box that sat on the deep shelf above the fire.

"Merry Christmas," he said.

After a moment, the box started to whistle "Good King Wencelas" in a melancholy but not unpleasant key. Cabal lowered his head and listened for a few bars. Something like a smile of happy remembrance flickered across his lips, or perhaps it was just the flickering firelight upon his face as the daylight died outside.

Abruptly, a sharp knocking at the door made his head snap up, the ghostly smile instantly replaced by his habitual expression of tight-lipped distaste.

Cabal wasn't in the habit of receiving visitors at all, not least because not many actually made it as far as the front door. The garden folk — pixies, sprites and fairies whose activities would have made Enid Blyton very sad — didn't usually permit it.

On the doorstep, Parkin waited patiently. It had been snowing earlier and he was wrapped up warmly. It hadn't surprised him at all to see that his were the only tracks that went anywhere near Cabal's house; quite the contrary. He rocked gently on the balls of his feet and blew out a cloud of hoary breath. In one of the flowerbeds near his foot, something small, fey and unutterably malign moved.

"Hullo, sonny," said Parkin, apparently sensing the movement by sonar and not even deigning to look down. "Before you get up to any nonsense with fairy-shot or the like, I think you really ought to know my boots are nailed with cold iron hobs." He looked down, his expression hard. "And I'm more than minded to grind buggers like you to dust with them if you get any bright ideas. Now," his expression softened to an entirely insincere smile, "how can I help you?"

After a nervous pause, the snowy hedges and borders chorused a shaky, "Merry Christmas, Police Sergeant Parkin."

"And a Happy Saturnalia to you, too. Now piss off out of it before I do you."

The door opened and Johannes Cabal stood framed there. He was a tall, lean man in his late twenties, blond hair cut sensibly short, blue eyes that had seemed nothing other than cold for a long time. He wore a white shirt but otherwise almost all black; trousers, socks, a black cardigan. Red tartan slippers and an enormous revolver completed his wardrobe.

"Herzliche Weihnachten, Parkin. Forgive the gun, I'd quite forgotten to expect you."

"Not at all, Cabal. Just chatting with your charming garden gnomes."

"Not gnomes!" cried the garden folk in horror at the slur, but Parkin had already gone in.

While Parkin made himself comfortable in the parlour, Cabal went off to fetch his annual bribe. He returned to find Parkin singing "Once in Royal David's City" with the box.

"Good voice, yon box," said Parkin, unabashed when he saw Cabal watching him from the doorway. "What's in it anyway?"

"Nothing you'd want to know, much less see." Cabal held out an envelope stuffed with banknotes. "Your, ah . . . remind me, how do we dignify this?"

"Your very kind contribution to the police benevolent fund," Parkin said as he tucked the envelope away in his coat. "It might amuse you to know, that's actually where eighty percent of it does go. I keep the rest as a Christmas bonus, buy something nice for the kids."

"I find your brand of honest dishonesty endlessly fascinating, Parkin."

"Aye, well. It's all in the degree, isn't it? There's plenty back in the village get their knickers in a twist every time this place is mentioned. Me and my tiny force of plods, though, we don't care because you keep your nose clean in this parish. The fact that you don't elsewhere is what this," he tapped the safely ensconced envelope, "is for smoothing over. Truth is, I don't see what it is that you get up to that's so much worse than what some of those doctors in the city do. It's all in the degree. Well," he started to draw his gloves back on, "I'd best be on me way."

Something stirred in Cabal. Perhaps it was the season and the memories, perhaps it was Parkin's non-judgmental view on Cabal's work and unexpected attack on the smug ranks of the loathsome medical establishment, but Cabal suddenly felt the need for some companionship, somebody just to chat to for a little while as the night drew in.

"Could . . ." Cabal floundered in the unfamiliar waters of social interaction for a moment. "Could I interest you in a drink before you go? It's a long walk back to the village, after all."

Parkin stopped. He weighed Cabal up for a few seconds, then sighed and said, "You're not going to poison me, are you? That would be a bloody silly thing to do."

"Poison?" Cabal was taken aback. "Ach, nein! I would not . . . I only kill in self-defence." He laughed.

Parkin had never heard Cabal laugh before, had hardly thought him capable of it, and its unforced nature did a great deal to reassure him.

"My laboratory is, that phrase . . . in mothballs for the winter precisely because it is such a difficult time to gather specimens." He shook his head. "You have nothing to fear, Sergeant Parkin. I do not kill casually. I abominate death."

So, abominating death, Cabal instead turned to the water of life for his guest. Specifically, a single malt that was very much to the sergeant's taste. Cabal was going to make some tea for himself but Parkin insisted that he would not drink alone and so Cabal acquiesced but insisted on adulterating it with a little water to the mock horror of Parkin although after a couple Cabal decided to forgo the water and so they went on and a little while later it was much later and a little while after that it was later still.

It was in the natural silence after Parkin had finished a strange little anecdote about a mad bull, a frightened constable, and a weapon usually intended to stop getaway cars by shattering the engine block. They sat listening to the sonorous ticking of the grandfather clock in the hall for a full two minutes. The whisky had given out by this point and they were now enjoying a good cognac. Cabal hadn't even known he'd had the stuff but Parkin's honed detective instincts had sniffed it out, along with the snifters to enjoy it in.

"So," he asked finally, "what's it like being a necromancer then?"

The alcohol had pleasantly warmed Cabal, but he was still some way short of drunk and that wasn't a question he cared to answer. Instead, he replied, "You've been kind enough to tell me some of your old war stories. Would you like to hear one of mine?"

Parkin was policeman enough to know when a question was being evaded, but he really hadn't been that interested in the answer anyway. This sounded far more engaging and he said as much.

"Very well." Cabal took a moment to recharge their glasses while he marshalled the distant events into a narrative order. "When I first decided to pursue this profession . . ."

"Why exactly did you do that?" interrupted Parkin. "Why did you decide you wanted to become a necromancer instead of, oh, I dunno, a train driver?"

"My reasons are personal," growled Cabal, the unfamiliar sense of bonhomie slipping slightly.

Parkin wasn't listening anyway. "I wanted to be a cricketer," he said wistfully as cigarette card dreams danced before his eyes.

Cabal decided to forge on regardless. "When I first decided on this course, I had no plan. There are no career plans for necromancers. One just has to guess. Extemporise. I decided to attack the problem from one aspect. Not that of the morbidity of the body, but of the longevity of the soul. I decided to become a ghost hunter."

Parkin looked at him askance. "Is this a ghost story you're winding up for, Cabal?"

Cabal shrugged slightly. "Why not? Christmas is a time for ghost stories, and mine has the distinction of being true.

"Where to begin? Perhaps with an observation. A word is a word is a word. But words have power and in my own profession I have long since learned to regard them with a cautious respect. Part of that power is that of remembrance. A single word can draw one back to another time and another place, as the scent of a flower can resurrect a lost summer from the sepia depths of the past. Other words, though, can chill the heart and take one straight back to an ugly time, a fearful place. My story starts with such a word." He said it slowly, a small effort of will apparent, each syllable forced over his lips as if he was using his tongue to evict cockroaches. "Pant-o-mime."

An adventurous production of *Mother Goose* in a small provincial theatre was not my first choice as a venue for spending my time a few days after Christmas [said Cabal]. This particular theatre, however, had its interesting aspects. Specifically, it had a death toll.

Actors are a flowery mob, given to exaggeration and hyperbole; but when they talked about dying on the stage in the con-text of the Alhambra, they were being very literal. In twenty years, four actors had died on stage in a variety of ways, all dramatic, some messy. The most recent case had occurred just before Christmas. The pantomime's plot — to dignify the excuse for a collection of bad puns, bad songs, and low comedy — revolved around a Dame, played by a man, who sells her magic goose in return for beauty. She realises her mistake and spends the rest of the interminable performance attempting to recover it. It is Faust for toddlers. The antagonist is the Demon King, a drunk in a red leotard and curling mustachios.

On the afternoon in question, a dull December afternoon with a sky the colour of oxidised magnesium, the play had reached the point where the Dame foolishly wishes out loud for beauty three times in the gloomy Dark Wood. Her wish is heard and the Demon King appears in a flash and puff of yellow smoke.

As an aside, summoning demons is actually a time-consuming and pernickety business. I feel this production seriously misled its audience. But I digress.

On this occasion, there was a flash and a puff, but no infernal materialisation. Only a muffled cry and sound like somebody taking an axe to a rotting tree stump. There was muttering in the wings. On the stage the Dame ad libbed as well as a man in a dress can when faced by an audience of primary schoolchildren who know damn well something is amiss. Then the manager made his way on stage, apologised fulsomely and said that due to a serious technical hitch, the show was being abandoned, full refunds would be made and the management regretted any inconvenience.

There had, indeed, been a serious technical hitch.

In case you are unfamiliar with the workings of this particular piece of stage legerdemain, I shall explain. The flash and smoke are primarily there to distract the eye while the Demon King makes his entrance through a trapdoor, a particular type known as a star trap.

The model the Alhambra had was octagonal in shape. Each edge of the octagon had its own triangle of trapdoor, the end vertices of each sector of trapdoor meeting in the middle. The trick is that the actor is bodily launched by the use of a rapidly rising platform up through the trap. The leaves spring back like the petals of a blooming flower on impact with the top of the actor's head, the actor shoots up through the stage and a little way into the air, the trap's leaves take the opportunity to fall back into place and the actor lands lightly upon them to shrieks from the stalls and cries of uncritical admiration from the circle. All this business is covered by the smoke and dazzle from the flash.

You will appreciate that the platform, a small item not much bigger than the star trap's aperture, must travel at a fair speed in order to accomplish the effect. The actor's safety is entirely dependent on the leaves moving up easily as he hits them. On this occasion, you will have guessed that they did not.

As far as could be ascertained, they had not moved a whisker. Not when the actor hit them, not when he cried out in the brief moment of surprise he was allowed, not when his neck snapped, nor even as his skull was crushed.

It was a mystery. The trap was checked daily as a matter of course and had always operated perfectly. The police were unable to find any sign of tampering or even of anybody who might have wanted to tamper with it. The theatre was shut for a fortnight as the trap was tried again and again and again and the police cast around looking for suspects, motives and the like. They found nothing; and as for the star trap, well, there's an axiom in science that an unrepeatable result is no result at all. The circumstances of the tragic event could not be repeated, and nobody had the faintest idea what could have happened.

Except me. Now I needed to prove my suspicions. That something was afoot was obvious to me. Chance may perform many peculiar acts and extraordinary happenstances, but I doubted that four apparently accidental deaths could be put down to mere bad luck. Not when successive deaths had occurred precisely two thousand, three hundred days apart.

The Alhambra was, as I have said, a small provincial theatre of the sort that was undoubtedly a music hall until a few years before. Now it put on rep productions of Shakespeare; travelling murder mysteries; and, of course, pantomimes. It lived a hand-to-mouth existence; and a fortnight's closure, even allowing for the days it would have been shut for Christmas anyway, was more of a drain than it could willingly manage. I expected to find the proprietor a desperate man, and I was not disappointed. Mr. Curry sat sweaty and unhappy at his desk as I introduced myself. In demeanour, he looked like a man whose dreams were haunted by the bailiff's knock. Physically, he looked like a shaved panda.

"You're an actor?" he asked after I had introduced myself.

Given I'd been delivering little other but lies in a convincing manner throughout my introduction, it seemed technically accurate to admit that I was, adding "I've come about the vacant rôle."

That froze him. "You know," he asked cautiously, "you know what happened to the last man who took that part?"

I blithely talked of a tragic accident, my understanding that the trap had been thoroughly tested, and finished with a statement to the effect that the show must go on.

"It's a major rôle," he said, as if it were Lear, "there's a lot to learn. Have you ever . . ."

"Ho ho ho," I intoned. "I am the Demon King! I come from where it's hot and wickedness I bring!" At this point, the audience should be booing and hissing. I am advised by the script to ad lib some responses." Curry looked at me, patently baffled. "I borrowed a copy of the script. I have an excellent memory. It did not take very long to learn."

Curry took a dog-eared script from his desk drawer and slowly chose a page at random, never taking his eyes off me the whole time. Finally he looked down and read, "Go away, you silly thing!"

"When I go down, Mother Goose, you'll be carried on my back. If I go below without you, then I'm sure to get the sack!"

I am attached to my dignity, I am well aware of it. Needs must, however.

Mollified, Curry closed the script. "Your delivery needs some work."

"I can deliver perfectly well. Organise a dress rehearsal. I shall demonstrate."

And so he did. The rehearsal was not an artistic triumph. I did not know my marks to 'hit them,' and there had been some

extemporisation on top of the original script. Further, the rest of the cast seemed loath to come near me. Perhaps they thought bad luck was now attached to the rôle. Theatre folk are indeed a superstitious crew, not to say vain, stupid, and unhygienic.

Perhaps, however, their reticence was due to my performance. Although this was in my early days and I was not even technically a necromancer at that point, I had already had the very mild fortune to meet a couple of demons. One had been weasely and apologetic but the other had been impressive in its air of wanting very badly to slowly shred every scrap of meat from my bones and eat my soul for dessert. Its every syllable had dripped with a patient malevolence, masking an incandescent capacity for brutality. I simply impersonated it. As we took our bows before an auditorium empty but for Mr. Curry, he clapped slowly and uncertainly. "Mr. Cabal," he said, "do you think you might tone that down a little? It's very good, very . . . original, but perhaps a little much for the kiddies?"

I was privileged to receive a changing room of my own. Actually, I think the rest of the cast insisted upon it. Almost all my entrances were through the star trap and the room was conveniently down in the cellar, by the props store and the trap platform. It smelt of damp and mice down there, but I wasn't intending to stay with the production for long, just until I had concluded my investigations. The whole acting conceit had occurred to me quite suddenly and, once it had done so, I appreciated the elegance of it. Curry was on the watch for reporters possibly defaming his theatre's safety record, and he would have given thrill-seekers and nosy types even shorter shrift. If he had got even the whiff of a possibility that there was a nascent necromancer wandering around his aisles, well . . . it would not have gone well for me.

The first night's performance was, I think, a triumph if a Demon King's triumphs are measured in screaming children being led out by the hand. Otherwise, the response was good. "Tone it down a little further," said Curry, looking the happiest I'd yet seen him as he peeked through the curtains, "but not much. A bit more 'delicious thrill,' a bit less 'bladder-emptying terror,' Mr. Cabal." I was happy to oblige, as long as I was left to my own devices in the theatre cellar.

[*Cabal noticed Parkin looking at him speculatively over the top of his snifter. Cabal narrowed his eyes. "You're imagining me in red tights, aren't you?"*

Parkin shook his head, letting the reverie fly. "No, Cabal. Trying my damndest to avoid imagining it, if you must know." After a moment he added, "Did you sing?" Cabal ignored him and continued.]

I was confident that the Alhambra was indeed haunted, but not by the usual chain-rattling suspects. There was a very distinct pattern here, a very ordered mind at work. The deaths had been a neat 2300 days apart. That's an ugly period measured in years — approximately six years and four months apart, a trifle over — but 2300 is a significant time span in arcane terms. Twenty-three times one hundred. No, there was magic here, of a perverse and corrupt kind; and it was lending power to a ghost that, I suspected, liked to kill. But one cannot theorise without data.

The theatre's stage doorman gave the air of having been

I there as long as the place had stood, possibly longer; it was easy to imagine them building it around him. I discovered him in his tiny office hard by the stage door, little more than a booth really, with a window and counter that allowed him to watch the comings and goings. I bid him a good morning and he regarded me like a dragon from a Nordic saga, reptilian in aspect and surrounded by fumes from his briar pipe.

"Good performance last night, sir," he said, his gaze apparently focussed on a smudge on the glass between us. "You scared the little tykes shitless, bless 'em."

"I try my best, Mr. Pensey, and thank you, I value your opinion. You must have seen a good few productions here over the years. How long have you been here, now?"

"Man and boy," replied Pensey, not really answering the question. Changing tack, I noticed two shelves of books behind him on the rear wall, each dated. They seemed to be theatre records and I asked him about them. "Oh, yes," he said, turning slowly to regard them. "My records, faithfully kept." He turned slowly back to me. The action reminded me somehow of a dead man twisting on a rope. "Never missed a performance through sickness, nor accident, nor holiday."

"They must make fascinating reading."

That slow turn again. "They do. I spend long hours poring over them." I imagined he did. It was far harder imagining him ever leaving that little office.

"All that history." I shook my head in admiration. "I wonder, Mr. Pensey, might I look at one, perhaps?"

He didn't turn his chair to look at me this time, but just his head in a slow and baleful movement. I was sure I heard the noise of scales moving. "You . . . want to look at my records?"

"Just out of interest." I pointed to one volume in particular. "Perhaps that one? That's the year of my birth. I wonder what was on the week I was born?"

He still looked at me suspiciously, but I now saw it was actually jealousy. He obviously didn't relish others thumbing through his annals, and who can blame him? Still, my open-faced interest seemed to sway him and he took down the book. "When were you born?" he asked, licking his thumb.

I gave him a date that was not my birthday and he spent an interminable minute paging slowly through. "Ah," he said. "That was a funny week."

"Oh?" I said, feigning innocent curiosity. "How so?"

"We lost an act. Halfway through a season, too. Very inconvenient."

I gently pressed him until he told me the tale. It seemed that a stage magician calling himself Maleficarus the Magnificent had been retained at that time. He was, allowing for Pensey's understatement, a remarkable proponent of stage illusions and close-up magic. "Went out to China and India," said Pensey, "learning tricks from those fakirs and other heathens. Must have done him some good because I've seen dozens of magic acts, sir, and not one of them held a candle to Maleficarus. He spent a small fortune getting things just the way he liked them so it was a surprise to Mr. Rumbelow, the manager back then, when one day Maleficarus doesn't turn up for the matinee. His digs said all his stuff was there but nobody knew where he'd gone. The police even dragged the river. Not a sausage. It was a shame. We'd had people coming from two towns over to see him, had to make refunds to them all. Very sad." Pensey looked off into the middle distance, lost in memory. "Working this side of the orchestra pit can make a man very cynical. You see how the lady gets cut in half, how Peter Pan flies, you see all the joinery, wire and armatures that makes the magic work. But Maleficarus, he was boggling, sir. Never could guess how he did half the things he did, not even seeing them from the wings." He brought himself back to the here and now, closing the book. "He did things that fair rattled the paradigms."

"Rattled the what?"

"Paradigms, sir. Conceptual frameworks. From the Greek para meaning beside or beyond and deiknynai meaning to know. Will that be all, sir?"

So, now I had the source of the haunt, I was sure. The date I'd given the worthy Pensey as my birthday was actually exactly two thousand and three hundred days before the first death. Theatricals vanish all the time, usually on the run from debt; and not a great deal is thought of it. I doubted that was the case here. Maleficarus had, if you recall, spent a 'small fortune' on bringing his act to the Alhambra's stage so I doubted money was the problem. I also had my worries about any illusionist that decides to call himself Maleficarus. It literally means 'evil doer,' but figuratively it is used to mean 'witch' or 'warlock' as in the title of Kramer and Sprenger's endlessly amusing idiot's guide to inquisition, the Malleus Maleficarum. There are mysteries to be found in the Orient that are not to be trifled with, and secrets that are protected by unforgiving and not always human guardians. I wondered if Maleficarus had roused something with his meddling, it had followed him here and dealt with him. And then, for some reason, stayed. More data still was required, much more data.

I returned to my dressing room and considered my next move. I remember sitting at my dressing table and looking steadily at the mirror, my chin resting in my palm, perhaps expecting my reflection to have a bright idea. And as I ruminated, the door opened behind me.

There was no drop in temperature, no feeling of unease, no warning at all and clearly, nor was there anybody on the other side of the door. I turned suddenly but the door stood open, the doorframe stood empty and there was nobody visible beyond. I rose slowly, walked quietly to the door and looked outside. There was nobody on the stair, nobody around the star trap mechanism, no sound, no signs. It was uncommonly quiet. Usually, there'd be somebody wandering around the stage over my head or the cleaners clattering around the auditorium or at the very least the skittering of the mice in the shadows. There was no sound at all. I doubted my senses and drew in a breath of air to test another. The basement usually had a musty smell, dust and rodents; but it smelled of nothing. I was aware of the coolness of the air upon my sinus and that was all. I touched my cheek and my face felt like cloth, a blurred, indistinct sensation. I knew, somehow knew, that my senses were being filtered through the perceptions of another. Something not quite dead, but a long way from alive. It was watching me, smelling me, tasting me; and I was minded of a python that I had once watched leisurely get the measure of a rat before engulfing it and devouring it. Far from meekly lying around while I examined it, I had become the object of its scrutiny.

As with demons, I have encountered two haunts in my life, Parkin, two ghosts. One was a pathetic creature, the fag end of a tragedy. I pitied it. But this one, this one caused my every hackle to rise. There was a slow, conniving malevolence about its presence that worried me, and an aching patience that worried me far more. What wonders could the humblest craftsman perform given a thousand years? And so what villainies could the palest, malign spirit engineer when time is nothing to it? Suddenly I knew that Maleficarus had not accidentally brought some guardian here in his wake. He had brought something here deliberately and paid the price for his hubris. What plans it now had, I could not imagine. Whatever they were, though, I appeared to be part of them.

The door to the prop store swung slowly open. I had little choice. Either it wanted to show me something or it wished me harm. Even the latter case would teach me something about it. I looked cautiously inside but the darkness was so complete that it was almost palpable. I tried the light switch but the ancient Bakelite clacked and rattled uselessly under my finger, its echo loud in the silence. I have had occasion to enter several tombs, but this place was quieter.

I went back upstairs to Pensey's office and borrowed a torch, a great practical thing sheathed in rubber that looked like it could double as a cosh. Its batteries were due for replacement, however, and the weak yellow light it produced did little to ease my misgivings as I entered the store. The prop store of any theatre makes fascinating viewing, but the catholic nature of provincial theatres make their stores all the more varied. In a few minutes I had passed Sweeney Todd's rotting barber's chair, a Chinese dragon, a plaster monolith, and a stand of French windows. There were chests and boxes galore, rolled up knights' pennants, a collapsing piano, Yorick's skull in a goldfish bowl, and the Duchess of Malfi's lover dangling from a beam. All intriguing in their way, but none had the slightest relevance to what I was doing. I was on the point of leaving when I heard the door shut with a bang. I hardly had time to react before my torch was snuffed as easily as blowing out an unguarded candle.

Abruptly, I was in the dark. Unfortunately, I was not alone.

"Cabal," whispered a voice in my ear. It was gentle and sibilant in the vowels. Human larynxes have difficulty doing that.

"Good afternoon," I replied. "You would be Maleficarus?"

"Your path lies elsewhere, Cabal," said the voice. I noticed that it had not answered the question. "Do not interfere."

"I seek only enlightenment."

"It is not here. Only death. Go now."

Perhaps it is a character flaw, but I hate being ordered around without even an introduction. "Why now?" I asked. "What is to happen?"

But there was no reply this time. My torch flickered back into life and the door swung open. I was being dismissed. Now, this I know to be a character flaw, but I refuse to accept warnings without being told the basis of the threat. If the phantom of the Alhambra wanted me to leave, it had chosen exactly the wrong way to go about it. I now knew that the next act in the haunt's little scheme would be happening very soon and not waiting the usual lengthy pause. That suggested that it was reaching some sort of fruition and that meant that it was worth waiting to see, warning or no.

This version of Mother Goose was a Demon King's dream. After a hefty appearance early on to broker the deal and a shorter one a little later when the Dame asks for the goose back and gets turned down, the king enjoys a very hefty absence from the stage, more than long enough to run around to the pub next door and wash away the old hopes for a serious acting career, before making a slightly unsteady entrance for the grand finale. This was useful to me too, as it provided a period in which I could prowl the theatre backstage without running into too many people who had the leisure to ask me what I was doing. As I made my second exit from the stage that night, I made my way to Pensey's office. He was characteristically delighted to see me. "Don't get too rat-arsed and back in plenty of time for your cue, sir."

"I'm not leaving the building," I said and enjoyed his mild surprise. "No, I was wondering about something you said about Maleficarus the Magnificent. You said he spent a small fortune preparing his act. What did you mean by that?"

"Mr. Maleficarus was a perfectionist, sir. He wasn't happy with the facilities so he paid for improvements out of his own pocket."

"Sounds unusual."

"It's unique, sir, at least in the history of the Alhambra. He was right, though, we certainly didn't have anything like that trap."

"The star trap," I said, knowing full well it must be.

"Yes, sir. He had some of the best stage engineers in the country in to construct that. Wanted it to be perfect. Beautiful craftsmanship, always worked like a charm. At least until your predecessor got his head smashed into jam by it." You will see that Pensey and tact were never likely to see eye to eye.

"But he designed it."

"Yes, sir." He wrinkled his nose as if he thought I was playing some childish trick. "How did you know that?"

"An educated guess." I left Pensey and walked down the steps to the basement with as much dignity as one can muster in red tights, cloak and artificial moustache. Oh, and those damnable horns. The spirit gum it took to keep those in place, blast them.

I examined the star trap closely. It was very clean, unsurprisingly. It must have had mechanics swarming over it immediately after the last "accident." I had researched the previous three deaths and they had been far less spectacular. They had all involved deaths on stage, though, twice written into the death certificates as strokes, once as heart failure. All three, I noted, had suffered their collapse in the same quarter of the stage. I was prepared to make a small wager that each of them had walked across the closed star trap immediately before dying.

The workings of the trap looked just as you'd imagine them; relatively simple but with excellent workmanship. I found the contacts that triggered the flash and smoke on stage as the platform passed a point, adjustable to allow for variations in the passenger's height. That was no major discovery — I'd been measured up for the trap myself right from the first dress rehearsal although I'd never known how they used the information until then. I found the panniers where sandbags were placed to counteract the actor's weight and launch him through the trap. I found the trigger mechanism, which ingeniously could be set off by the actor on the platform, a stagehand standing outside the frame of the platform lift, or even from the wings using an electrical relay. All very clever, all very irrelevant. There had to be more to the trap than I was seeing, but I was damned if I could find it.

I finally spotted Maleficarus's little secret as I examined the collar of wood and metal that held the top of the frame rigid immediately below the trap itself. It seemed over-engineered to my eye and the closer I looked, the more redundant the collar appeared. A few seconds' work with a screwdriver allowed me to remove the inner wooden hoop and exposed the metal band that lay sandwiched between it and another outer wooden hoop. It appeared to be brass, but I had my suspicions that it was a far rarer alloy. I could not find any weld or joining mark but there were imperfections; slight ridges that were just visible in the obtuse light of the electric torch and to the gentlest brushing of my fingertips. I went back to my dressing room and got some paper. I laid the paper around the inside of the hoop and gently shaded it with an eye pencil. Don't look at me like that, Parkin. It's perfectly normal theatrical accoutrement.

A few minutes careful work gave me a map of the ridges. They didn't mean anything in themselves, but I followed the strongest ridges with a greasepaint stick and returned to my dressing room to hold the paper up to the light, viewing it from the reverse side. You see, the ridges were just where the metal had been pushed back by characters being driven into the metal of the outside of the hoop, driven in at the tip of a cold chisel. A particular type of chisel sanctified in a process whose details have no business being repeated in a tale for a Christmas Eve.

The characters were easy to make out, all the more so as I'd been expecting them ever since I'd seen that hoop with its characteristic sheen of the metal of Leng. It's a difficult metal to lay hands on. No forge in this world can make it. You have to go . . . elsewhere. It is very necessary for some effects that, even by a necromancer's standards, are unsavoury.

The metal hoop constituted something called the Maw of the Clathik. A clathik, for your information, is an ugly beast with the body of a bull, the face of a boll weevil and a hide that can only be described as rugose. It eats spiritual energy, quite literally draining souls through its tubular mouth. The hoop used the name only partially figuratively; its function was essentially the same. Once every 2300 days, the hoop would become active, looking for a soul to devour. Standing on it was as deadly as travelling through it. Setting it under a stage was an inspired touch. These things always work better with an audience, usually of cultists. It's to do with empathic resonance, the more observers you have the better. Having a poor hapless theatre audience to generate an empathic wave was ingenious, I'll grant him that.

Oh yes, Maleficarus had certainly picked up a few new tricks on his travels. Conjurors getting ideas above their station is far more common than you might think. They usually start young, performing minor vanishes and transmutations in the parlour to the wonderment of their families. There's something in the bafflement of an audience that is intoxicating. It is the faintest scent of power. A few go further — the illusions become grander, the audience becomes larger. Finally, they're being paid to perform, but the real reward is the gasps and the sighs of disbelief, the slightly nervous laughter of people seeing things that cannot be. But smoke and mirrors can only take a man so far and he gets to thinking, if an audience will respect this fakery, then what might be possible with true magic? How much larger the audience, how much deeper the respect?

It is a madness, of course. To meddle with such profound and dangerous forces simply for personal gratification is pure folly, worse than suicidal. But vanity can do it to a man; and Maleficarus was such a man, it seemed. He had pulled too many rabbits from too many hats; insanity had claimed him.

Show me a stage magician who values the writings of Dee over Houdin, the works of Simon Magus over John Maskelyne, and I shall show you a disaster in the making. In this case, alas, the disaster had already occurred two decades before.

The dressing room door swung open and there was nobody beyond it. It appeared the late magician was summoning me for another interview. Late in a very loose sense if my suspicions were correct. I folded up the piece of paper and pushed it in my pantaloons for safekeeping before walking outside. The door to the prop store was already opening as I picked up the electric torch by the star trap mechanism and walked into the darkness. The torch was almost no use, its tired yellow beam seeming to grow weaker by the second as the batteries exhausted themselves.

The magician's spirit didn't waste any time with pleasantries. "You were warned," it whispered harshly in my ear.

"Yes. I believe I was."

"You will die."

"We all do, Maleficarus. Even you, despite your best efforts." It seemed that this wasn't going to be one of those chinwag sorts of séances. I decided to leave and walked unhurriedly to the door.

I had just reached the door when a massive blow caught me between the shoulder blades, picking me up and carrying me ten feet or more before dumping me to the floor. It's difficult to describe the nature of the force that struck me. Although it carried the force of a bull's charge, it didn't strike me quite instantaneously. There was a sense of being borne aloft as if picked up by a high wind. I felt more like a kite than a victim right until I crashed into the floor and was sent sprawling. I was on my feet again in a second, whirling to face the open door to the prop store. But there was nothing there.

"You were warned," the voice repeated, its anger grating over my bones. It seemed foolish to argue the point. Instead I ran for the stairs. I didn't even get close.

The force of Maleficarus's wrath entwined around my legs like a quicksilver cat and I fell again. This time it held me and I was dragged back across the floor. As I tried vainly to stop myself, I noticed movement out of the corner of my eye. Can you imagine a sandbag walking, Parkin? That's what it looked like. Like rats in sacks, sandbags were processing from their pile in the corner and into the pile on the cradle of the star trap. It took me a moment to understand Maleficarus's intention, but when I did, I redoubled my efforts to escape. The weight in the cradle had been carefully calculated to impel me with just enough force to make a dramatic entrance through the trap and no more. Too much weight meant too much acceleration. If I hit the star trap too quickly, my skull would crumple faster than the leaves could move aside. Maleficarus was engineering another accident. This one wouldn't be on his schedule and would doubtless be less efficacious than the previous sacrifices to his ambition, but I don't think that really concerned him very much by that point. Almost below the limit of hearing, I became aware of a throbbing of syllables; an incantation delivered with the sheer melodrama only a stage artiste would feel necessary. He was awakening the Maw. Not only did he intend to kill me, he also meant to burn my soul for his greater glory.

I am a necromancer. At that point in my life I was a necrothologist. The difference is largely technical to the layman and I won't bore you with definitions. I was already aware of many different methods of "raising the dead" to use a vulgar term and also very aware of their shortcomings. Maleficarus had lighted upon a technique of granting immortality and decided that the great cost was acceptable to him. In a real sense, after all, he wasn't paying it himself. Usually, the sorcerer wishing to use the Maw is dependent on having reliable servants who will carry out the rituals and sacrifices over an extended period to give him his second life. History has shown that the servants are far more likely to take the money and run rather than get involved in a drawn out series of murders. Very wise of them, too. Maleficarus had undoubtedly shown great ingenuity in dispensing with the servants in favour of a machine placed in such a place that the sacrifices would willingly line up to die on his behalf.

I wasn't familiar with every nuance of the ritual he was using, but taking a soul once every 2300 days seemed to increase its effectiveness. If he'd decided to kill me a thousand days into the cycle, I doubt he would have been so keen to use the Maw to finish me. As it was only a few days, he didn't seem to mind using it and then starting again. Just my luck.

I was abruptly pulled into the air and hung windmilling ridiculously in that silly costume for a moment before I was thrown headlong into the star trap's frame. I managed to twist so that I didn't crack my head against the supports and took the blow on my upper back instead. There was a fierce pain and a

sense that something had given way; my scapula as it turned out. Pensey's electric torch fell from my hand — I'd utterly forgotten I was holding it — and rolled across the platform. It was strange that, at the moment before my utter extinction, even as I saw the safety case around the trap's lever swing open with no hand upon it, it was strange that I should be thinking of Mr. Pensey's torch and its remarkably rugged construction. As Maleficarus pulled the lever, I moved my foot and kicked the torch so it rolled up against the support at the edge of the platform. The catches disengaged and the platform shot upwards.

Very nearly five inches it got before the torch hit the underside of the lowest horizontal strut and the whole thing stopped dead.

I lay, silent but for my laboured breath, bundled in the frame of the trap. Maleficarus was silent, his fury scenting the air like ozone. Above me I could hear the pattering of the actors' feet, the laughter of the crowd. Behind me, I could hear the faint buzzing of the cue warning from my dressing room. Then, in front of me, from the open door to the prop store, I heard knocking.

It shouldn't have surprised me. This whole rigmarole — I almost said pantomime — had been in the pursuit of immortality. Immortality as a creature of flesh and blood, not a ghost. It made sense that he was keeping his body somewhere near. I felt his presence fading from the air as his wretched excuse for a soul condensed and curdled back into the body he'd abandoned a generation before. I suspect he'd been planning a more triumphant return to his mortal coil than the hasty one I'd forced upon him, but needs must when the devil — or at least a demon king — drives.

I tried to get to my feet but the pain from my shoulder was agonising and I slumped back down while it stopped battering me. I had come close to fainting from it and that — given an imminent visit from a mad revenant — would have been inconvenient. In the prop store, the knocking became a pounding. It only served to confirm my suspicions, although I might have preferred a less threatening form of endorsement. I determined to get up and out of there, injury or not, and cautiously started to get out of the trap cage. I'd hardly begun when the pounding terminated with the sound of, somewhere in the darkest recesses of the store, a theatrical chest being thrown upon. It seemed that Maleficarus had finally managed to get out of bed. I redoubled my efforts to escape.

I could hear everything through that door: the clumsy staggering fall as he clambered out, his body not nearly as responsive as he remembered it; the slow, scraping advance as he half walked and half dragged himself towards the door; his hissing voice as he heaved air in and out of lungs as dry as coral on a museum shelf. "You were warned! You were warned!"

Well, yes, I had been. The irony of it was that I'd had no intention of halting his experiment. I just wanted to understand what he'd been up to, observe his progress and then leave him to it, perhaps with the occasional follow-up visit. His current exertions and my broken shoulder blade were all the result of a misunderstanding and of Maleficarus jumping to the conclusion that I'd wanted to stop him. Silly man.

A tattered, semi-mummified hand gripped the doorframe of the prop store, yellowed bone showing through the parched skin. I didn't entirely understand how any further sacrifices were going to repair the damages of time, but I guessed Maleficarus hadn't really thought that part through in any great detail. Perhaps he wanted to look like a scarecrow. People are strange, after all.

I had the strongest feeling that things were going to become very unpleasant very quickly. I managed to get onto all fours in the bottom of the cage — all threes, that is — and started to crawl out. I was very conscious of getting too close to the Maw; it glistened and lights swam beneath the iridescent surface of the metal. It also seemed to be salivating, but that could have been an illusion of the light. I looked up as I got halfway out and saw Maleficarus bearing down on me. He was a terrible mess; at some early point of his voluntary death, parts of him had liquefied in the way that putrescent flesh does and made awful stains on his clothes. He'd decided to entomb himself in his stage clothes, naturally. I was glad the top hat was missing, but the dinner suit suitable for a minor dignitary at an ambassadorial function and the opera cloak with silver clasp were in evidence. Not in evidence were swathes of skin, muscle tissue, his lips and his eyes. He didn't seem to need any of them but if he was expecting immortality to get him an indefinite season at the Palladium looking like that, he'd been wasting everybody's time and a few people's lives for no good reason.

Despite being dead, he still had a good turn of speed and I realised that I could not hope to outrun him while injured like that. Instead, I held my position and waited to see what he intended to do. If he'd just brought something heavy or pointed from the store, he could have killed me then and there but, as was apparent from his whole scheme, he was prone to the idée fixe. He'd awakened the Maw, and that was how I was to die. He ran at me and I raised myself to a sitting position better to meet his charge. Then I changed my mind and ducked.

Maleficarus hit me at a dead run and his shin caught my shoulder. That wasn't pleasant. Despite the sensation of having two disparate slabs of bone that were theoretically meant to be one and the same grate against each other in my upper back, I heaved myself forward and out of the cage, slapping Pensey's

torch clear with a harsh blow as I passed. My feet were still on the platform as it started its ascent, but my chest was on the floor and I felt the platform scrape up my instep and clear.

Of course, Maleficarus was aboard. Of course, he weighed less than me being semi-skeletal and all, and the platform had been counterweighted for my mass. Of course, he'd been adding more sandbags still so the platform rose like a shell from a mortar. Of course, the Maw was waiting.

Maleficarus had a deal with the Maw. He would feed it once every now and then, it would supply him with much of the energy it harvested and keep some back for itself as a retainer. This arrangement had never been drawn up with the possibility of Maleficarus himself being fed to the Maw. The Maw devoured his spirit and then, as per the deal, gave most of it back. It then took it again and gave most back. And again and again and again. It's a small miracle, I've always thought, that calculus allows an infinite number of operations in a finite period of time, that Achilles can catch the tortoise after all, just in time for them to shin up the asymptote together. Being devoured by a Maw is reputedly agonising beyond belief. You can draw your own conclusions as to what it feels to be devoured an infinite number of times in perhaps a quarter of a second. And good riddance.

What happened to him?" asked Parkin.

"What? After he exited the other side of the Maw? Why, he was shot through the star trap and showered over the entire stage and the first three rows of the audience in a hail of desiccated body parts. The parents were not impressed." Cabal examined the bottle. "Oh. We've run out of brandy, too."

"I'm very sorry, Cabal." Parkin pulled himself up from his slump and stretched. "I've drunk you out of house and home."

"Oh, not at all." Cabal was more than ready for bed. He felt like he was going to be sleeping a long time. "It's been enjoyable, I suppose. In a cathartic sort of way. I don't get many opportunities to discuss my work."

"No, I imagine not. It's been interesting. Horrible, but interesting."

Cabal saw him to the door. Parkin stood on the doorstep and drew on his gloves as he looked into the black sky, the stars twinkling as harshly as glass splinters in the freezing air. "Goodnight, Sergeant Parkin," said Cabal, stifling a yawn.

Parkin took a step forward and enjoyed the sound and sensation of the freezing snow crunching under his foot. He checked his watch and raised an eyebrow. It was past midnight. "Merry Christmas, Johannes Cabal," he said turning. But the door had already closed and he could just make out the clicks of the bolts being thrown. Moments later, the downstairs lights started to flicker out. Parkin smiled. "I hope you have a Merry Christmas one of these years, Cabal. I really do," he said to himself. Then he turned his face to the direction of the village and started the long walk home, a home of warmth and of family. ☌

Jonathan L. Howard is currently working on an espionage game called In Cold Blood *that he swears has nothing whatsoever to do with Truman Capote. Another adventure of Johannes Cabal appeared in the very first issue of this magazine.*

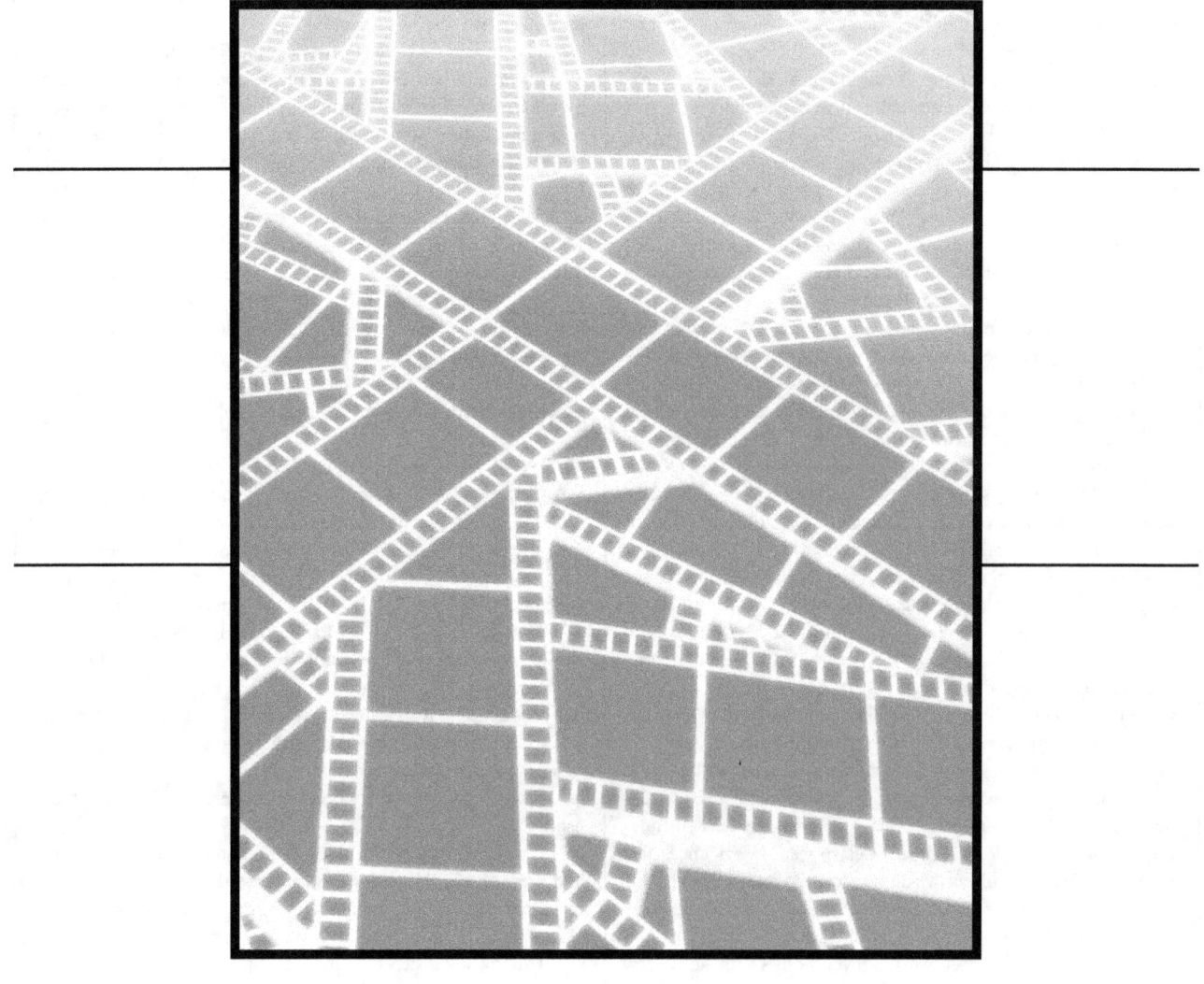

ILLUSTRATION BY DARREN WHITTINGHAM

The Paramount Importance of Pictures

by Lynne Jamneck

> *". . . who'll come to find you first*
> *your devils or your gods?"*
> — *Tracy Chapman,* Crossroads

J *ust look at the silly bitch.*

Mike shook his head, one hand clutching the megaphone he used to direct the insipid sheep some liked to refer to as actors.

Who had he pissed off to deserve this torment? Wasn't it enough that he had to shoot this claptrap of a movie on a shoestring budget, second-hand remodeled sets, a piss-poor script and shoddy special effects?

Mike narrowed his eyes at the so-called star of the show, her brow furrowed in consternation and confusion. What had the producers been thinking when they suggested (no, practically threatened) Denise Barrett for the part of a cynical, down on her luck, futuristically evolved space pirate?

No, this definitely wasn't about acting prowess, rather the impressive pair of silicone babies she sported underneath the ridiculously revealing costume which looked like a leftover from a *Xena* shoot. Probably was.

Yet, every so often he couldn't help but feel a small morsel of sympathy for her. Everyone knew Denise Barrett couldn't act her way out of a can, but hey — at least she had perfect legs and tits that were insured for millions.

"Cut!" Mike's voice sounded metallically across the crowded lot. The actors dropped their professional facades, some opting instead for irritation while others adopting a more resigned approach.

Denise Barrett, star quality positively gleaming from her accompanying attitude, threw her copy of the script on the floor and stalked out from behind the fiberglass of her spaceship cockpit.

"How the fuck am I supposed to pronounce this garbage?" she fumed at her director.

"Denise, honey, it's science fiction."

"It's unpronounceable!"

Muted titters from the peanut gallery.

"Calm down, for God's sake," Mike responded. His momentary sympathy had vanished along with possibly the last tether of patience he still had left. Haven't they tried this scene fifteen times already? Felt more like hundred and fifty.

"Everybody take five." Mike fiddled in his shirt pocket for a crumpled pack of cigarettes. The actors dispersed within a mutter of insult and slander.

Denise slouched into a chair marked BARRETT next to him, pouting.

"You signed up for this, Denise." Mike smoked, trying to remain stable. He had three weeks to wrap this disaster before post-production was scheduled to start.

"It's a ridiculous story, Mike. Fucking *Star Trek* meets *Indiana Jones*, for chrissakes."

She had a point. However, his previous two films sank at the box office (despite artistic and critical praise), and he had a wife and three kids who didn't take money, but rather bled it from his thinning pockets.

Thinking of Clarissa made him flinch inside. Mike suspected his wife was having an affair.

"Mike, lovey?"

The director cringed inwardly at the high-pitched, succulent voice of his make-up artist.

Freddy Finkelstein was an old-school Jew with a horn of a nose, and a love for young, bruised-looking boys surpassed only by his affection for powdered train tracks on mirrored surfaces.

He sniffed tellingly as he minced in Mike's direction.

Denise rolled her eyes. Both she and Freddy were queens who didn't like to be upstaged by the presence of the other.

"Mike, dear, I'm having a bitch of a time doing Fran's hair for that scene with the lightning storm. The bloody tart is drunk again and won't keep still. I'm telling you, if she comes out from underneath these hands looking like Elsa Lanchester's Bride of Frankenstein it'll be her own fault."

Mike bit his lip in a bid to quell the anger bubbling in the pit of his stomach. Why couldn't something just go right for a change on this Goddamn set?

Just last week, one of the sound engineers was almost decapitated when a mistimed explosion sent the Ark of the Covenant's lid propelling across his makeshift dessert.

Denise was right. The story was ridiculous. How the hell did God's Ark end up in space in the first place? Then again, a script

that actually made sense seemed to be the exception these days rather than the rule. Money didn't mind loopholes. In fact, loopholes were what sequels thrived on.

Denise muttered something unintelligible but decidedly rude before storming off in the direction of her trailer.

Freddy piqued his nose.

"What's up with Ms Thing? Having trouble pronouncing all those big words? Moreover, what am I supposed to do with that lush Fran?"

Mike flicked his cigarette onto the ground, crushed it underfoot.

"Go dump her in the fucking tank they used to shoot *Titanic* for all I care." He hooked his jacket from the back of the chair and walked off.

"Just where the Hell are you going?" Freddy reprimanded.

Mike didn't answer.

Exit one fed-up director, stage right.

Mike instructed the barman to take money from the heap in front of him on the bar counter. The young punk took more than was necessary, but it didn't bother Mike. He had other things to worry about.

Mike was thinking about Terry Macmillan, the screenwriter whose work was the basis for his new film. Lately he'd been thinking about Terry a lot. Maybe it was because things hadn't been going so well on the *Universal Covenant* shoot that he'd been thinking of the guy so much.

Two weeks after he'd been connected as director for Covenant, Terry had shown up on his doorstep, at two in the morning. Terry had been rambling, speaking in fragmented sentences, giving Mike the impression that he had been drunk.

Not so.

He wanted to buy the script back from Mike, which of course was impossible since it wasn't his script to sell. Terry wanted him to talk to the Producers, remove himself from the project.

Naturally, Mike refused. He even made a joke about it, something concerning artistic integrity that he couldn't remember now.

Terry'd become agitated, and Mike finally had to let a security guard escort him off the property. A couple of times after that Mike had tried to phone him, but Terry's landline seemed to have been disconnected, as was his cell number.

Mike shook his head, trying to clear the cobwebs, and tipped his finger for another whisky. Why did he always dwell on the past when he drank?

The cell phone in his pocket rang.

Mike could only let it go on ringing for about ten seconds before he finally had to relinquish and answer.

"Where the hell are you?"

Waiting for the bar man to pour his fourth straight double whisky, Mike recognized the distressed voice of his personal assistant. "As long as I'm not on set, Ellen, I couldn't give a flying —"

"Are you drunk? For God's sake, Mike . . ."

"What? I can't have the luxury of some time on my own? Besides, I'm not drunk. I'm angry."

"Did you forget your appointment?"

He ordered another double and didn't answer.

"Mike, you're half an hour late for your meeting with Otto Klemper. Ring a bell?"

Mike remembered.

He muttered a silent shit into the phone and hastily stopped the bartender from pouring the drink.

"You did forget," Ellen sighed audibly.

"Jesus Mike, do you have any idea what I had to go through to pull this off in the first place? The man is practically a recluse. He even refused a meeting with Shyamalan."

"Ellen, relax. I'm putting my jacket on; I'm walking out the door. Wait — give me the address again?"

He jotted the information on the back of his hand, hoping he got the spelling right and thanked Ellen profusely.

Truth be told, he expected something a little more . . . gothic. Bates Motel, maybe.

Otto Klemper lived in a small, compact suburban house. Inconspicuous, whitewashed walls and petunias blooming in solid trays below the windows greeted Mike as he stepped from his car onto the curb. For a moment he even thought he might have the wrong address.

Then a frail looking man, carried by nothing more than old age and a knobby cane appeared in the doorway.

He neither smiled nor waved. Just watched.

Mike finished chewing the last of his peppermint before approaching up the paved driveway. "Mr. Klemper?" he asked, smiling his best director smile.

"You're late," the old man replied without the slightest inflection to his voice.

"I know, and I apologize. One never can predict these movie shoots."

The apology didn't lie itself quite as well as Mike would have wished for. He hoped Klemper didn't smell the lingering trace of booze from the sweat underneath his armpits.

The old man said nothing, just turned his back on Mike to proceed back into the house. So much for the welcoming committee, Mike thought as he followed Klemper inside.

The house was immaculately neat — a welcome, cool respite from the heat outside. There was still the decidedly musty smell of maturity lurking about the hallways, but not like when he used to visit his mother in the old-age home. This reminded him of something more raw . . . like unearthed rock and soil. Maybe the old guy liked toiling in the garden. Like that actor he once directed — until said actor's nosy neighbor informed the cops that his afternoon of supplanting seeds had turned into frantic midnight slogging.

They found the guy's wife and kids buried amongst the daisies and other assortment of pottings. Crazy son-of-a-

"I assume you came here to ask me something, not daydream in the middle of my lounge?"

Mike snapped from his reverie.

"It's the least you can do after the harassment I had to endure from your secretary," Klemper continued.

Mike studied the old man's face. His skin seemed parched and stretched, in dire contrast to the icy blueness of his eyes. He found himself apologizing once more: "Oh, Ellen, yes. She's very

driven. I keep telling her she doesn't work for Spielberg."

His feeble attempt at a joke went unnoticed. If Klemper actually noticed the humor in Mike's quip, he wasn't laughing. Instead he turned his attention to the liquor cabinet and poured two generous dollops of Scotch from an expensive-looking decanter. He gave one to his guest before taking a slow seat in a faded lounge chair.

Mike sat down opposite, noticing the low tick-tock of a grandfather clock somewhere in the back of the house. He waited for some sort of invitation to start talking. None was forthcoming. Klemper watched him from where he sat, sipping whisky, cane balanced against his knee.

Mike thought he looked older than he initially considered, but it might have just been a trick of the muted lighting. He was about to say something when the old man jumped the gun on him:

"Let me guess: in a last-ditch attempt to inject some . . . respectability into your hoary little film, you've come here today for some juicy quote. A small morsel of supposed truth that will hook your audience to the 'creepy' feel of your attempt at passable entertainment, mmm?"

Mike swallowed the liquor, silently scolding Klemper in the reprieve. Don't try and put me down old man; remember, I work in an industry that invented the concept. He decided to ignore the comment completely.

"I have just one or two questions. Contrary to popular belief, not all movies want to belittle the importance of their subject matter. I'll do my best not to waste your time, Mr. Klemper."

"You're already wasting; might as well tell me what this picture of yours is about."

Klemper still wasn't smiling, but Mike thought that he caught the tail end of interest in his last words.

Briefly, he filled the old man in about his tale concerning a group of futuristic space pirates who return to Earth two hundred years post nuclear-holocaust in search of the lost Ark of the Covenant.

"Bah!" Otto Klemper harrumphed at the mention of Mike's chosen relic. "Not that Pandora's box again!"

Mike frowned as Klemper steadied himself on his cane to pour more whisky.

"There haven't been that many movies dealing with the Ark. Come on, give me some credit."

"Sure, sure," the German sneered. "But that didn't keep the ones that eventually got made from distorting the truth."

He gave Mike a disdainful look. "Why do you think I balk every time one of you people telephone me? You never listen to what I say anyway."

Mike briefly thought to question Klemper about his previous Tinsel town visitors, and then decided against it. He got the distinct feeling the man belonged to the kiss-don't-tell stable of kooks. Ellen might put stock in the old fart, but Mike was starting to feel all the more that Otto Klemper was nothing more than a well read misanthrope, with a persona concocted around the combination of his ill-temperateness and Nazi-inspiring name.

"In my version," Mike continued, "the heroine finds out that the Ark has been in space all along, guarded by the original monstrous, godlike inhabitants of Earth, who ruled the planet way before the Dinosaurs — way before anything we have knowledge of."

He leaned closer to Klemper's chair, winking conspiratorially. "Very Lovecraftian, don't you think?"

Even in the muted light of Otto Klemper's shade-drawn lounge Mike could see the red blotches blooming on the old man's cheeks.

"You cannot do that!" Klemper exploded, almost spilling his drink.

"Oh balls!" Mike chuckled, having finally had enough of the old miser's higher-than-thou attitude. He knocked back the rest of his whisky and rose from the chair. This had been a complete waste of his time. Who needed the fucking movie to be 'historically accurate'? As long as it has a couple of decent explosions and copious, uncalled for shots of Denise Barrett's million dollar body — who cared about facts? Mike heard Klemper shuffle after him as he made for the front door.

"You'll regret this," he seethed at Mike's back. "They won't like this, not one bit!"

Mike laughed as he stepped back into the sunlight, and then stopped to offer a parting shot to Otto Klemper:

"Moviegoers don't give a horse's ass about plot or logic; not the one's who'll be lining up to see Universal Covenant. That's the beauty of Hollywood."

As he drove away, muttering to himself, Mike caught a last glimpse of the old man.

Standing in the doorway, surrounded by deceptively uptown bliss, he couldn't be a hundred percent sure whether the expression on Klemper's face was one of relief, resignation — or a queer, unsettling mixture of both.

DENISE BARRETT. With the prerequisite gold star at the top.

As she stood wavering in front of the trailer door, Denise couldn't help but feel that somehow she still wasn't where she wanted to be. Worse yet, she knew that some things would always be just outside her acting grasp.

For one, she'd never be Meryl Streep. Some days she wondered if she was even Cameron Diaz.

But she had a body you could pour into the tightest, smallest piece of costume, breasts that made men think of their mothers, and legs that went on for the proverbial mile. Yes, the Honchos of Hollywood loved her, their hard-ons profuse evidence of the fact.

Ignorant bastards.

She unlocked the trailer and went inside. Once the door was closed she fell into a tired pile on the unmade bed, still dressed in the ridiculous costume that was supposed to make her look like an Amazon from space.

An urgent knock made her sit upright.

Christ, she hoped that wasn't Mike again. If it was, he was going to be drunk for sure, and then the come-ons would start. What the hell was he thinking anyway — that she'd willingly have an affair with her director?

That would be the ultimate chestnut to her bumpy record of a résumé, and she wouldn't have it. Denise Barrett might not be Oscar material, but she sure as hell wasn't a cliché either.

She mustered some sparkle, and reached to open the door.

It wasn't Mike, thank God.

It was his wife.

At first Denise wasn't sure what to say to the dark-haired woman standing five small trailer-steps down. And Clarissa Palmer didn't offer anything either, just stood there looking at Denise, hands pitched to her hips like she had something to tell her.

The hooter of a car sounded not far off, making Denise start.

"Well, are you just going to let me stand here or can I come in?" Clarissa waited, eyebrows cocked dangerously. Denise smiled nervously as she stepped aside to let the woman in.

Clarissa made sure the door was locked before taking Denise's face in her hands, and kissing the star of her husband's latest movie.

"I just couldn't wait until tonight," she said slyly.

"What if Mike saw you?" Denise asked.

"I looked around the lot for him before coming here. One of the set designers said he did a walkout again."

Denise nodded.

"I think he knows," Clarissa said.

"The set designer? Knows what?"

"Mike — I think Mike knows," Clarissa corrected. "That I'm having an affair."

"If he knew with whom, it'd be pretty ironic, seeing as he's still trying his damndest with me."

A loud thudding noise interrupted their speculation, followed by a moment of uninterrupted silence. Then a slow, deliberate knock on the door.

Who's that? Clarissa mouthed. Denise hitched her shoulders. Someone moaned.

Denise grabbed the door handle and turned back the lock, but when she eventually opened the door, the sight that greeted her made her wish she hadn't.

Doubled-over and twisted on her trailer-steps lay Freddy Finkelstein.

He seemed to be in a severe state of shock, and appeared to be bleeding freely from every pore and orifice of his body.

His eyes looked like collective rockets about to pop, while a bloodied hand tried in vain to cover up a grim, gaping hole in his chest.

"Wa—wa—" he gurgled.

Both women stepped back and could do nothing but watch in revolting horror and fascination.

"Warn Terry . . . it's looking for Terry . . ."

The last word blew from Freddy's lips into the wind as he collapsed on the ground for good in a messy pile of twisted tissue and blood.

"Ellen! Ellen, damnit . . ." Mike pushed through the crowd of set people that had gathered around the lot in the half hour since he got the phone call.

"Mike, thank God you're here," his assistant breathed as they managed to meet up amongst the chaos.

"What happened? I got a hysterical call from Denise just as I was leaving Klemper's house. What's happened to Freddy?"

A cynical looking woman in a faded suit walked up to them. Mike noticed the Police badge around her neck.

"Are you Mike Palmer?" she asked.

"Yes — Denise Barrett, where is she?"

The detective directed somewhere behind her. "One of the paramedics are with her. Don't worry, she'll be fine. Just a little shock, imaginable after what happened." The statement was accompanied by a perfunctory smile.

Mike waved his hands. "Just — exactly what did happen, Detective . . ."

"Jones. From what we've been able to gather, it looks like Mr. Finkelstein was murdered."

"Oh shit." Mike couldn't really think of anything else to say. Part of him felt sadness over Freddy's death. Another was already worried what this new development would do to his filming schedule.

Detective Jones scrutinized him, noticing his trembling hands. Ellen excused herself to comfort Denise.

"I understand Mr. Finkelstein worked for you, Mr. Palmer?" the detective asked.

Mike nodded, extracting a beat-up looking cigarette from his shirt pocket.

"He is . . . was my principal make-up artist."

Jones nodded sympathetically. "Who is Terry McMillan?"

Mike's forehead squeezed a frown between his brows.

"Terry wrote the script for the movie I'm currently working on."

"The same movie Freddy Finkelstein worked on?"

"Yes. Wait a minute," Mike pondered. "Are you telling me Terry had something to do with Freddy's death?"

"Well, we don't know that yet. But Ms. Barrett told us that, just before he died, Mr. Finkelstein said something about warning Terry . . ." She flipped casually through a small notepad.

"Warn Terry; it's looking for him." She looked up at Mike. "I believe those were his last words. Any idea what that could mean?"

"Not a clue."

"Okay. We sent two cruisers to the address Ms. Barrett gave us, just to make sure Mr. Macmillan is safe. Or not trying to flee the country."

Mike nodded. Was this the reason he never felt comfortable around Terry?

The man always had an edge of anxiety about him, like that night he showed up at his home. Forever looking over his shoulder as if expecting something to catch up with him. But the screenplays he wrote were always good box-office, even if they were a tad on the clichéd side.

"Freddy said, 'it's looking for him?' What did he mean by that?" Mike said, thinking out loud.

Detective Jones turned away as a loud voice called her name. Then back at Mike: "As soon as we know more Mr. Palmer, you'll be sure to hear. Excuse me."

Mike looked round the busy lot. He spotted Denise on her way towards him, still visibly shaken from her experience. He met her halfway and she collapsed into his arms, crying. He wanted to ask her what, where and how, but figured that he wouldn't get anything helpful from her in the state she was in. Better to wait. Who knew — maybe there was still a chance for the two of them if he played his cards right.

From across Denise's shoulder, Mike saw Detective Jones approach once more. The look on her face didn't bode well.

"We just heard," she informed them. "It seems Terry McMillan committed suicide in his apartment. The call came in from the cleaning lady just minutes before the officers arrived on the scene."

Denise started crying afresh while Mike rubbed vigorously at his aching temples. The detective continued:

"The cleaner said she just talked to him this morning to confirm that she should still come in, so if it is suicide it must have happened within the last couple of hours. We'll know more after we get the forensics people in there.

There is however, another point of concern."

"Oh God, what now?" Denise moaned.

"The police found a note, presumably written, presumably, by Mr. McMillan. It was addressed to you, Mr. Palmer."

Mike froze momentarily. He always suspected Terry knew about his feelings toward Denise. Was this to get him back for all the changes he ended up making in the script? Or for going ahead with filming anyway after that peculiar late-night visit?

"It's a warning of some sort. Said that it was coming for you now. That you were the only one who could still dispatch the secret. Do you know what he's talking about, Mr. Palmer?"

Mike felt the raw deal of uneasiness flutter its way 'round his stomach. He shook his head slowly. He tried to remember some of the weird (sometimes unsettling) conversations that he and Terry sometimes had at three in the morning, both drunk (or stoned) out of their minds. If only he'd paid more attention.

Detective Jones handed him a card.

"I suggest you go home Mr. Palmer. Get some rest. I'll have an officer escort you home and stay overnight until we know more of what's going on. If you think of anything helpful, please don't hesitate to call me."

He nodded numbly, mind far away. Thinking of Otto Klemper's last words:

"They won't like this, not one bit."

Mike was finally, mercifully drunk.

He'd been fighting off investors and the wrath of producers all evening, all wanting to know what the hold-up was with *Universal Covenant*.

So the make-up artist got killed — everyone has enemies in this town. Get another one. The screenwriter offed himself — those moody (loony) types always did. If you need changes to be made, hire a hack. Just get the fucking thing in the can, Mikey!

Denise finally fell asleep on his couch, courtesy of Prince Valium.

There had been the fair amount of joking and mockery when that prop almost chopped the engineer's head clean off his shoulders.

Then the glue they used to keep some of the faux tomb-pillars in tack melted underneath the spotlights, almost caving in on Denise and three other actors.

All of a sudden the set was cursed, ha-ha, very funny. Mike didn't worry about it. This sort of thing only inspired people to come and see a movie even more.

Everyone was insured, he was covered.

Now someone was dead. Think of how many people would come to the cinema now. Mike wasn't sure whether he should cry or celebrate. The whole thing made him feel very uneasy.

He ducked into the liquor cabinet for a refill, and when he came back up saw a face that scared him so bad he almost dropped his drink.

Probably because he had been thinking about the old man ever since speaking to the police that Mike now nearly had a heart attack at seeing him again. More importantly:

"How did you get in here?"

Klemper looked troubled, yet resignedly so.

"Surely, more pressing should be Mr. Palmer — what am I doing here?"

Mike waited, wondering if he should try reaching for the pistol two drawers away.

"I was right, wasn't I?" Klemper continued. "You didn't listen, because you're so used to getting your own way. What you fail to realize is that you're not working with people here, Mr. Palmer. Some things . . . some things are so much bigger."

Mike thought he heard something move close to his right.

His head jerked, and he gasped.

There were . . . things in his room.

He couldn't form a clear picture, but he recognized forms, shapes, claws . . .

Had he been snorting cocaine? Something worse?

But then it touched his leg. It squeezed. Mike yelped.

"Sometimes I'm amazed at where the intellect come from," Otto continued jadedly. "All these people writing books about Ethiopia, Axum and soldier-priests. What drivel." He leaned forward in Mike's expensive camel-hide chair.

"And then some Hollywood wash-out writes down something he dreamt, sells it to be made into a movie and whammo! Hits the nail square on the head."

Mike noticed that the thing on his legs had fangs; huge, sharp pointed things full of gunk.

They glided into his flesh like a steak-knife through sirloin. Mike found himself unable to move, to even scream. His mus-

cles refused to respond.

The beast began to suck. Something warm was attaching itself to his neck.

Klemper watched, fascinated.

"It's self-defense, you see. The instinct to protect its home is paramount. Too many people trying to use it for the wrong reason." He seemed momentarily off-kilter, somehow guilty and uncomfortable at once. Klemper continued:

"Somewhere, someone will see this movie and start to get ideas. If more people believed the theories of washed-out archeologists we'd be in deep, deep trouble, Mr. Palmer."

It was inside him.

Both of them, Mike thought as he felt a sharp sting at the base of his neck. His vision became blurry. What was that . . . something big coming in through the door . . . Jesus, what . . . was that its mouth…?

"Oh they know that others suspect the truth. Naturally they can't go and kill them all. That might provoke its own study and investigation. But you were going to let millions of people see this, Mr. Palmer, and they cannot have that. All we can hope for is that after your death this film gets shelved in a very dark room. Preferably right at the bottom of all those other piles of films which never got made."

Klemper rose from the chair, unwavering support from his cane.

Mike began to feel light and somehow loose, as if parts of him were slipping away. He looked down. Blood, everywhere.

"You chose to tell a good story, Mr. Palmer. Pity that someone out there doesn't want anyone to know about it. Didn't think about that, did you? Well, not to worry; you wouldn't be the first." He leaned in and winked:

"Pretty Lovecraftian, don't you think?"

As the old man turned and walked away, more shapes started to coalesce in the room, closing in on Mike.

He knew he was dying, that there was no hope for him. He also remembered why he didn't want to recall those conversations with Terry. He knew that there was truth to the whole art-imitating-life debacle, and was now convinced that indeed, truth was stranger than fiction.

But then, how could it not be?

Wasn't it the very experience of our day-to-day lives that inspired so many strange things to leap forth from the pages? ⑥

"This story came about after watching the most recent Academy Awards. Here were all these people, glitzed and glammed to the nines, accepting their little statues for all the movies offered to us in the year before. But what if the movie-making process involved something more — something the people involved weren't even aware of? And if they knew — would they still be out there collecting awards for it? Aye, therre's the rub. Plus, of course, it gave me a wonderful opportunity of taking the mickey out of an industry that's been entertaining me for 27 years. Bless Hollywood's greedy, opulent heart.

"Ahem. So. After you've read this, read more of my work in Raging Hormones *(Lethe Press) and* Darkways of the Wizard *(Specificworld/Cyber-Pulp Books)."*

WINNER OF THE ANUBIS AWARD FOR HORROR
JUDGED BY T.M. WRIGHT
ACCLAIMED AUTHOR OF *A MANHATTAN GHOST STORY* and LAUGHING MAN

PERSONAL DEMONS
A JAKE HELMAN CHILLER
BY GREGORY LAMBERSON

Ex-cop Jake Helman risks Heaven and Hell to stop a serial killer who steals the souls of his victims.

"… a heady, *scary* brew."
-- **T.M. Wright**

"…expansive, phantasmagorical, and very creepy…"
--**Roy Frumkes,** *Films in Review*

"…an irresistible, scary, action-packed horror novel full of intrigue and deep thoughts on life and death. "
--**Nick Yak,**
The Horror Fiction Review

"… compelling and well written."
Scott Johnson, *The Horror Channel*

"... one whopper of a story that almost any reader will find irresistible."
--**Chris Welch,** *Hellnotes*

"…an intricately constructed, genre busting descent into a hellish noir sci-fi nightmare with an unexpected spiritual dimension."
--**Filmmaker Larry Fessenden,** *HABIT* and *WENDIGO*

PERSONAL DEMONS
Trade Paperback and Limited Edition, Signed and Numbered Hardcover
Available from Broken Umbrella Press:
www.brokenumbrellapress.com
Also available at Shocklines

www.slimeguy.com

ILLUSTRATION BY NICOLA GAVIN

SCHOOLBOYS. MAGIC.
MYSTIC TEAM SPORTS.
NOT WHAT YOU THINK.

Class of 666

by Andrew J. Wilson

Some folk call your schooldays the happiest of your life, but it's funny how they never talk about the nights. Every night's a school night here at Boleskin House, because you're never allowed to leave the grounds—the staff make sure of it. The gates are all locked and the windows shuttered by the final bell. I'd still try and make a break for it if I could, but the ghouls begin to stir just beyond the playing fields when the sun goes down.

Mister Wood was still trying to teach us basic astral projection when Fat Malky Fairbairn managed to nail Woody's hand to the blackboard with a well-aimed set of compasses. Woody wasn't in the mood for it at all that afternoon.

"Gugger!" he shouted as he tried to pull the spike out of the wood of his hand. "Witch one of you did this? Squeak uck!"

We all stared at the scratches of runic graffiti on our desktops and kept our mouths shut. It's not much of a code to live by, but no one wanted to get branded a clype and wake up spontaneously combusting in the night.

Woody managed to wrench the compasses out of his hand and brandished them menacingly as he jumped down from his stool. He began to hobble arthritically between the rows of desks, his wooden joints creaking with each halting step. At three feet, Woody was by far the smallest of our teachers, but no less threatening for his lack of height. His speech impediment was amusing only until he began to talk directly to you.

"Come on, goys," he screeched, his voice sharpening like a knife being ground on a whetstone, "I want a gloody answer! Who the 'uck threw this?"

Mister Wood was one of those notorious ventriloquist's dummies with a mind of its own. He had possessed his owner and driven the third-rate performer to commit suicide. Actually, Woody didn't do it because he wanted to take over his partner, he did it because the silly twat couldn't throw his voice properly. He hated being made to look stupid. Unfortunately for the little homunculus, he was left with the speech impediment and couldn't get his Equity card.

For his sins, Woody ended up teaching at Boleskin House. Occasionally, other teachers would point at him behind his back and whisper, "That's what killed Variety."

"Tinker!" he shrieked at me. "Did you do this?"

"No, sir," I mumbled. He usually picked on me because he could pronounce my name.

"Well, tell me who did!"

"Dunno, sir."

Woody's glossy face seemed to redden with fury, but his varnish might just have been reflecting the sunset.

"Yes you do, you little gastard!" he shouted. "Go to the Head right away. You can tell him this class just volunteered to field the team for Saturday!"

Everybody all gasped at once, all except for me and Poor Wullie. Wullie's head was still jammed into the dunce's bucket so he couldn't hear. My chest was so tight I couldn't breathe.

The Head is just that — a head — nothing but a great big flabby ball of hairless flesh. He's the size of a bouncing bomb and floats in an enormous glass vat full of bubbling green fluid. His office is filled with the tangle of copper piping that circulates his environmental broth. It smells like boiled cabbage juice from the school kitchens.

Some of the kids say the Head is Aleister Crowley. The rumour is, some acolyte decapitated the old pervert after his death and kept the skull in a fish tank filled with preservative. After that, it just grew. And if you believe that, you're a knob. I think the Head has always been just a disembodied bald lump floating along throughout his unspeakable half-life.

"Tinker, isn't it?" the Head asked, his voice gurgling through the underwater microphone inside the tank and dribbling out of the speaker on the mould-spotted wall.

"Sir."

"You were sent to us after murdering somebody, weren't you?"

"No, sir."

"Well, boy, what led you through our doors?"

"I put an older laddie in a coma."

I didn't mean to do it, but Tam Duff had been asking for it. For months, the big bastard had been nipping my head, bullying me, hitting me, making me look stupid. I'd tried to ignore him just like everybody said, but that just made him want to break me all the more. I'd tried to fight him too, but Tam was a year older than me and huge with it.

Finally, he cornered me in the woods on my way home from school. Duff had an air pistol and wanted to use me for target practice. Something snapped inside me — suddenly I could feel his spongy, festering thoughts with my mind. I couldn't read them, but I could sense their poisonous texture and turgid flow.

So I grabbed Tam's mind with my own and pushed. The big tube just collapsed like a demolished cooling tower and I ran away.

I hadn't touched him and nobody saw me, so I thought I was home free. Tam was found by a man walking his dog and ended up in intensive care. Two weeks later, the Government men pulled up at the door in a flash car with no number plates and I was on my way to Boleskin House. There was no trial, no children's panel, no social workers. I was busted and that was an end to it. I didn't even know I had supernatural talents until I was locked up here in the bad boy's black-magic borstal, locked up like a monkey in a cage.

The Head cleared his throat, his jowls rippling like the bell of a jellyfish. "I remember now. You might as well have killed that boy, Tinker. The only thing you can do with someone in such a persistent vegetative state is turn them into soup."

Who knows when the Head is making a joke? I wouldn't put it past him to be deadly serious. Something pretty rank goes into his vat.

"Well, my lad, why did Mister Wood tell you to report to me?"

"One of the other boys threw some compasses at him," I told him and explained what Woody wanted to do with us.

The Head pursed his flabby lips and hummed for a while. He rolled around in the bubbles from the air pump and eventually turned completely upside down, his poached-egg eyes never leaving me.

"No one admitted to the offence?"

"No, sir."

"And no one would tell who had done it."

"No."

"Well, then, fielding the Blitzkrieg team on Saturday seems a suitable punishment for you all. Report back to Mr Wood. Your classes tomorrow will be cancelled so that you can all concentrate on training for the game against St. Baphomet's with Mr. Smiley."

I said nothing. The Head floated to the top of his tank and began to nibble at the crumbs of god-knows-what floating there. I was dismissed.

I WOULDN'T HAVE SAID that things were looking good at that point, but they got downright ugly in the dorm after lights-out.

"It's gonnae be a massacre," said Jonah Jones. "They Baphomet boys are dead good. And if they dinnae actually kill us, we're as good as dead at the final whistle. This is aw your fault Malky, ya big balloon!"

"Shut it, Jonah!" Malky snarled back. "Those posh public-school pansies might have won the championship last year, but we can bury them. Or don't you have the stones for it, you inbred fish-fucker?"

"Basturt!" Jonah sprang out of his bunk and laid into Malky with his webbed feet. "Ah'll show ye whae's got the stanes roun' here!"

Jonah is pretty sensitive when people wind him up about the part of the country where he grew up, especially now that it's under ten fathoms of water. Still, he should have seen the funny side of Malky's nonsense. After all, his folk can hardly be inbred if the rumours are true and they mate with deep-sea abominations every equinox.

"Mumble mumbledy mummy mum?" asked Wullie, his head still stuck in the bucket.

Malky made the Voorish sign, and Jonah backed off. Everyone in the dorm could feel the palpable sense of blasphemous power hanging over the room like a thundercloud. The smaller boys and those with less well-developed powers pulled the covers over their heads and started praying.

I took the name of a dead god in vain and got out of bed myself.

"Stop it!" I growled as loudly as I dared. "Much as I hate to admit it, we're going to need both of you on Saturday."

Malky waved his spell away and I shivered with relief.

"But he's why we're in this mess," Jonah moaned.

"Jonah's right, Malky. You're a stupid radge and we're all going to get it because you can't keep your fat head down. That's why you're going to need all your power for the game." While he settled back into his bed and rubbed his bruises, I turned to Jonah. "Don't get too cocky. Malky may be a big divvy, but this bloody place is purpose-built to screw us up one way or another. Do you really think he's made one bit of difference?"

Jonah shook his head and went back to bed.

"Everybody has to pull together if we're going to get through this," I told the whole dorm as I slipped under my threadbare blanket again.

"Hey, Tinky Winky, who died and left you in charge?" Shuggie Bain shouted across the dorm.

"You did, you numpty," I reminded him.

The Shug's memory hasn't been up to much since his accident and we have to keep pointing out the obvious to his decomposing face. His whimpering kept me up late into the night.

There's something called nominative determinism. That's when someone grows into their name. For example, a Mr. and Mrs. Pratt name their son Wally, and he grows up to be a complete fuckwit. We had to learn about this because of its significance to the black arts.

Mr. Smiley, our P.E. teacher, obviously hadn't heard of nominative determinism, never mind learned to spell it. I've never heard him laugh or even seen the corners of his mouth turn up in a smile. His vicious streak is long enough to reach from here to Hell itself. I don't think you can call him a sadist because Smiley doesn't even seem to get any joy out of his relentless brutality.

We spent all Friday out in the freezing autumn mist that hung over the muddy playing fields. The numbing monotony was only broken by the occasional shower of frogs. It wasn't a good sign, but at least Jonah got to have a snack.

Smiley kept shouting "Wards!" the moment after he hurled a spell or mystic talisman at us. Half the boys had sustained cuts and bruises by the middle of the afternoon, the Doppler twins had gone into shock, and the rest of us had screaming migraines. It was a hell of a way to prepare for the match. After this, we were going to be toiling just to walk on to the pitch. "You are a disgrace," Smiley told us at every opportunity, "an absolute embarrassment to this establishment! What do you think you are playing at?"

We all knew better than to answer back.

"The rules of Blitzkrieg are very simple — the winning team get to fight another day. When you go out there tomorrow, you will play for the highest stakes that you pitiful little losers can offer — your miserable lives."

Jonah put his hand up. "Sir, will we be allowed any weapons?"

"Didn't you hear me, Jones? There are no rules against anything. Use what's in the stores and wear any armour you can find." He made his point by banging Wullie's bucket with his fist. The metal clanked and Wullie fell over, probably feeling a little pale. "Cast any spells you can manage. Just make sure you win!"

"Please, sir, what kind of ball will we be playing with?" I asked.

Blitzkrieg is very loosely based on rugby football, with a little bit of shinty mixed in for devilment. A monstrous egg is used as a ball. The teams do whatever they can to get it through the other side's goal posts. The match ends when the egg hatches. The losing team is sacrificed to whatever is inside.

Smiley licked his lips. It was not a pretty sight. "Oh, that's going to be tomorrow's little surprise. . . ."

AS SOON AS our class walked into the assembly on Saturday morning, some supportive school chum yelled, "Dead men walking!" Rumour had it that the teachers were running a book on the result of the match and the odds against us were supposed to be astronomical and astrological.

Woody, Smiley, and the rest of the staff all sat on the stage, looking down on us like gargoyles. The Head wasn't in attendance, but his portrait hung from the wall and his puffy eyes followed you round the room anyway.

The Reverend Glaister rose to give us a little pep talk. He's ordained by the Esoteric Order of Dagon, but I don't think that's actually a recognized church. The Rev just lifted it out of an H.P. Lovecraft paperback and got his doctorate of theology from a post-office box in Tennessee. Religious plagiarists are always the worst.

"You are scum!" Glaister screamed at us, his oily black toupee flapping on his head like a panicking crow. "You are the silt of the earth, lower than vermin, less to me than the worms of the earth!"

It was going to be one of those days. I focused on his agitated wig and tried to will it to take off for the rafters.

"You have all been sent to Boleskin House because you are evil! You were lucky enough to be born with special talents, but you have abused them and that is why you have ended up in our care. We are here to contain you, and either break you or train you, if we possibly can. Many of you will die during this process. You will not be mourned! A few of you will graduate with your minds and bodies intact. You will then be conscripted into this country's sorcerous and philosophical special forces. If you succeed in surviving long enough to join a unit, never forget that you will still be nothing more than cannon fodder in the war with the Other Realm."

Glassy Glaister paused to catch his breath then chuntered on like a kettle boiling itself dry.

"Today, one class among you will face the fine young men of St. Baphomet's on the Blitzkrieg field. You are unworthy of this honour and I am sure you will prove it this afternoon. The pupils of St. Baphomet's are of the officer class, our brightest and best. You don't stand a chance."

Fat Malky flamboyantly broke wind and amazingly managed to shut the old windbag up for a moment. Glaister eyed us as if we were specimens on a microscope slide before continuing.

"Those of you who are about to die, we salute you," he hissed. Then the Rev made a mystic pass at us and all thirteen members of the class went into convulsions.

When we came round in pools of our own vomit, the rest of the school had gone. Mops and buckets had been thoughtfully provided so that we could clean up our mess.

Games of Blitzkrieg don't start with a whistle. The referee fires a starting pistol loaded with live ammunition. Half the time he needs the remaining rounds for self-defence during the match. Sometimes the gun also gets used to pick off deserters.

We trooped out of the Portaloo that served as the changing room and did a final stock-take on our kits. The Doppler twins had half-inched some armour from the main hall, and it was too late for anyone to take it off them now. If they survived, the punishment would be worth it. The rest of us had scraped together the sharpest garden implements we could find and divided them up among ourselves. Poor Wullie had the tinsnips we'd used to cut a slit in his bucket so that he could see what he was doing. Pathetically, the mops we'd used to clean up after assembly were among our most impressive weapons. They weren't exactly broomsticks, but they had potential.

The boys from St. Baphomet's had changed on their Mercedes coach. They were strong, fit, and well fed. Most of them had floppy blond hair and perfect teeth — they looked like Vikings who'd pillaged a health farm. Their kits and uniforms were expensive stuff: American football helmets, Kevlar vests, tungsten baseball bats, and magician's wands.

The basilisk crawled out of its horse box and waddled to the centre of the pitch. The beast didn't look at all well. Its scales were flaking off and its putrid flesh hung loose on its bones. The monster gurgled in agony as it laid its egg in the pentagram painted on the grass, then gasped its last poisonous breath, rolled over, and died. Half the staff were needed to drag the carcass away.

The egg that we were to play with seemed almost completely black until you got close up. Then you could see the speckles of star sapphire embedded in the shell, flecks that pulsed in a hypnotic sequence, simultaneously echoing distant constellations and obscene curses in forgotten languages.

"This is gonnae be the Kinder Surprise tae end them a'," Jonah whispered to me. "Whit d'ye think wis the faither?"

I kept my mouth shut because I really couldn't guess. All I knew was that it certainly wasn't another basilisk or cockatrice, or any kind of heraldic beast I'd come across.

Stands had been erected at the side of the pitch, and the staff and other pupils lurked behind the razor wire and electric fencing. The Head had not deigned to attend, but he might have been getting a live feed direct to his tank from the video camera that Woody was setting up. The Reverend Glaister showed his support for the home team by making the sign of the evil eye at us as we walked onto the pitch. The betting against us was still

going on among teachers from both schools.

Smiley was acting as referee, and I got a bad feeling as I saw the captain of St. Baphomet's slipping him something that looked like a wad of cash. The whole thing was a set-up. Maybe it had been rigged even before Malky got us into trouble: like the patsies we were, we were always meant to take the fall.

The sense of impending doom got worse as our P.E. teacher ordered the Doppler twins off the field to sit on the bench instead of our chosen substitutes. Finally, I noticed that the coin Smiley was going to use was double-headed.

"I presume we're tails," I grumbled.

"That's right, Tinker," Smiley replied as he made the toss. "And heads it is!"

"You bloody cheat," I hissed.

He raised the pistol above his head to start the game, then dropped his aim and shot me in the head.

I WOKE UP on the bench at half time. Smiley's bullet had creased my skull, but I wasn't getting a sick note that easily. The Reverend Glaister had bandaged my cut and brought me round by pouring absinthe from his hip flask up my nose.

We were 25–0 down and had already lost three players. The captain of the Baphomet blonds had torn off Shuggie Bain's arm and smashed his rotting corpse to pieces with it. Another couple of kids had been eaten by the opposition in a scrum just before the end of the first half.

"Get out there and play, Tinker," the Rev spat. "Let's get this over with. I want my money, and the less time I have to spend watching you and your scummy classmates getting killed the better."

Enough was enough! I whistled a little snake charm and Glaister doubled up as his intestines locked his other organs in an excruciating grip.

Then I staggered onto the pitch to join the others and prepared for the worst. A few seconds later, St. Baphomet's rolled over us like a juggernaut with eleven heads and scored another try.

"Ah'm gonnae run for it!" Jonah wailed, wiping the blood from his eyes.

"Don't be stupid," I told him. "I've got an idea."

We huddled and I explained the plan. Malky and Jonah picked up the two mops and got ready. The Baphomet team took their positions with nonchalant strides. I muttered the spell.

As the other side charged again, first Jonah, then Malky, launched their mops like skyrockets. They might not have been broomsticks, but our cleaning tools flew straight and true. Two Baphomet players called Speirs and Pearce went down with the mops sticking right through their hearts. Nominative determinism had come into its own.

"Get intae them!" screamed Jonah, and we went for it. The rank smell of discharged spells hung over the pitch like dispersing tear gas as Malky made our first touchdown.

After that, it was war. Both sides reanimated their dead and stitched players back together with bootlaces in the best tradition of battlefield surgery. We weren't in St. Baphomet's league, but we knew how to play dirty and there were no rules to stop us. The Doppler twins managed to possess half the other team for nearly ten minutes and the scores began to level.

Jonah equalized when the game was in its dying seconds. The crowd were getting nervous. Blitzkrieg doesn't have many rules and there were certainly none about a draw because there never had been one before.

Woody and the rest of the staff all started yelling at Smiley, who turned on the Baphomet team in turn.

"You've got to win, you idiots! Have you any idea of the consequences if you don't?"

Now we knew that all bets were off. Whatever was about to hatch from the egg we were using as a ball would probably slaughter everyone if somebody didn't lose.

The public-school boys tried to rally just as Poor Wullie summoned an electrical storm out of nowhere. St. Baphomet's forgot the ball completely as the cream of their side were struck by lightning and had to roll in the mud to put out their burning strips. Wullie took a bolt himself, but it blew the bucket off his head and he staggered up the field to put us into the lead, his straw-coloured hair spiky with mud and static.

"I don't know if we can hold it together much longer," Malky said, his face slack with exhaustion. "I'm sorry I got us all into this."

"It's not over till it's over," I replied.

The game bogged down from then on. The ball moved up and down the centre of the pitch, but the Baphomet survivors couldn't get through us. Nevertheless, we were finding it increasingly difficult to keep our defensive ward spells up. Time seemed to slow. It was like playing in treacle.

Inevitably, the opposition broke through and the ball was punted deep into our half as their fastest player ran to catch it. We were done for.

"Who's the daddy?" screamed the Baphomet captain in triumph as he reached for the ball. A crack like a pistol shot rang out and the egg began to hatch in his hands. The captain's face turned from passionate red to terrified white as the thing within the shattered shell came out to feed.

Its body seemed to expand like ectoplasm as it smothered its victim, growing by the second as it fed. The monster unfolded like a fan as pinions burst out of its mass and leathery wings unfurled. A hundred eyes popped up across its twisting body as if being blown into existence like bubbles. Jagged beaks snapped open and shut and the monster shrieked like an air raid siren as the captain of the losing side came apart in its claws.

The rest of St. Baphomet's team ran screaming in all directions as the creature swooped up and round, expanding all the time, and began to search for more prey. One by one, they were plucked from the pitch like party snacks and dismembered in showers of blood. The game was a bogey all right.

Jonah and I put our arms around Malky's shoulders to steady him and the three of us collected the rest of our survivors. We were in the clear, but we could tell the thing from the egg wasn't finished even as its beaks and mouths ravenously consumed the last player from the other side. The monster was voracious but fair, and the game — its game — had been rigged.

Smiley fired his pistol wildly as the creature flapped its now-enormous wings and swooped towards him. Smiley ran for the benches as he emptied the gun.

"It's his fault!" Smiley screamed, pointing at Woody who was still taping the action. "It was the dummy's idea!"

"Watt's your 'ucking game?" Woody wanted to know.

But Smiley grabbed Mister Wood from behind his video camera and hurled him at the monster.

" 'Uck you, you 'ucking gastard!" screamed the dummy as the thing from the egg turned his wooden frame into sawdust.

It made no difference. Smiley never made it to the magical defences of the stands and the flapping beast caught him in mid-stride. The abomination was nearly sated, so it began to play with its food, pulling off thin strips of flesh and tossing our teacher in the air. Smiley screamed for nearly twenty minutes.

As we staggered back to our Portaloo to dress our wounds, the Head floated past us like the Great and Terrible Oz. Sacs in his jowls were distended with some lighter than air gas to keep him in the air and his pallid flesh still dripped with the green gunk from his tank.

"Well done, my lads," the Head burbled, "You're through to the quarter finals."

We never did find out what had fathered the egg-monster with the basilisk. The creature is being kept in the stables "for a rainy day," according to the Head.

Speaking of heads, those of Smiley and Woody have been stuck on spikes at the doors of Boleskin House. Smiley's flesh has rotted away, leaving little more than a skull, so he's grinning now all right. Of course, Woody was never technically alive, so he's still rambling on about "Gloody guggering gastards," but nobody pays any attention any more. My class is just waiting for our next game of Blitzkrieg. Everybody else thinks we're going to lose — but I wouldn't bet on it. ᕼ

Recent stories by Andrew Wilson have appeared in Gathering the Bones (Tor) and the Thackery T. Lambshead Pocket Guide to Eccentric and Discredited Diseases (Night Shade Books). He is of course aware that the above tale of character-forming edification bears a passing resemblance to the H*rry P*tt*r stories, so some readers may be surprised at how much of it was taken directly from his own childhood.

ILLUSTRATION BY LYNNE FURRER

Sugar Skulls

by Chelsea Quinn Yarbro

The day after tomorrow would be el Día de los Muertos, the Day of the Dead, the Feast of All Souls. Today was the Eve of the Feast of All Saints, when children in the big country to the north put on foolish clothing and went to take food from their neighbors, or played tricks on them for refusing their demands — it was one of the many strange customs that prevailed among those people with their big houses and big cars and yellow-haired women.

Refugio shook her head as she followed her grandmother's instructions and continued to mix the shining white sugar into the whipped egg-whites that would permit them to shape the mixture into the hard-set celebratory skulls. Already most of the candies were made, ranging in size from that of a cup to a few as large as a real skull, with scenes inside them when you looked through the frosting-outlined eyes. Many had names of the loved dead written on the skulls in her grandmother's square letters made of red or black frosting. Refugio wanted to write some of the names herself, and imbue them with her emotions as she did.

"Abuela Concepción," she said, reaching for another bowl of whipped egg-white and starting to measure in the sugar. She had been helping her grandmother since shortly after dawn, knowing that this was the only day on which they could prepare these candies, and wanting to make as many of them as possible.

"¿Sí?" her grandmother answered, not taking her eyes from the small molds she was filling; these would be the smallest skulls, hardly larger than a thumb and given minimal decoration. They would be sold five for a peso, and consumed by the handful. So far there were three hundred of the finished skulls sitting out on trays in the dining room, their licorice dots for eyes and missing teeth making them seem unusually stark. By the next morning, there would be at least double that number waiting, like small versions of the stone carvings of racks of skulls that stood at the end of the main street, next to a wide avenue of old, old stones that led to a crumbling mound behind the cemetery, and the first tangle of trees, many perched on hillocks said to be haunted. These sugar skulls seemed pale echoes of the overgrown stone ones.

"Tell me, how much longer do we have to work before we eat? The mid-day bell sounded a while ago. Can't we stop for a moment?" She summoned up all her nerve to ask, for Abuela Concepción took her skull-making very seriously and begrudged every single moment such mundane tasks demanded. "I'm hungry. I'm sorry, but I am."

Abuela Concepción sighed. "It is almost time for it, you're right. But I will have to work through siesta to get all this done. There's a lot left to do. I must have the skulls ready before first Mass tomorrow, or sin by working on the Feast of All Saints. No. We make skulls today and sell them tomorrow. That is the only day people will buy." She put her hands on the table and leaned forward.

"I'll stay up through siesta if it will help. But I need to eat and have a little chocolate to drink, or I won't be able to help you the way I should." She turned her melting dark eyes on her grandmother. "Please, Abuela." She hoped her grandmother couldn't read her thoughts, or take notice of her dark intentions.

It took Concepción Molero a little while to decide what to do. "All right, chica, but it will be nothing fancy. For all it's almost a feast-day."

Refugio laughed. "That doesn't bother me," she said with all the confidence of her eleven years. "I will honor the saints as best I can by helping you sell the skulls tomorrow. That should make it all right."

"Don't you want to join the celebration in the evening?" her grandmother asked. "There is going to be a fine gathering in the square."

"Not particularly," she lied heroically; she loved the excitement of town festivities, for it was the only time she could feel herself expand beyond her limited world and embrace everything that lay beyond the town market of Santa Luz, which was what tempted her more than anything else she could imagine. "I know you need my help to finish."

Abuela Concepción moved to the ancient stove on the far side of her kitchen. "Soup and tortillas with a little cheese and a cup of chocolate, then," she said, using a match to start the stove.

"This was easier when Mama was alive to help you, wasn't it? You miss her being here?" Refugio asked in a small voice as she went to wash her hands in the old zinc basin immediately below the pump. She worked the worn handle vigorously and made sure she used soap as well as water, as her mother had taught her.

When Abuela Concepción answered, her voice was muffled. "Yes. This is the hardest year, since it is the first we have had to make the skulls without her, and you miss her as much as I do. It is difficult for both of us."

"If Papa weren't in prison, he'd help," said Refugio, although she doubted it.

"If your Papa weren't in prison, he'd be off in the forest with his friends, pretending to be soldiers fighting the government, and we should have to leave this town," Abuela Concepción said bitterly. She plunked the lid on her soup-pot with more force than usual.

"Well, I'll help you as much as I can," Refugio said, and meant it in more ways than her grandmother guessed.

"I know you will. And you're a good girl for it," said her grandmother, going to pump water into her kettle, then returning to the stove to set it heating. She had made tortillas the night before and there were still a few left for their lunch. She wrapped them in a damp cloth and put them in the warming oven in the pipe above the stove. The gas was working well today, and the soup warmed quickly, its fragrance filling the kitchen with a heady mix of herbs, onions, peppers, garlic, and goat. Concepción went to find the wedges of cheese in the cooler, and brought them out, one pale as milk, the other a light golden shade and slightly firmer than the first; she cut a portion from each and reached for the grater. "Here, Refugio. You do this. I have to finish these skulls." She offered a shallow dish to her granddaughter. "Use them both."

"All right," said Refugio, and set her bowl of sugared egg-whites aside. Grating cheese was a pleasant change, so long as she was careful not to scrape her knuckles on the sharpened holes in the grater. As soon as she was done she wiped her hands carefully and turned to Abuela Concepción. "There."

"Very good. I'll make chocolate for you, but you have to get back to your mixing." She sighed as she looked at her tray of molds. "I have to get more of these. They always sell better than the rest."

"Because they are small," said Refugio, "and you sell them for so little."

"Because they are the cheapest of all I make." Abuela Concepción shrugged, accepting the iron rule of poverty.

Refugio went back to stirring the skull-making mixture. "Will we need more eggs?"

"I hope not," said her grandmother, now busy with making chocolate. "I don't think Jorje or Ysidro have any to spare, and Lupe charges too much."

"I could ask, if you like. They might let me have one or two more they can spare for us," said Refugio. She had begun to notice that she was able to persuade her neighbors to help her on the strength of her youth and misfortune. It was a beginning, she thought, a first step to her freedom. "Let me go ask."

"I don't want you trading on tragedy, chica. You should have more pride than that." Abuela Concepción was sternly disapproving. Her busy hands kept at her work, independent of her speaking.

"Padre Cazdor says pride is a sin," Refugio reminded her with a hint of mischief in her smile. "A very bad sin."

"And so it is, when it flies in the face of God. But pride that is born of dignity is entirely different. You want the respect of your neighbors, not their pity," said Abuela Concepción, stirring the chocolate in the small saucepan.

Refugio thought about this as she continued to stir the con-

tents of her bowl. "What if I offered to work in exchange for the eggs? I could tend their chickens."

"I doubt they'd let you do that," said Abuela Concepción, continuing to fill the molds. "Not their chickens; they'd worry you'd filch eggs or take one of the chicks or some such prank. If you'd be willing to milk their goats for two or three mornings, they might accept a trade." She looked aside, suddenly ashamed. "No. You should not have to get eggs for me that way."

"Well, we must have them, and you cannot spare any time. It makes sense that I should do it," said Refugio, feeling suddenly very grown up. "Everyone knows you make the best skulls in the town. If you have a few more to sell, you will make a little more money. And I will only be doing what Mamacita would do, if she were here."

"But I don't want you to bear this burden, chica, nor did your mother. It shouldn't be yours. Your mother wanted you to have a chance to continue in school and to make something of yourself. Of all of us, you are the one with the ability to do it, your Mama told me. She knew you aren't like most of the children in Santa Luz; you're clever, not like the others. You ask questions no one, not even Padre Cazador can answer. Everyone knows you're smart, that you could go a long way in the world if you were taught properly. You could have a life very different than the one your Mama had. I pray it will be longer and much better than hers." Abuela Concepción stopped her labor for a moment. "I promised your mother to give you that chance."

"The bruja has said she'll teach me her skills," said Refugio.

"No!" Abuela Concepción held up her hand almost as if to strike Refugio. "You should have nothing to do with her — nothing!"

"But she'll teach me for nothing. She wants to teach me. She said so," Refugio felt her confidence slipping away. She knew her grandmother disliked the old witch-woman who lived near the ruins beyond the graveyard and was said to commune with ghosts there.

"You won't learn anything worthwhile from her, chica," Abuela Concepción threatened. "She is a superstitious old fool."

"But everyone is afraid of her, aren't they?" Refugio asked.

"That means nothing! You must not let the foolishness of others —" She crossed herself. "That old woman preys on those who are not wise enough to realize that — I'll hear nothing more about her!"

Refugio knew it was useless to argue; they had been over this very question many times in the last six months. "But I want to study something, Abuelita. Yes, I like school. It is good to learn. But most girls my age leave school and learn to manage a household. There isn't much more I can study here in Santa Luz if I can't learn from Viuda Estrella."

"Yes, most girls end their schooling at your age. But you must not, and you must not become a student of Viuda Estrella, for that would be worse than sending you to be a house maid in the city," said Abuela Concepción. "Your mother would have done anything to see you be properly educated, with a degree and good employment before you. She said if you were not educated, smart as you are, it would be a great injustice. Padre Cazador says you are the brightest pupil the school has had in years. Not that you should boast of it, for it is a gift from God, not anything of your doing. It would be a sign of ingratitude for what God has done if you were to turn away from learning, which Viuda Estrella would be the epitome of insult. Padre Cazador says that you deserve a good education, not the superstition and sorcery Viuda Estrella professes."

"If he says so, then he should help me get one," Refugio exclaimed with more emphasis than she had intended.

"Refugio!" Abuela Concepción admonished her. "This isn't a wealthy town. The parish cannot afford to give money to children who will not devote themselves to the Church. Everyone knows that." She finished with the skull molds and stepped back. "If you had a vocation, it would be otherwise, but you haven't one, have you?"

"No, Abuela. I couldn't be a nun, with those hours and hours of praying," said Refugio apologetically. "I can't live as they do, all my time set out, order in everything, and accusing myself of sins I can only imagine." She angled her head upward in defiance. "You can tell Padre Cazador if you think he has to know."

"I wouldn't do that," said Abuela Concepción. "He wouldn't be surprised in any case."

Without warning Refugio grinned. "No. I ask too many questions in class — he's told me so. He says some of the questions aren't proper at all, but I can't help it."

Abuela Concepción nodded. "I know. That is your nature. A pity you weren't a boy: more could be done for you. But it doesn't matter — you have to follow where your curiosity leads. Your mother made it clear to me how it is with you."

"Yes," said Refugio. "And what can I do?"

"Mayor Arrugaverde isn't likely to pay any attention to people like us — we have nothing he wants, and we know none of his friends. He never has extended himself on our behalf in the past. He is not interested in the poor except when he needs someone to vote for him, and then it is only a sham fellowship he offers. The richest man I know is the mechanic, Justino Caida, and he has six children of his own to provide for." She went to rinse her hands and took down two white stoneware bowls. "Get the spoons, chica."

Refugio set her bowl aside and followed her grandmother to the pump. She dried her hands on the hanging scrap of towel, then took two steps across the kitchen and opened the drawer in the worn cabinet, removing two soup spoons, a knife, and two frayed napkins. She went into the alcove that served as a dining room and put the spoons and napkins flanking the bowls, and laid the knife on the smaller clay trivet. "I'll fetch the butter," she said, and went back into the kitchen to the cooler. Taking out the small tub of butter, she stood aside to permit Abuela Concepción to carry the soup-pot to the table.

"The tortillas will be quite warm by now," said Abuela Concepción as she set the pot down on the larger trivet. She returned to the kitchen to retrieve them.

When Abuela Concepción returned, she and Refugio sat down and bowed their heads for the short prayer of thanks: "God, Who gives this food, let it nourish my body as Your Word nourishes my soul. Amen."

After echoing the Amen, Refugio waited for Abuela Concepción to ladle out her soup. The steam rising from it was delicious, and Refugio licked her lips in anticipation; her long morning of working with food had made her hunger sharper, and she anticipated eating with appreciation. "This is wonderful, Abuela."

"It's good of you to say so, chica," said Abuela Concepción, pleased that Refugio had such good manners, for they both knew the meal was very simple. "Take a tortilla."

Refugio did as she was told, cutting a few curls of butter from the tub and spreading them carefully on the golden cornmeal round. She rolled this up and took hold of it as if it were an edible cigar. "Jorje will have more goat for sale soon."

"And after this Día de los Muertos, we'll have money enough to afford some," said Abuela Concepción.

"It is all to the good," said Refugio, who knew she was expected to speak only of pleasant things at table.

Abuela Concepción tasted her soup and let the spoon drop back in the bowl. "Too hot," she muttered, and opened the small bottle of mineral water that was her usual drink at lunch. "I will set up my booth first thing in the morning, while you attend Mass. Then you may keep the booth while I go to the second Mass."

"Of course, Abuela," said Refugio, and bit into the roll of her tortilla.

"You're not to bargain with anyone, or to promise what you cannot deliver. Tell them you cannot do it because I order it so," said Abuela Concepción. "Everyone in town knows me. They will believe I would tell you such things."

"Sí, Abuela." Another bite of tortilla and Refugio dared to test her soup. It was very hot but not scalding.

"Be pleasant to everyone, especially the important families. They always buy skulls from me, and if they do, everyone else does, too." She took a tortilla and rolled it up without the luxury of butter; she dunked one end into her soup, then chewed thoughtfully on it for a short while. "I must find some way to get a patron for you, chica. You cannot go about the world nothing more than a peasant when you have it in you to be much more." She stared toward the small window where a wedge of brilliant

light made the little alcove glow.

Refugio knew better than to interrupt her grandmother's thoughts. She continued to eat her meal, saving the chocolate for last. Finally, as she buttered a second tortilla, she looked toward the front door on the far side of the scrupulously clean main room. "The special skulls — who is coming for them?"

"Dominga Caida. She should be here after siesta, unless she sends one of her children — she's almost ready to deliver, and it isn't easy for her to get about just now." Abuela Concepción frowned. "If only she would introduce me to her uncle in Cedro Cima, something might be arranged. He has money, and to spare."

"Why would she do that?" Refugio asked with an innocence she did not feel. "Doesn't she have children of her own to look out for?"

"She does, and two of them are already promised work on their great-uncle's land. He has orchards and a mine and he raises cattle, pigs, and goats." Her brow darkened as she continued to think. "His sons have been sent to university."

"That doesn't mean he'll send me," said Refugio, suddenly struck with a new plan. "We could do as they do in the north — dress up in demons' clothing and demand help or promise to blow up their houses. Viuda Estrella says that much can be done on this night." She grinned as she weighed the options this could give. "I could walk to Cedro Cima this afternoon and I could waylay Dominga Caida's uncle after sundown."

Abuela Concepción looked outraged. "Refugio! Never even think such evil thoughts. That is an affront to our faith! You ought to go to the church and confess at once!"

But Refugio was too enchanted by the idea to accept the reprimand. "He wouldn't know it was me. I'd talk in a big, deep voice, and I wouldn't let him see me very well. I'd tell him I came from Los Ángeles and I expected him to do as men in Los Estados Unidos do, taking care of those who are intelligent and making them rich and powerful, just as was done for Carlos Istmo — he has three restaurants in Texas. The same could be done for me." Her grin widened. "I'd say he had to do this or else!"

"You mustn't. That is worse than going to the witch-woman — which I forbid you to do! Promise me you won't do anything so foolish. Promise me you won't even think about it again." Abuela Concepción was truly worried, for she knew her granddaughter had great determination and a recklessness that could easily mean trouble for a girl.

Refugio could see she had gone too far. "I wouldn't do it, Abuelita, not really. But it is fun to wonder what might happen."

"No, it isn't. It's wrong and it could bring you into great trouble." Abuela Concepción was still very much worried about Refugio. "What sort of satisfaction could you take in anything so . . . so criminal?"

"I said I wouldn't do it," Refugio reminded her, beginning to pout. "Do you doubt me, when I promise you?"

"I worry about you. I worry you'll let your disappointments drag you into trouble," said Abuela Concepción.

"You have no reason to worry," said Refugio, relieved that this, at least, was the truth. "I will not do anything that will harm me."

"Very well; I will trust you," said Abuela Concepción. "You and I will forget you have ever said such things. I know you are not an evil child. You will stay away from Viuda Estrella, and abandon such dreadful thoughts as you've told me today. I will take this as the power of the saints, who are very near now. So, in the presence of the saints, you swear that you will bring no disgrace upon our family. Do this for me, and for the memory of your Mama." She tried to resume eating but found her own cooking now to lack savor, and she soon found an excuse to stop eating. "You have the rest of your meal. I have to get back to making skulls."

Knowing she was still in disfavor, Refugio only nodded and added some grated cheese to her soup. There were some things she had learned from Viuda Estrella already, and she could use them without her grandmother knowing. She made plans as she ate. When she had finished, she took her bowl and utensils to the sink, worked the pump, and washed them, then added the last of her grandmother's soup to the slop-bucket and cleaned her bowl and utensils as well. Only when she had dried the flatware and bowls and put them away did she speak again. "I'm sorry, Abuela."

"Be sure you are," said Abuela Concepción as she worked on filling another tray of molds. "I don't want you to put yourself in danger."

"You can't blame me for wanting to do something to make things better for us," she said in a small voice.

"No. But if you do something wrong it will make things much worse," said Abuela Concepción. "Isn't having your father in prison enough?"

This stung Refugio, and she blinked back sudden tears. "I won't go to prison, Abuela. I wouldn't do that."

"Well, pranks like the ones you proposed can get you there," said Abuela Concepción. "Come on, chica. We have many more skulls to make." This was a peace offering, and Refugio accepted it as such.

"I will," she said with relief, and went to resume whipping sugar into egg-whites.

"I know you say these things to cheer me," Abuela Concepción said a bit later. "But, chica, they are not easily understood by most people, who may think you are serious if you talk of these things where you can be overheard."

"I won't blather," Refugio promised, all the while trying to think of some means to gain the advantage she sought in a way that would not upset her grandmother.

"No, I don't suppose you will," said Abuela Concepción, her face long and serious as she interrupted her labor on the skulls. "I will need more licorice."

"There is still a lot in the pantry," said Refugio. "Do you want me to fetch it?"

"No. I'll attend to it myself," said Abuela Concepción, and set her immediate work aside to retrieve a handful of licorice strings for making eyes and lost teeth for the skulls.

"They say that if you have some hair from a rich man, and you write his name on a skull and then he eats it, his treasure will become yours," said Refugio as she watched her grandmother ornament the sugar skulls.

"That's nonsense. Only old people believe such things," scoffed Abuela Concepción. "Old people and Viuda Estrella."

"You don't believe it," said Refugio.

"No, and for good reason," said Abuela Concepción. "I don't want to hear any more nonsense out of you, chica. Not today, not tomorrow, not ever."

"Oh, very well," said Refugio, but her mind continued to play with all the various stories she had heard about ways to draw good fortune to you on these special feast days. There had to be something she could do to end the hard life she and her grandmother had been living. Perhaps, she thought, I will make a skull of my own, and make sure it has everything to bring me money so I can continue to study. That idea thrilled her, and she let her imagination wander while she prepared more sugared egg-whites. Suddenly she dared to speak. "Abuela, tell me — would you permit me to make a skull of my own? I'd do it when we've finished for the day, and I wouldn't make a very big one, not a little one, but the teacup size. I just thought it would be nice, for Mama. So I can remember all that she wanted for me." She felt a little uncomfortable with this little lie, but told herself it wasn't so far from the truth. Her mother wanted her to be educated, so making a skull to do a fortune spell wasn't exactly a lie.

Abuela Concepción stopped her work and stood quite still for a short while, then said, "If that would please you, then keep out enough mix to make a skull. Not the very smallest, but not the largest, either."

"Thank you, Abuelita," said Refugio with her most winsome smile. It would be a fine thing to cast such a spell as the skull would contain.

"But you must continue to work now. There's still more to finish, and time is getting short." She sounded almost gruff, as if the reminder of her daughter had taken her by surprise and left her feeling bereft.

"I will," said Refugio, and resumed her labors with renewed energy as she thought of how she would prepare the skull for its magical purpose.

"Very good," said Abuela Concepción, preparing more molds. "You are being a great help to me today, chica. I want you to know how much that pleases me."

"You're good to me, Abuela," said Refugio. Her grandmother blinked, and Refugio could see tears on her lashes. "Don't be sad. Please don't be sad."

"I can't help it, Refugio. I don't want to see your life go to waste as so many others have done. Your father has been reckless, and some of it is in your nature as well. It is one thing if children are foolish or have no capacity for study, but you are bright and you are happiest when you're reading. I should be able to do something for you. If your father hadn't got himself on the wrong side of the regional government, something might be done. But with him in jail and no money, and that awful Viuda Estrella hoping to bring you into her —" She blotted her tears with the hem of her apron.

"I'll think of something," said Refugio, making it a promise.

"I hope you will, for I haven't been able to," Abuela Concepción admitted as if confessing to a great sin. She shoved Refugio away gently and then wiped her hands before going back to her work. "When you make your skull, ask God for help."

"I'll do what I can," said Refugio, and went back to the tasks her grandmother had imposed upon her.

By the time all the molds had been filled and the skulls were drying on the narrow racks, it was dark. Dominga Caida had come and gone, taking the special skulls away with her, and leaving behind full payment with an extra peso for having the skulls ready on time. Now, as dusk thickened, there were four lights in Abuela Concepción's house, one in each room — bare, glaring bulbs set in the ceiling, lending their brightness to the encroaching night. Abuela Concepción finished washing up all the bowls but one.

"Shall I make my skull now?" Refugio asked as she looked at the last small egg waiting on the table. At least she hadn't had to go out to try to get another.

"Yes, if you still want to," said Abuela Concepción. She didn't want Refugio to know how tired she was or how much her feet hurt, so she declared, "I'm going to listen to the radio, to find out if there's any news."

"Oh, all right," said Refugio, paying less than half her attention to what her grandmother said. She was thinking about her skull, and what she would do with it. Working with great care, she took the second-largest mold and began to spread the egg-white-and-sugar mixture on it, pausing now and again to write down what she wanted from the spirits that hovered over Santa Luz. Whispering her invocation, she worked with great care, remembering how important it was to show respect for the spirits whose aid she sought. It would be very late when the skull was ready, but Viuda Estrella said that tonight of all nights she would be awake almost until dawn. Refugio was careful to follow the instructions the witch-woman had given her to the letter, for if she botched any part of it, the results could be calamitous. "This is for money so I can study," she said, pressing a tiny round of gold-colored foil from a candy-wrapper. " This is for protection." If Abuela Concepción knew what Refugio was doing, she would forbid it and would destroy the skull. She looked about as if expecting to see her grandmother watching her from the doorway, but no, Refugio was alone. When she had finished filling the mold, she set it on the windowsill, facing the east, where the moon would shortly rise. Viuda Estrella had been most specific

about that, and Refugio complied. "There," she said to the skull that had her own name on it. "Let the moon see you."

By the time Abuela Concepción turned off the radio and made her way to bed, Refugio had already donned her good white-cotton dress with the lace edging, just as Viuda Estrella had told her to do. She had a flashlight and a sack for the skull she had made, and she loaded it carefully before letting herself out through the narrow door at the back of the pantry. Thinking of how much her life was about to change, she almost skipped with excitement. She kept the flashlight off until she was on the road outside of Santa Luz, for she didn't want anyone to see her as she made her way toward the ancient, tumbled stones and the house where Viuda Estrella was waiting to work her most potent conjuration on Refugio's sugar skull on this most magical of all nights. Her future would be so much better than Abuela Concepción feared. Viuda Estrella would teach her all she needed to know to make her way in the world, to be a woman of importance. Then she would go to the school in Guanajuanto, and after that, she would venture out into the wider world, with the education her grandmother wanted for her and the strength of Viuda Estrella to give her power.

As she walked, Refugio sang to the skull wrapped in her handkerchief, telling it of all she wanted, confident that the saints and her mother heard her. The beam of the flashlight was a cone of brightness in the dark, lighting her way. She felt deeply happy, and for the first time in her life, she believed she would be able to achieve all she wanted, for the skull and her industry, combined with the might of the saints that could be invoked on this night, would remove all obstacles before her. There was so much to look forward to, she thought, and took the path to Viuda Estrella's house. ⏾

A professional writer for more than thirty years, Chelsea Quinn Yarbro has sold over seventy books and more than sixty works of short fiction. She lives in her hometown — Berkeley, California — with two autocratic cats. When not busy writing, she rides her Norwegian Fjord horse Pillu or attends the symphony or an opera.

www.ingramcontent.com/pod-product-compliance
Lightning Source LLC
Chambersburg PA
CBHW081148170626
46809CB00010B/3132